PARIS PAGES

BY THE SAME AUTHOR

The Confession of Stella Moon (Saraband, 2016)
—what are you like—
(Postbox Press, 2019)

PARIS PAGES

A NOVEL IN A HUNDRED FRAGMENTS

SHELLEY DAY

First published in 2023 by Postbox Press,
the literary fiction imprint of Red Squirrel Press
36 Elphinstone Crescent
Biggar
South Lanarkshire
ML12 6GU
www.redsquirrelpress.com

Layout, design and typesetting by Gerry Cambridge
gerry.cambridge@btinternet.com

Cover image/design © Nicolai Sclater
@OrnamentalConifer

Copyright © Shelley Day 2023

Shelley Day has asserted her right to be identified as the
author of this work in accordance with Section 77 of the
Copyright, Designs and Patents Act 1988.
All rights reserved.

A CIP catalogue record for this book is available from
the British Library.

ISBN: 978 1 913632 58 8

Red Squirrel Press and Postbox Press are committed to a
sustainable future. This publication is printed in the UK
by Imprint Digital using Forest Stewardship Council
certified paper.
www.digital.imprint.co.uk

to Trey, Barney, Maddy, and little Lola Gray

to very dear Anni

&

*to Tal and Seal, intrepid inspirers,
who went to help in the 'Jungle'*

I do, I undo, I redo

Louise Bourgeois
Installation at Turbine Hall, Tate Modern,
May 2000

PART 1

I Give everything away
I Distance myself from myself
from what I love most
I leave my home
I leave the nest
I am packing my bags

Louise Bourgeois, 2010

1

You start the story many times. You never know how to go on. The story is confused and confusing. Its characters are ditherers, there's nothing compelling about them. The tale is fragmented and can't tell its beginning from its end. You've created a snake and you allow it to swallow its own tail. Now you expect us to read it… Come on.

Ta gueule, László.

2

Wet Sunday Morning in Paris, November 2019

This is the street I walk down on Sunday mornings. Today it is raining and cold as I step out into the rue de Seine, pass La Palette where I'd like to have breakfast but I don't have the cash. One of those green parakeets is screeching from up high in that Indian bean tree in the little Square Gabriel Pierné.

Then the great dome of the great Institut de France is rising on the *quai* and the buildings of Paris are the colour of oyster shells, today darkening with weather. Here and there they've been cleaned restored renovated renewed, windows repainted re-puttied preserved; *le patrimoine culturel* is important, especially in times when you need threads that connect. See the great colonnades of the great Institut, how the shape of it looms and encloses, looms open its arms; heavy and safe, it dominates, holds.

I cross the Seine at the Pont des Arts, my tread soft on the old wooden boards. I walk on to the Église St Germain d'Auxerrois and shelter under the porch from the rain. The organ is playing, I hear it through the open door.

Outside, behind those plastic barriers they put up, some road works are underway. A small green tent is pitched under a horse-chestnut tree that has all but lost every leaf. It must be unstable without guy ropes, I see only one, flimsy, tied to the tree. Parked up are scooters, a bike, a few cars. Tourists in silver quilted jackets come past dragging silver suitcases, following phone-maps, heading home, unsteady, in their new Paris shoes.

Over the road, over there, that's this end of the Palais du Louvre.
Saying the name to myself I hear the word *ouvre*
and the church door where I'm standing is open and it says *poussez poussez*
and over there the curved zinc roofs of the apartment buildings are darking with rain.

And the Louvre is open
and the church door is open
and the oyster roofs of Paris are darking with rain.

Now it is singing that emerges from the open door, voices in unison singing, are praying. I know what they're saying.

Two grey pigeons strut one after the other along the dark iron fence. A clock strikes the quarter hour. Tyres hiss wet on roads.

The miracle that humans can mark pages with thoughts.

I walk on. The great bells of the Église St Eustache clang clang clang as I cross rue St Honoré. I pass the great glass fortress of Les Halles. Christmas lights are going up and Beaubourg at the end of the road looms bits of blue plastic and perspex and scaffold, its gaping vents open throats that scream silent across the oyster roofs of Paris.

From up there on top you can see right across the city to where the Sacré Cœur lifts herself up from the slopes of Montmartre; Paris otherwise is such a flat city, easy to get everywhere by foot. I write these notes on-the-hoof, it's become a habit, I pencil them in with my Blackwing pencil on the lined pages of my notebook; these the joys and comforts of walking alone, directionless, *une flâneuse*, in Paris.

Some people have not much sympathy with this building, the Pompidou Centre, but for me it was formative, for me it was Paris. I was married to an architect once, so Beaubourg was Must, and me being from the dog-end of an abandoned city in the North of England, I'd never seen anything like it, never dreamed anything like it, like made of Lego and all those tubes, like the chutes they sent money down in our Co-op. Paris, full of not-Paris reminders.

I tried shruggingly then to look like everything was normal, but inside I was craving sick with longing, longing for everything, anything that might ever even be possible, a life different from the one I was cut out for; all that began at Beaubourg. We walked the streets of the

Marais. We sat sketching in the Place des Vosges. We stared up at the apartment of Piano and Rogers, where they lived while they did the work. The house of Victor Hugo over there in the corner. It's free to get in and there's a café in the courtyard now.

You might say I grew up in Paris, I grew up in that plastic moment gaping up at the Beaubourg; me, a clumsy late-comer to Art, Architecture, Literature, owing to circumstances beyond my control.

See all these people now in all these Paris places
where they choose to walk in this life
the styles of shoes that they pick
see them all
their Paris coats
the walking style they deem appropriate
for this fool street we all are on.

3

I'd been thinking about word paths when László shows up.

Mark pages with thoughts, he mocks.

László. The doubter. Disbeliever.

He warns of the poison distilled from the words you've followed all your life, the secret words, the secrets of words, the words behind words; the small axes they hide among the crisp clean sheets you laid on the bed of your 'unfathomable marriage,' the sharps concealed under the crisp white cloth you laid on the table.

You gaze out through the kitchen window as you used to do when the children were small. It is autumn, recently arrived. You are in another country. A low sun slants across the grass and lights up the beech tree whose leaves are yet to fall; leaves cling to the beech the longest of any deciduous tree, it is said, they refuse to be cast until they give the say-so.

The happy sound of children playing drifts in across time through the open window; all grown up now, they carry on their tight shoulders what words they have managed to salvage without stooping.

In memory, for Maria Stepanova, the real and the invented appear as equals.

Indistinguishable, says László,

You sleep alone now, you eat alone. You look out at the white sheets and the table-cloth, how they billow on the line, sails for the ships that wait in the harbour while you navigate your course by unreliable stars.

4

The towelling coat hangs limp on the bathroom door, its bones removed. And me, heading out, boneless too, into the rain with my umbrella. It's 09h30, Saturday, St Germain des Prés.

People are gathering for morning coffee on the terraces of cafés all along the Boulevard and up and down the little streets that run west to St Sulpice or east towards the river. The plastic latticed chairs and small round tables with their red and white check cloths spill out across pavements and cause pedestrians to step out into the road.

The most famous cafés—the Café de Flore, Les Deux Magots, La Brasserie Lipp—their terraces fill up quickly even on a rainy morning like this. These places were favourite haunts, back in the day, of aspiring writers: James Baldwin, Hemingway, Joyce, Beckett, Jacques Prévert; all dead now, all famous, and seats on the terraces where they acquired their writer-hoods are highly sought after.

Back then, artists in the 6th *arrondissement* were mostly a poverty-stricken bunch. Between the wars, this now chic quartier was poorer, the cafés were warm and, for people with hardly a sou, *pas chers*.

With World War 2 came the Occupation and the *Résistance*. Then, later, post-Occupation Paris was alive with politicos and philosophers, all hard at it, reforming and rebuilding the world and literature with their words and their pages and it was all happening on these same terraces. Literature—radical, subversive—magazines, books, essential bricks for a grand rebuilding. Sartre, de Beauvoir, Camus, Richard Wright, Ionesco, Duras, Nathalie Sarraute—new movements, new visions, new hopes, all taking shape right here on these streets, on all these pages of Paris. And Beckett, who'd worked for the *Résistance*, now devoting himself exclusively to literature, claiming he was not political.

Clara can hardly fail to feel the pull of it, the great old-fashioned pull of that sense of the new, the vast possibilities of the as-yet undiscovered. Clara's not alone in wanting to touch just a bit of it, but she's yet to choose a café to be her personal base. She's been given to understand that you have to have a café. Three Paris essentials: a room in your *quartier*, a café, *un resto*.

Take Patti Smith, when she's here, she's usually headed straight for the Flore. Clara saw her in there once, twice actually. She was tempted to say Hi but couldn't think how and whether it'd be invasive, so she'd ended up walking on by which she now regrets though she still can't think what words would have been appropriate.

Clara follows Patti on Instagram; the Queen of Punk, now in her seventies, is still wowing folk across the globe with stage performances. When in Paris, Patti makes Insta posts of writerly photographs showing the Flore-branded thick white cup—she says it makes her think of a baptism font—with its black *allongé*; a pen (biro); a notebook (moleskine-type), all arranged artfully on the Flore disposable-paper-illustrated placemat they put out fresh for each new customer. Everything is Art or in the service of Art. Clara is envious. Of that kind of devotion. She's half aware of being envious. She takes screenshots for keepsakes. Patti wouldn't mind, she believes in keepsakes.

In her Insta pictures Patti sometimes includes a book, something she's currently reading. There was Dante once, Gogol, Rimbaud. Lately Clara has noticed the tone getting more spiritual which is starting to ring a bell with Clara. Clara could monitor her own earthly progress by her changing attention to matters of the soul but she will usually push such thoughts aside.

Sometimes, as Serendipity would have it—Paris is a city for Serendipities—it turns out that Clara and Patti have something in common: one time it was a mutual liking for the Ghent altar-piece, the van Eyck triptych *Adoration of the Mystic Lamb*. Johannes had pooh-poohed the connection when Clara saw it; she'd told him about it in a wave of excitement, but it was shortly before they left London and they'd both been tense.

Pff, Johannes said, *Oh Clara, Clara. A lot of people will admire that particular work of art I think you can find.*

Johannes, Clara felt, had dismissed her excitement in such a superior way—the apparent superiority exaggerated, she now realises, by the fact that English was not his first language. That day, belittled, Clara had gone straight to the box they'd packed and she'd retrieved the Ghent book from the bottom of the pile, messing up all the rest. She'd flicked noisily through the pages to locate the double spread of the triptych; she'd walked out to the copy-shop on the corner, returning half an hour later with an A3 colour photocopy which straight away she pinned up roughly on the living room wall—all other posters and pictures had already been taken down. Johannes watched her but said nothing. When Johannes said nothing, that meant something mattered; in her almost four years with him, Clara had learned that much. Then, weeks later, when they finally

left the London apartment to go their separate ways—
Clara to Paris and Johannes back to Oslo—Clara had
left the picture, curling now at the edges and dangling
on the diagonal by a single drawing pin.

All things considered, Clara has decided the Flore
won't be her café after all, even if Patti Smith does go
there. She'll choose something less well-known, more
individual, more her, et *moins cher*. The Café Fleurus in
rue de Fleurus—Gertrude Stein lived in that street for
thirty-five years at number 27 and held her famous sa-
lons there—is a good candidate. They serve a fine apple
pie and have *décor* that steps naturally out of the 60s;
there's nothing pretentious or famous about it and *les
deux patrons* always make Clara feel welcome. If you
have to have a café, well this is probably going to be
hers. The rue de Fleurus is a good street, right by the
Luxembourg garden, even if Clara's still not sure what
she thinks about Gertrude Stein.

It has been said that Stein was a 'conservative with an
increasingly reactionary bent' which information Clara
finds difficult to assimilate, given all the claims for the
revolutionary-ness of her writing and her support for
artists. Clara is a little afraid of her fascination with Gertrude Stein, unsettled by how she's drawn to someone
but doesn't know why. She's stood several times outside number 27, gazing up at the stone plaque, trying
to formulate her opinion about the woman, her life, her
writing. The psychoanalyst inside Clara assumes the
failing to be her own, that she *could* find some sense
in Stein's work if she looked hard enough, if she could
treat the writing as expressing extreme condensation,
as in dream. She's read a lot about it, but she still has

not reached any *rapprochement* with—as Janet Malcolm describes it—the 'almost audible clash of wills between Stein's divided selves' in her work—that is what both fascinates and repels Clara.

Clara has scanned the windows on the first, second, third, fourth floors of the building where lived Gertrude Stein the writer, the art-lover, lesbian lover, friend of Picasso, wielder of such power and influence in the literary world of Paris. She'd felt nothing but an absence, nothing beyond the initial adolatory awe she's manufactured in accord with some local Blue-Guide stone-plaque recipe. Clara's pilgrimages left her emptier than she'd been before, her inability to connect with the great woman confirmed a chasm inside her, the great canyon of nothingness that divides each of us one from the other...

and each of us from ourselves, says László.

... God knows, it had been impossible enough for Clara to connect with Johannes—living, breathing, passionate Johannes—let alone the long-dead cold goose Gertrude Stein whose work she still can't fathom.

And what of Max Zuniga, another of the once-admired long-dead, he who left behind only words; by what means could Clara hope to connect with him? She so desperately wants to write The biography, the definitive biography, the story that gets inside, really *inside* the man, *inside* his mind, his shadow mind, his history, his shadow history, his *true* story—that's what she's here in Paris for—but as Clara knows very well, some thresholds are difficult to cross.

You need a passeur, László says. *Someone to take you over the border...*

Zuniga. *Passeur.* Clara doesn't usually pay attention to László but this time she punches a line into her phone Memos app:

Z. : creativity as Passeur.

Standing now on the Boulevard St Germain, on the corner by the Café de Flore, Clara replaces her phone in her bag and quickly checks that she's brought a book with her. She likes to have a paperback with her. She can panic if she forgets to bring it. Books are props, they hold you up. What you read reveals your character. Books are signs, emblems. Clara likes to have a small Folio text in French for times when she is not in a hurry; she reads French slowly, closely, often has to look up words, always trying to deepen her understanding. In her bag, ah, here it is, she locates with relief *Ecrire* by Marguerite Duras. And ah, Parisian serendipity at work again, Duras' own *appartement* was down this very street, rue St Benoît, just down there, near the bottom, on the right. And the man who's buried beside her at Montparnasse was installed just across the way.

Clara likes books. She looks forward to the suggestions Patti Smith makes in her writing and on social media; since leaving London, Clara finds anglophone books keep her connected to a world she has not altogether left however much she might wish to. If Patti mentions something, Clara will make a note or take a screenshot; she might Google a review, perhaps find a copy occasion at Berkeley Books or at Gibert; she likes to go pre-loved, if she can, not only for her budget, but also for the planet. There's Galignani for new, or Penelope at Red Wheelbarrow will order it in, it's important to support indies too.

Clara looks forward to encounters with books, where they will take her, where Patti might guide her next: Rimbaud, Bolaño, Robert Walser. She appreciates these vicarious anchorings now she's in this new city, now she's alone, Clara is grateful for all the moorings she can get. Books are friends she doesn't yet have, and soon she'll be writing her own, the biography of Max Zuniga, the book that will rescue the man and his theory from the oblivion to which they have wrongly—in Clara's opinion—been consigned... Yes, books have power, they can be great liberators; Clara looks forward to the journey to (or with?) Zuniga, and will it also be an anchor to herself, she will soon find out...

Outside on the Boulevard, people emerge into the open air from underground via the stone-stepped *bouche* of the Métro St Germain. On the corner with rue Bonaparte, there's a stall selling *crêpes* and the aroma of hot pancakes fills the air. Paris at this hour on a Saturday in late autumn is calm and quiet and Clara likes it this way.

A sole traveller hurries by, his coat flapping, he skips up the steps into the Église St Germain. Clara knows a beggar will already have already installed himself under the archway there, as he does every day.

We must take up our places early, says László. *You can wait a long time in the line.*

For now, though, if you pass the Zadkine sculpture on your left, and carry on down towards the river, go down rue Bonaparte and, on your right, look for the shop where they sell those ouroboros rings and bracelets; look, see the snakes swallowing their tails in the jewellery shop window, see how someone's placed real apples among the snakes to ripen in the autumn sun.

Move in closer and you'll see your own reflection.

Look at you, Clara, hovering there among the snakes and the apples, like Eve reborn.

Or like the bathroom coat, hanging there limp and waiting.

5

I'm very glad to have this key to this small studio Frédérique has lent me in the rue des Canettes. I'm glad to be able to walk these streets, to feel the unevenness of the cobbles through the soles of my boots. These red boots, these Fly boots, I call them my city boots, I bought them for Paris.

I'm glad to stand in the mist from the fountain that centres Place St Sulpice where the great grand church towers behind me like a relative. Or I gaze up at the pale stone apartment-block-streets and count the *étages*—rarely more than seven. Patrick Modiano lives somewhere round here, I'm not sure where. I've sometimes wondered if I am gazing up into his window, like Clara searching for a window into Gertrude Stein.

I have seen a literary-looking man taking his constitutional in the Luxembourg Gardens and, convinced it's Modiano, I've been tempted to follow him the same way his enigmatic characters are apt surreptitiously to follow the meandering trails of other enigmatic characters, weaving on his pages from street to street, *quartier* to *quartier*, in and out of moments, across the times and the spaces of Paris.

In Paris you always wish you could draw. I brought Sadie here to make art. She's a photographer. I wanted to help her out of the *impasse* she'd got herself into. I wanted to be a sort of Clara and help Sadie.

If I could draw I would sketch this long narrow rue Visconti that is more like a passage-way, I like how its walls keep leaning in, one towards the other, making nonsense of perspective. This little street links rue Bonaparte with the rue de Seine. If you look on Wiki you'll see how long and narrow and tall it is. You can find out how, over hundreds of years, this tiny *rue* has been associated with so many artists—Delacroix, Balzac, Voltaire. The realisation that those feet have trodden these same stones where your own insignificant toes now tread can overwhelm you when you first arrive, before you manage to push all that to one side and make Paris your own. History is a good counterbalance if you have any foolish sense of your own personal significance. Equally it's a comfort to feel part of it at the same time as you know that you aren't part of anything at all.

If I could draw, I'd make a map of my Paris, of all these streets I know. I'd make collages and mark them up with colours and words and snippets of tickets. I'd stick things on with Pritt Stick. I'd draw doors and windows and statues, gargoyles and caryatids and round cartoon people like Agnès Varda marching alone along rue Daguerre to her pink *atelier*, all wrapped up in her winter coat.

Autumn is on the turn now and coats have become a thing in Paris. They're in all the shop windows, there are coats everywhere and suddenly everyone is wearing them and that's us, headed for winter, all wrapped up in our warm *manteaux*.

6

Sadie arrives back at her petite *chambre* de bonne in the rue de L'Arbre Sec and her phone is ringing—she had deliberately left it behind when she went out to get the *gougère* at the *traiteur* down the street. She sighs as she picks up the phone to see who it is that's calling.

Everyone's nervous just now, there's a fragility in the air, Sadie's not sure where it comes from, but people do seem to be feeling it, it's not just her. In UK it's the hateful Brexit thing, and here in Paris every Saturday the *Gilets Jaunes* are marching, and in other cities too. Sadie had tagged along to start with on one or two of the *manifestations*, just to see, but it was hard to make sense—so many issues, discontents, factions... Then she'd seen on TV bits of the demos turning violent as frustrations boiled over. She'd backed off, continued to be interested, but from a distance. Plus the refugee crisis across Europe continues unabated and there's still no co-ordinated policy for helping the displaced and desperate. It's shameful, to Sadie's mind, how the UK propaganda machine has exploited the plight of displaced people to its own Brexit ends.

Sadie had been working at the so-called 'Jungle' at Sangatte near Calais when it was finally destroyed more than three years ago. A volunteer, helping with food distribution, her experience at the Camp had all but broken her. She'd taken photographs during her time there, but hasn't since been able to bring herself to look at them. They've remained in encrypted folders on an external hard drive. She'd taken photographs and recorded testimonies from the displaced people who clamoured to talk to her, clearly hoping to have their lost voices restored, their silenced and denied stories heard.

Sadie—then—had believed her work could make a difference, could reveal—through Art—the personal consequences—often so tragic—of conflict, of the persecutions and global poverties that drive desperate people to leave their homes and flee their countries... Like Marguerite Duras—who, alongside many writers of the time, had worked with the *Resistance*—Sadie had believed a primary role for any artist was to bear witness at every level—personal, familial, social, political—to the human consequences of a society's chosen means of functioning...

Naïvely—as Sadie now sees—she'd sought to produce 'evidence' to counter the misinformation about migrants, refugees and asylum-seekers that continued to dominate the UK news media. But misinformation was, and is, systemic and systematic. The mainstream narrative is all about division, all about creating an Enemy out of a group of voiceless desperate people, demonising and scapegoating them, effectively erasing their humanity…

People said she was just being paranoid, but it all smacked to Sadie of the sort of thing that should never happen again; she found such ideologies abhorrent. Her response had been to volunteer at Sangatte, to make her art unashamedly political, to put her talents into the service of the needy. But Sadie hadn't been able to see things through. Personal issues had meshed too easily with political ones and together they'd spilled into her art and stopped both her and it in their tracks. She'd filed her work away and hasn't been able to look at it since. Sadie wasn't strong enough. She'd been destabilised. She'd been defeated. In trying to remind the world of the humanity of others, Sadie had become dangerously close to losing her own.

Then, arriving in Paris, Sadie found herself not safe or saved as she'd anticipated, but overcome by a terrible sense of dislocation: once again an Outsider—to the place, to herself; the old repetition, reasserting itself:

I do, I undo, I redo.

The mantra artist Louise Bourgeois lived by now places Sadie beside herself, detached, unhitched.

Sadie is unsteady. Things are serious. She tells Clara of another instance when she is unable to locate herself in her own mirror image.

Mirror mirror on the wall...

Clara nods, leans in, invites Sadie to say more, but Sadie hesitates, says she doesn't have the words...

Images? Clara ventures... the mirror...

who is the fairest of them all...

Not Sadie. She looks like me but she is not me.

Who...

She's a shadow that moves... she's an echo...

Can you bring her back? Clara asks.

I want her to leave. But I can't let go. I'm afraid to let go...

Afraid... Clara says.

Of being in pieces, broken in pieces, fragmented.

Sadie puts the flat of her hand to her chest and tries to steady her thumping heart. Paris was supposed to be the way to a new life, a way to begin again, a safe life. Clara was supposed to be the road to salvation. But the old demons are still there—if anything, intensified—ever dismantling away at the roots of her, *do, undo, redo*

Clara is saying something, but Sadie's no longer listening. That thing in the mirror won't ever listen.

Every day Sadie lives the futility, the absolute futility, of any engagement with Art. Aesthetics: what is the point of it when human beings the world over are suffering and dying needlessly. How can Art 'bear witness' in the geopolitical mess where the lessons from history are regularly unlearned, actively supressed or ignored.
Sadie knows she should be thankful for Paris, thankful for Clara, thankful too for the Academy of Art and Design and the second chance they've put her way. She doesn't want to let them down, she already has more than enough guilt to deal with.

Clara says it is a 'crisis of faith' Sadie is going through. But crises of faith are religious and Sadie's crisis is different, it's not even secular, it's something else entirely. Faith in humanity, that's what I mean by crisis of faith, Clara had corrected herself, but by then Sadie had stopped listening again. Sadie switches off when Clara starts telling her what's what. To be told what's what is not what you pay a therapist for.

Today in her tiny *chambre de bonne* Sadie listens to the phone ringing, she watches it vibrate against the saucer on the table. She takes the *gougère* out of its bag and sets it on a ceramic plate. She goes to re-heat the coffee in the microwave. Is there even any place where ethics and aesthetics coincide?

Sadie leaves her phone unanswered, lets it ring and ring until it flicks onto answerphone. She checks her text messages: two from László, one from Clara. She doesn't open any of them. The missed call is her tutor at the Academy. He's left an answerphone message, saying she's behind with a deadline. Sadie doesn't want to know. She switches her phone onto 'silent' and lays it down again among the mess of papers, pens, sketchpads, unopened letters, books wedged at pages she's forgotten what was being marked or why, wedged open for so long the pages will never again close properly together. She takes a bite out of the *gougère*, wishes she'd warmed that up as well.

Come on, Sadie.

Ta gueule, László.

7

She lined up all her shoes and not a single pair stood out as actually her own. She wore them, pair by pair, religiously, even though they didn't fit.

It's not as though she needed shoes, more shoes, more shoes, but more that she was a gambler who could not resist, compulsive, could not resist, in which, she resembled her late friend Evie who ate apples, only apples and nothing but apples, who couldn't stop herself from eating apples.

If there were shoes, she'd have to walk in them. Give me those shoes, she'd say, for I am compelled to walk in each and every shoe every day of my life so help me G-d, every shoe on this earth other than my own. To which extent, I have none. I live among the loaned ones, the borrowed ones, the formerly loved and loathed; the temporary, the tested ones, the tricksters, the habits, the worn-out or worn-away, all of them lined up along my hall, stacked up against my red red walls. My walls are lined with borrowed shoes, their soles worn down their leather tilted split and spoilt.

You know, when you stop to think, there must be many broken shoes, discarded shoes in this world of ours. Close your eyes and think of them, the sad ones, the forgotten the dismissed ignored, the abandoned ones, they all once held feet.

Now line them up, those sad shoes, a few pairs, a singleton, pick them up and put them in a line. Now, there they are, lined up along your hallway floor. Or if you don't have a hall, line them up anyway, in your room, along a wall, any wall, line them up, side by side, near the door, as close to any door as possible. Line up those shoes along that wall. Count how many there are. Keep counting.

8

Clara is in Paris, learning a new language, writing a book for which she does not yet have a title. Well, she's not quite writing the book, but she will, this is the research phase, the early months…

With an acute sense of discomfort Clara realises she should really by now have got more to grips than she has with project Max Zuniga. She should—as the semi-official biographer—by now have, at least, the arc of Zuniga's life, the evolution of his work on the creative process; she should have skeleton-mapped the story of the man who made the theory, the man mysteriously missing from Freud's inner circle, and missing from history…

Clara looks down the list she made months ago in the back of her diary, a time-line; she sees how far behind she is. There are no ticks against any of the items: the sources of Zuniga's motivation, the roots of his genius, the reasons for his (apparent) failure, his (evident) disappearance. Clara underlines failure, makes a few pencil notes in the margin of the first of the *feuilles doubles* she's bought at Gibert's for this project. She does have a dedicated notebook, but starting in there would be too much of a thing. She highlights 'failure' with an orange pen. She imagines herself inching forward, onward, among the under-linings, curses, erasures.

Oh Clara.

Clara has never written a biography before, but she's done plenty of Case Studies and, well, they're practically the same thing are they not.

Clara is a writer now, a biographer. She's no longer a psychotherapist. Her heart has shifted. Imagine though, if she was invited out to dinner and someone asked, 'and what do you do?' she wouldn't know what to say… She could hardly say she was a writer, let alone a biographer… They'd ask what she'd written and say things like, 'oh, are you famous, should I have heard of you …' What do new writers call themselves when they haven't published anything… when they've not actually started to write anything yet …

Clara, you need not worry about this now because

there is no danger of anyone inviting you out to dinner.

Oh, Clara.

And the fact is Clara is not quite done with being a therapist. She has Sadie coming twice a week for a start. Since arriving in Paris, Clara has deviated from her exclusive biographer plans and taken on a couple of clients, in a transitional kind of way. Nothing too demanding. Sadie, though, she's not exactly easy. Clara needed to avoid doing too many endings all at once…

too many losses

… plus she's read that Zuniga was seeing patients at the same time as he was writing his theories. Indeed, his patients must have been facilitating insights, inspiring his writing. Plus, being a therapist pays the bills. Clara can't make ends meet with only the tiny advance the publisher indicated they might offer her—they haven't actually paid her anything, neither has she actually signed any contract—which means she's relying on her savings which are not huge.

Today Clara is walking in the Luxembourg gardens as advised by her friend Moira for the purpose of taking care of her own mental health. Despite her professional training—possibly because of it, Clara now reflects—she hadn't foreseen the impact—what people now call Challenges—that would come in the wake of the changes she'd made to her life / lifestyle/ geographical location / job / relationship / income/ social status, etc. Clara had picked Freedom from the range of options available to her, she'd picked Paris and the life of a writer, chosen the things her dreams had for so long been made of. It all makes Clara unsure of the precise origin of her current angst.

Oh Clara

9

Those times, when things threaten to get the better of her, Clara will take comfort in walking aimlessly—today in the Luxembourg gardens—being a *flâneuse*, just watching other people doing their own things, keeping her feet on the ground, her body moving in the Real.

A Japanese man
on a green tin chair
under a plane tree
meditates
in the lotus position
eyes closed
palms up.

A boy learning tennis, his coach's black jerkin, up zipped, the soft alternate thud of the yellow ball, the quick scrape of white sneakers on tarmac.

A bunch of lads playing basketball, jumping, laughing.

Ponies in a lazy line, heads down, resting, ropes trailing, waiting for children.

Mothers speaking languages to babies in buggies.

Children doubled up on *trottinettes*, their voices excited enough to put their hats askew.

People learning that strange fast walking with those special power sticks; a bored-looking man-coach yelling instructions, checking his watch.

Low autumn sun.

Distant traffic.

Sirens.

People wrapped up in coats and hats in case winter arrives while they're out and about.

Mothers talking in tongues to babies; they repeat and repeat in rhythmic high tones that fall, like the leaves, one by one, one after the other, *les feuilles mortes* that drift slowly to earth, land silent on sisters already fallen, silent those who have passed this way and passed on.

Clara puts in her ear-phones, listens to Yves Montand, *les feuilles mortes* as she walks.

Oh, these sinewy paths strewn with leaves
these layers of memory
all these pages and pages of lives
unwritten.

10

Today it's Saturday and the *Gilets Jaunes* are out in force in the *quartier* St Germain through which Sadie is now walking towards Berkeley Books in the rue Casimir Delavigne. There's an event on at the bookstore, the installation of the new stained glass, which will turn out to be a bit of a 'do,' if she knows Phyllis. The artist, Alison, she'll be there, maybe Lisa with her poems and keyboards, Herenui with songs and her ukelele, perhaps a few writers from the AWOL group sharing words. Sadie's been looking forward to this. She's even been wondering whether she'll dare share some of her own work if the opportunity arises. Artists of all sorts are always welcome at Berkeley Books.

She probably won't take them out of her bag, but Sadie has brought with her a few small collages she's recently made, trying to capture the moods of the city in the grey, zinc, pearly and oyster tones of the buildings. They're all she's managed so far, it's been so difficult to get started and she's not sure if her idea is working. Perhaps she's using colours, shapes and shades that will remind people of French *cimetières*, all stone and severe, hard-surfaced, colourless. Anyone who knows Paris knows this city has moods, each *quartier* its distinctive *caractère*; and the light, the light, always shifting. So perhaps they're too static, these little amateur collages Sadie has made…

Sadie loves the cityscapes of Paris as they cluster around the snake-winding river in all their moods; she loves standing on the Pont Neuf looking west to watch the horizon turn deep evening red as the Eiffel Tower lights up and sends out its beam and sparkles. And to the east, Notre Dame, encased among towers of scaffolding since the fire that threatened the entire edifice and demolished the spire. She'd been close by, that day in April, she'd watched, like others, with incredulity, then horror, watched as a scene unthinkable unfolded. People near her on the bridge were crying as the realisation dawned that it was the precious cathedral that was burning. Sadie had stood and watched as the spire collapsed in flames. But for the skilled actions of the *pompiers*, Notre Dame would be no more. Sadie had stood there, overwhelmed by so much emotion flooding into her. Now, thinking about her collages, Sadie knows she is nowhere near capturing the multiple spirits of this city she wants to make her own.

Still, she would love to see her little works on display in Berkeley Books. Perhaps they're too personal to be Art. Clara had said as much, well almost. Sadie had realised, in the making of the collages, how the moods of the city paralleled her own. Clara had smiled when Sadie told her this, then Clara said what she'd said without even asking to see any of the collages. They'd stayed in Sadie's bag that day, as no doubt they would today.

Clara doesn't understand what it is to be an artist. She says she has a special interest in creativity, and that man Zuniga she's supposed to be writing about, Clara's obsessed with him, he had a theory of creativity. Clara had given Sadie some internet links, said they might be some good in getting Sadie going with her work mojo, getting over her current creative impasse, but Sadie hasn't followed them up. Clara really has no idea about what it's like to be an artist. It occurs to Sadie that her little collages would be considered by most to be bland and depressing. She was foolish to imagine they could be anything else. Because that's how she's seeing the world at the moment, even Paris.

Art doesn't have to be beautiful, Sadie, says László. *Just truthful.*

11

On that Saturday of the *Gilets Jaunes* Sadie is crossing the Place St Sulpice and is jolted out of her reverie by loud bangs and whistles and a sharp realisation that the *manif* is getting closer. She hears crowds and shouting as she turns at the Café de la Mairie on the square and into the narrow rue des Canettes. By the time she's nearing the junction with the rue du Four she's in the thick of it, can't hear herself think for the noise, and anxiety is starting to take hold. The huge shouting crowd goes back far as she can see. Sadie doesn't know which way to go to avoid being swallowed up in the hollering mass.

She could retrace her steps, but won't.

This is not Sangatte, Sadie, this is not Sangatte. Keep going.

This is not the first time Sadie has been among the protesters—they're out every Saturday, taking different routes across the city. She does tend to keep away from crowds like this which can act as triggers. Clara has advised they're best avoided.

It is with trepidation that Sadie views the groups of chanting 'yellow jackets' now thronging at the intersection, the crowd swelling into adjoining streets. The traffic has stopped. As fast as police put up barriers, demonstrators undo them, throw them aside.

Everywhere Sadie sees the forces of Law and Order are massing. It's not for no reason they're called 'forces'—armed police, *gendarmes* on horseback, CRS with riot shields, helmets and breathing masks are unloading from lines of white Transit vans... the red *pompiers* and SAMU vans are lining up, making ready for casualties and fires. Blue lights are flashing on every corner. Whistles. Sirens. And the massive crowd getting more and more agitated, chanting in unison in response to someone shouting incantatory through a loud hailer. It's impossible not to feel the insistent urgent energy of it. Now drums, like the Drummers of Burundi Sadie once heard at WOMAD, begin to beat their rhythm; Sadie can't see them but she can hear the boom boom boom of the drums and it is stirring up such restless emotion in the crowd and

...it *is* just like Sangatte...

Panic wells up inside Sadie. She thinks of László. She puts on the determined air he'd approve of, she tries to keep on walking, *keep on going the way you're going, keep on breathing, steady, determined, breathing.* She reminds herself that this may look like a terrifying horde but, in reality, these *Gilets Jaunes* are just ordinary people. Not very different from herself. Discontented, yes. Some downright angry, yes. But the bottom line, these are ordinary people. Frustrated, they want change. *Manifesta-*

tions like these are a tradition in France, an accepted part of life in a *république*, an essential element of democracy. The right to peaceful protest. It's a human right, and this scene is testimony to how a country values those values, the right of citizens to make their voices heard. There's nothing in any of that to be afraid of.

But Sadie had witnessed such violence at Sangatte. At Sangatte she'd seen a side of the human character she'd rather not have seen. She'd seen a side of herself she'd rather not have seen. Humanity is flawed. She doesn't need reminding.

Sadie backtracks up the rue des Canettes, takes a sharp left into rue Guisarde. She'll cut through by the Marché St Germain, avoid the main road. But the road's blocked there too and she's forced back down to where another crowd has gathered at the corner by the Mab Café. It's a student café and has large windows the length of two sides. Sadie notices with some alarm that the windows have been completely boarded up with plywood, the door of the café is locked with a huge padlock, and the crowd is blocking the entire junction there as well.

Sadie takes a right into the little street where the soup kitchen is. László volunteers here on Wednesdays. It's amazing how he finds it in himself to volunteer, finds the means to give, when he has so little himself, when he doesn't even have a stable place to live. László, *sans domicile fixe*. The sign on the soup kitchen door says *Ouvert* but the door itself is closed. Across the road the plate-glass windows of both the Apple shop and Uniqlo have been closely boarded.

It's impossible to get to anywhere near the Berkeley Bookstore. Sadie just about reaches the Boulevard but sees the police are moving in a synchronised cordon, the helmeted and masked front row behind riot shields, canisters of something are being thrown—flash bombs or tear gas, she can't tell. Smoke billows up from where they land. The sirens are continuous. A helicopter circles.

This is not a mood of Paris Sadie wants to know. This one is ugly. She's showed nothing of this in her silly little collages yet it's as real as the light she was trying to capture. Then she sees what could be causing this seachange. A small, angry, tough-looking group, all men, all in black, in balaclavas, they're dragging bikes and *trottinettes* and bins and bags of *ordures* into the middle of the street and setting them on fire. Is this what the News media calls *black-bloc*? There's a loud explosion in an adjacent street—possibly the rue de Buci—Sadie looks up and sees clouds of dark smoke appearing above the rooftops.

The crowd is dense around where the men in black are now engaged in open combat with the police. The sirens are continuous. Sadie is pushed along by the crowd down streets she hardly knows. Some people are trying to get away, others are rushing and pushing in the opposite direction.

At the top of the road Sadie manages to break free, she runs into a back street only to find herself in the middle of a group of Police and CRS unloading from more white vans, evidently mobilising to deal with the changed atmosphere on the Boulevard. She looks about her, trying to take it in. Then the police are marching off like a regiment, it's as if she wasn't there at all, they just walk around her, so intent are they on a singular purpose. Sadie is left standing alone in the narrow street, the riot carrying on but a few blocks away. And she thinks how young these police are, how very young, not much more than the kids you see at the gates of the *Lycée*, how odd to see them marching off chatting like they were going for a game of basketball.

But it's not a game. Off they march, all dressed the same in dark anonymous uniforms, carrying shields and firearms, each a bit-part in the giant state machine, they move off in unison, marching in time, their strides all the same length. To have absorbed that regimental mentality and be not even twenty. To be acting as one, like an army, ready to pitch itself against people just like itself. A body. Of one mind. Of one intent. To dehumanise, dominate, quash, oppress, destroy.

Like at Sangatte.

Beware the single story, Sadie, says László, quoting Chimamanda Ngozi Adiche.

Sadie does know there is another, an alternative, a parallel story, she'd seen that too at Sangatte. Fearing to be trampled, she'd let the police pull her from the angry crowd, she'd let them pull her free, she'd let them help her. Sometimes it's impossible to reconcile two opposing stories, both firmly anchored, each as true as the other.

How many stories do you have, László? Which is the

story that brought you to Paris, which is the story that keeps you here…

We, each of us, he replies, *we each come out from under Gogol's Overcoat.*

The courage to be yourself, you mean?

Read it whichever way, László shrugs, *is all the same to me. It's how you read it that counts to you.*

The courage to do what has to be done. To do what you can do, however small. To accept who you are. To be true to yourself, to what you in your heart believe.

László turns to leave. *Hiding can only be a temporary solution, Sadie*, he says. *Even when it is yourself you are hiding behind. Or from.*

12

Sadie decides to go 'home' after all, give Berkeley Books a miss this Saturday.

How odd to have thought of that little room, that tiny attic that doesn't even have a proper window or a toilet, how strange to have referred to it as *home*. She's never done that before. Home. Now she just wants to get from the *rive gauche* back to the safety and peace of her *petite chambre de bonne* on the *rive droite*.

She's lost all appetite for political protest as well as for artistic endeavours. These days, her mojo so quickly fades. And those collages she did, still there in her tote bag, how lazy they are, how futile, they don't go anywhere near capturing the realities of this city, these silly sentimental little efforts don't reflect at all a Paris that is even capable of these moods she has just witnessed. They reflect a Paris in denial.

A Sadie in denial.

It always comes back to this with Sadie, since Sangatte: Art is foolish and superfluous in a world as troubled as this. A complete waste of time.

Heading back to her *chambre*—it's more difficult to refer to it as 'home' now the impact of that word has entered her consciousness—Sadie makes her way back via the rue des Canettes and, on impulse, steps into the Bar Chez Georges. A white-haired man in orange trousers and a pink sweater is coming out of the door as she prepares to go in, he smiles *Bonjour* broadly and holds the door open for her. The man with his smile and his colours and his bright *bonjour* has the effect of restoring Sadie to the Real.

Inside the Comptoir des Canettes it's warm and busy and there's a feeling of yesteryear, a disorienting sense of displacement in time—disorienting in a nice way, not discomforting—it's a resurrection of an older Paris, a post-Occupation Paris, optimistic, artistic, singular, determined, radical. Sadie looks about her, adjusting to the change in atmosphere. Around the walls, photographs, black and white, from the fifties and sixties she guesses and, on one wall, a big print of a couple dancing; she moves in to take a closer look. It's a Doisneau.

She'd thought it was. How lovely. How very lovely. Sadie sits down.

How uplifting art can be. In the right place. At the right time.

Beauty is truth, truth beauty...that is all you need to know. That's Keats, says László.

Surrounded by these photographs—and particularly evident in the black and white *Dancing in the Street*, it comes to Sadie how both dark and light are necessary, how they depend one upon the other, you can't see one without knowing the presence of the other, the one the reverse, the absence of the other, each only existing as a negation of the other...

How a single candle both defies and defines the darkness, an observation attributed to Anne Frank, but Sadie's not sure a child could think like that, but Anne Frank was an extraordinary child, so maybe she did.

The *patron* comes over when he sees Sadie examining the picture. He introduces himself as Hugo and tells her the photograph was probably taken in this very street in 1949. Doisneau, he explains, was a friend of this bar, a regular; and, after the War, in the fifties and early sixties, artists, writers and politicos like Guy Debord, Jean-Michel Mension, the Lettrists, the Situationists—Hugo gestures around the photographs—radical groups like that, he tells her, met here to discuss and plan how to make the world a better place. Musicians too, he smiles a warm smile. And people from Hungary, he adds, in '56. His mother, he says, remembers those times well.

Before my time, though, Hugo laughs. His grandfather, he tells Sadie, was the eponymous 'Georges' who opened this bar in 1952.

Sadie looks around her. There's hardly a piece of wall that doesn't have a picture pinned up on it. Sadie has walked into her spiritual home, more important to her than an actual home. She takes off her coat and lays it on the bench beside her. She is sitting under the Doisneau. He can look down at her, he can sprinkle his magic dust onto her collar, if he'd be so kind.

Sadie orders a *grand crème* and a cheese platter and, while she is waiting, it occurs to her that she could ask if it might be possible to display one or two of the little Paris collages she has in her bag on one of the walls, she can see a couple of gaps where something of hers could fit... But no, she reminds herself for the umpteenth time, her little efforts are naïve and foolish, they're too static, too sentimental, too complacent, yes, foolish, immature, uninteresting, unidimensional, compared to these photographs with their directness, their air of urgency, their movement, these black and white snapshots—she peers more closely at the ones nearest to her, a female vocalist, open-mouthed, in a clingy satin dress, leans up against an upright piano; a man is blowing a trumpet, his cheeks distended, sweat running down from his temples; and now the whole jazz band in full swing, they're in a vaulted cellar, swirling smoke is clouding the lens... yes, many of these pictures are indeed snapshots, quick poses, actions captured in the process of completion—each one emitting the vital energy of a time that is passed and gone yet lives on.

The wonder of these photographs, the aliveness of them after so many years, shocks Sadie back into life, awakens her desire for Art that has for so long lain dormant. She'd give anything to create work that could have such an impact. It's so long since she's been able to even think anything like that.

Truth, Art, Politics, conscience, shame, guilt, all fighting it out within her since Sangatte.

Sadie, her art fighting for its very life inside her.

13

Her *café crème* arrives and a little bowl of tiny pretzels. Sadie smiles, and dares, for the first time in a long while, to feel herself begin to relax, just sitting there, in Chez Georges, absorbing the atmosphere.

She is just finishing her coffee when the phone rings its 1960s tone. Hugo—who's been busy behind the bar washing glasses, wipes his hands on a tea towel and steps to one side to pick up the phone. Sadie watches him as he listens to the caller, she sees him raise his eyebrows, then frown, he leans across the bar to look out of the window, says a few words before replacing the receiver. Straight away he goes outside and begins closing the shutters. In a few moments the bar is dark. Sadie watches with increasing alarm as Hugo shuts the door and locks it from the inside. *Nous devrons peut-être tous passer la nuit ici*—We may all have to spend the night in here—he laughs, as he drops the key into his pocket and switches on the lights.

Hugo is no sooner back behind the bar than there is a sharp rap at the door. Someone is rattling at the locked door and talking with urgency but Sadie can't make out the words. Hugo goes back to the door and opens it. The man with the orange trousers and pink jumper comes in, closely followed by a woman with black hair and wearing a long black coat, she reminds Sadie of Edith Piaf, *petite* and all in black, Sadie is so enchanted she almost expects the woman to burst into *la vie en rose*. Hugo locks the door behind them and this time he hangs up the key on a hook behind the bar.

Sadie is uneasy, knowing she is locked in. The old claustrophobia. Gone is the pleasantly relaxed feeling she was enjoying a minute ago. She should leave, leave now, but the woman in black—Marie—is introducing herself, sitting down at the next table and gesturing insistently for Sadie to join her. Sadie shakes her head, finds herself instead standing up, gathering up her coat, heading towards the bar to settle her *addition*. Marie continues to try to engage her, *mais tu es belle*, she's saying, *tu es jeune… comme tu es adorable…* But Sadie has only one thought, increasingly insistent, to get outside, get away from the rising panic within her, step out into the open air. She settles her *addition* but Hugo is reluctant to open the door. He explains that the *manifestation* is likely to be passing close by the rue des Canettes very soon and unless Sadie wants to get caught up in that a second time…

Sadie is sweating. *Il est tard et je dois rentrer à la maison*,

Sadie says, aware of how lame an excuse this sounds, how amateur her French sounds. *Je voudrais prendre un taxi...*

The man in the orange trousers—his name is Guy— stands up and comes to her rescue, helps her on with her coat, lays his hand on her shoulder, tells Hugo he will accompany the young lady to a taxi. He holds out his hand and receives the key for the door.

Guy lets Sadie lean on his arm as they walk up the little rue des Canettes to where the taxis are lined up opposite the bus stop on Place St Sulpice. She's exhausted with emotion. Guy's silence indicates that he seems to understand.

À demain, he says; as she steps into the taxi, he touches her on the forearm, *à demain?*

À bientôt, Sadie says, realising she means it. *Et merci pour tout.*

C'est normal, Guy smiles as he turns to go, *c'est normal.*

14

I believe that if I could land on a plan all my problems would be solved. Possibly every artist thinks this. It would be like landing on Park Lane in Monopoly and building hotels and life is suddenly perfect.

I mean a writing plan, a schedule for my writing days. Then I think a plan for each and every piece of work would not go amiss. So, an overall plan, and lots of sub-plans. To bring order to chaos. Then comes the idea of a whole life plan, that could be even better. When I was a kid I used to wish I had eyes that could see round corners.

You've been writing on-the-hoof and being a *flâneuse* and criss-crossing Paris and writing and standing on bridges and walking in museums and peering through shop windows and writing and rattling long-distance on *métros* and buses and writing and now you have all these small pieces mounting up and one day it occurs to you that you are, in fact, writing, and therefore you probably don't need an actual plan.

You're writing. Some kind of book. *Paris Pages*. Provisional title. You write in curly-cue pen on the outside of your notebook. You think of Clara. How she wrote *Zuniga* on the front of hers and will probably live to regret it.

Then you think, if it's a book you're writing, a novel, then you really do need a plan. Because working to a plan is a good way to write a book. But nothing of yours fits ever into any plan and isn't/ wasn't written with any plan in mind and never has been.

László looks at you and shakes his head in that way of his.

I don't mean a plan in the sense of Plot. It's okay to have no plot. Not all readers expect plots. Some do but some are content just to tag along. Which is a good thing because not all writers do plots either. Plots can come from characters and from places, you don't have to make them up because the story can do that on your behalf.

You think a plan will make you feel safe, is that it?

If I could make an effective plan I would write exquisite prose, multipl-y embedded, like W G Sebald, Modiano, Per Petterson. I'd tell it like it is, like Ernaux. I'd knock people over like Beckett; soothe like Tove Jansson; counsel, insightful, brave, and strong, like Maya Angelou; go dark-deep melancholy desperate beautiful like Plath. I'd meditate poetically like Toni Morrison, tantalise and annoy like Gertrude Stein. Like Clara, I'm never certain how well I get on with Stein; perhaps I see her more as a pivot, a queen bee, choreographing minions. I'd lead myself astray like Malte Laurids Brigge, or Anne in *Astragale*. I'd be capable of cruel shocking things, like those twins in Agota Kristof.

Or I'd just be plain engaging, like Patti Smith. I don't know if with her it's the actual prose or the fact that she's famous and well-loved already, and/or is it the kind of art/life she stands for, but when you read her (I'm thinking of M-Train) it feels like you're hanging out with her and I'd like my words to do that, or some of them.

That's Patti Smith, not you, László chips in. *How about just be yourself.*

My dad said the same when I was a kid. *To thine own self be true*, he wrote it in the front of my Bible, lest I forgot. I didn't get the 'thine' thing then but I do now and I still have the Bible lest I ever do forget.

I was watching David Lynch on You-Tube, it was a masterclass for film students but I watched it anyway because I thought Sadie might get into film at some point (she hasn't yet). Be true to yourself, Lynch said, convincingly. Find your own voice. Be true to the ideas that come to you. Don't walk away until you have it correct.

15

Hi.

Agnès here

OK, so, I've started on the book and I've changed my name to Agnès. I'm not yet sure what my surname will be. I wonder whether I'll need one. I know it's the usual way of things, to have two names, a first name and a last name, but I can't think of any reason other than custom or habit why two names have to be the thing. I did know someone who had a name and a number, but he was unusual. My friend's grandmother said there's no dignity in numbers, she said any fixed identity can be dangerous and she hates tattoos.

I had to buy a ream of paper for the book. It was heavy and I wasn't feeling up to much that day but I managed to lug it back from the shop on the Boulevard to the apartment. Then when I got home I noticed they'd overcharged me. I didn't go back. Even though I am making every cent count at the moment, I didn't go back. I can't stand the burden of going back which is not something I want to tell people. Besides, any day now my cards could cease to function and it would be just my luck if I went back and the ceasing-to-function was, unbeknown-to-me, already underway. I don't know how their functioning system works in banks or how their pricing system works in Office Depot so I just gave up and decided not to think about it or anything related. In the apartment I put the paper on the shelf then moved it to a different shelf. Nothing is as it's meant to be at the moment. It could have been me who mis-read or mis-remembered the price it said on the shelf, like maybe I'd been overtaken by wishful thinking, I mean if your perception can be altered by dread or trauma or curses or spells, why not by wishful thinking.

Someone, I thought she was a friend—well a sort-of friend—she got exasperated with me in a writing group and it's been praying on my mind. I joined a writing group to help me get on with the book. I found it on that #Meetup app. It meets in the Café de la Rotonde in Montparnasse on Wednesdays for three hours. This person in question had already got a bit upset at the beginning when one of the guys corrected her and said Hemingway and Scott Fitzgerald more often went to the Dôme and not the Rotonde, then when I read my piece out for the crit she was already fired up and she said I was being philosophical and it wasn't fiction and wasn't this supposed to be a fiction group.

Only she didn't say it like that, calmly and measured, the words didn't come out smooth and neutral and interested or even purely observational. No. She spat out the words like someone had forced her to have oral sex. Her face was pulled into this grimace and her eyes were weird like staring but kind-of absent. It was like my being philosophical (in her judgement) had offended her.

Then I made the mistake of using the word 'representation' in seeking to explain/defend myself and she didn't like that even more. I was talking about the closure of the refugee camp near Calais where I had been in real life with work and which happened to be the current subject of an expo in the basement at Beaubourg; for her that wasn't a suitable subject for fiction and, correct her if she's wrong, but this isn't supposed to be a memoir group either. She was livid, she actually did go grey.

I didn't know what to say. I just looked at her but it was like she wasn't there any more, there was something sad and ugly had taken her place and I felt hurt and annoyed to be judged and to have my work judged and dismissed from some standpoint I didn't recognise, and I started to think her hairstyle was no good and I almost thought bad things about her clothes and her shoes but I stopped myself because thinking like that made me mean and not like myself and I already have problems with that without adding on any more but all the same her whole persona altered before my eyes when I heard her say what she said.

Actually, I felt acutely vulnerable and I remembered reading somewhere that the criticisms that hurt most are the ones we already secretly believe about o   urselves.

I didn't know what to say so I didn't say anything or I don't think I did, but when you have trauma like that your mind goes a blank and so can your memory so I can't tell you how anything or what happened after and it made me wish I'd said to her well what's fiction anyway, hats off to you good lady if you can define it, and I could have thrown in a few quotes if I'd been able to remember any. And later again after I got back to my apartment and I went to lie down for a bit I had to ask myself: was that real or not or did I misperceive and misremember and did the world itself shift. I don't know the answer.

I do know one thing and that is I've changed my name, I'm Agnès now and my surname is going to be Grey.

I'll give the philosophical Calais piece to Sadie or Sadie via László because they have no problem with representation, well Sadie does, but she comes at it in a different way.

16

Most often you cross at the Pont Neuf where the river divides into two or narrows and closes two into one depending on which way you're assessing. It's hard to tell the direction of flow from your current personal angle.

You focus instead on the turbulent wakes of the *bateaux mouches, les batobus*. One after the other, the other, they approach the bridge and the trippers look up and some are waving, then they go under, disappearing under.

You stand and you wait and you waiver, hoping to see if there's some kind of flow to follow, some kind of sign to indicate where you are headed, this time or next time or any time or if you are coming this way or that way or your own way or outward or inward or which direction.

Ton propre chemin.

Christmas things are stacking up already in the big BHV store. You gaze west down the length of the rue de Rivoli, see all the people walking home and away, see La Défense looming up through where the mist is rising.

We could all say something new or different.

Or we could be like that old man there, dressed in tatters ingrained with dirt, his feet tipping out of his shoes; but look at him intently cleaning and cleaning round the edge of that rubbish bin with some grubby napkin.

*There but for the…*László says.

Sadie must be hearing things; there's no sign of László.

17

Along the Quai de Gesvres, three gendarmes in waterproofs, the sound of their horses' hooves on tarmac. The sight of the crumpled lady in spent rubber boots who steps out into the road without looking, crosses at the wrong time, the wrong place, who goes diagonal by the Hôtel de Ville; cars pull up quick but nobody hoots. The lady hobbles towards the Carousel which is not yet lit up, not yet playing its candy music.

Now the old man, wrapped in torn plastic, his feet bound up with cloths, he's bent double, he's dragging two overloaded supermarket trolleys tied in convoy but each is straining to go its own way. He stops to feed the pigeons; he has bags of seeds and broken bread and crumbs. A crowd of birds swoops and lands and masses around his feet, pecking about and strutting and making noises.

Les jeunes filles voyagent insouciantes en trottinette sur la rue du Renard; elles parlent, elles rient, elles regardent leurs portables.

The terrible queues hungry for the Pompidou Centre are taking shape as Sadie passes, a human snake ravaging two whole streets, no kidding.

A small blue tent is pitched at the door of the disused barred-up BNP Paribas, a pair of trainers neat by the zipped-up door.

They travel in pairs, the dark blue guards with their truncheons who patrol Paris on behalf of the *Mairies*. László can't stand them. He'll not go anywhere near them. Clara says he's paranoid when Sadie mentions it, but what does Clara know. Sadie can't bring herself to eye them suspiciously. On the contrary, and against her better judgement, they make her feel safe.

László told her she's an idiot, a blind stupid idiot, she should open her eyes. *Remember Sangatte*, he says.

Sadie shrugs. Sangatte was different.

Sadie crosses the rue du Grenier St Lazare and walks on through the Quartier de l'Horloge. She arrives at her café Unicorners on time and all is good. Adriana welcomes her as she comes in the door. Adriana comes from Romania. She tells Sadie she misses home, that she's saving up to make a visit, that Sadie is her favourite artist-customer. She hands Sadie a coffee. Adriana remembers Sadie likes to take oat-milk.

She'd invited Sadie to hang one of her little Paris collages on the wall in the café, but Sadie is stalling, she keeps thinking she'll wait until she can offer something better, something that contains more of herself. Adriana has told Sadie so many stories of her life before Paris. Sadie wants to reciprocate but she also wants to wait. Sadie's stories are all half-formed.

Adriana and Sadie would like to be friends but neither knows how to. Today it occurs to Sadie that perhaps they already are.

She takes off her coat and opens her laptop. When the coast's clear she'll ask if anyone's heard from László.

18

Zuniga it turns out is all but AWOL and Clara is sorry and not sorry. At least she still has Sadie and the other therapy clients. They need her. Sadie won't leave. Clara will keep going. But she's faltering on Z. Clara can't afford to be faltering. Zuniga is why she's here. He's supposed to be her life.

Clara needs more time to get to grips with biographical method, really get a handle on what she is doing before she starts on the actual *magnum opus*. She's determined to do the great man justice. Best not go diving in too soon.

Plus, there are issues.

Problems, corrects László. He can't stand how Clara uses words to sidestep other words, to corral ideas and cajole herself into corners, how she sets up all this re-framing which piles denial upon denial. *Problems*, he repeats, *Problems*, he says it louder.

Clara hears him but she refuses to call problems *problems*. Concerns. Issues. Challenges. What it means to write a life. What it means to know another person, let alone one who died in 1939 and whom you never met whilst they were living and whose archive she has discovered is all but empty and that latter is the biggest, the main actual problem that she's facing—OK it is a *problem*—the looming possibility that she will find no material about Zuniga's life that she can work on…

Work with, corrects László.

Before she came to Paris, Clara's researches at the British Library had suggested she'd find what she wanted—chiefly Zuniga's papers on the Creative Process—in the Archives Nationales in Paris. But the Zuniga file—which turned out to be just a tatty-looking box—when they finally located it, there was very little in it, and nothing at all about his work on Creativity. The librarian was *très gentille* and had directed Clara to the Bibliothèque Nationale where she did find two manuscripts, but neither was annotated, and neither had anything to do with Zuniga's theory of Creativity. No letters, no notebooks, nothing personal.

Clara had been pointed some time ago in the direction of La Galcante, a private *librairie de la presse ancienne* in the rue de L'Arbre Sec but she hasn't yet followed that up, primarily because of its location in the very street where Sadie lives. It would be just Clara's luck to bump into Sadie in Sadie's own *quartier*. That would be awkward. Ever mindful of preserving the therapeutic transference—which already with Sadie is fragile and unpredictable—there'd been an embarassing moment the other day when Sadie had called her Sara, that being the name of Sadie's long-dead mother. The most awful aspect was that Clara hadn't noticed straight away but had only realised the slip when Sadie stumbled and backtracked on what she'd said and apologised profusely. So, for good reason, Clara has so far steered clear of La Galcante, telling herself that a press archive wouldn't have anything on Zuniga anyway.

When she'd first had the idea for the Zuniga biography—which was a while before she'd decided to leave London—Clara had a vision of herself living high up in a tiny garret in the *quartier Latin*, occasionally dining in the same little brasserie where the likes of Hemingway ate. She saw herself seated at her little writing table working late into the night, her darkened room illuminated only by the single halo from an angle-poise lamp while the lights of Paris flickered on the street below. This image—a dream, a fantasy—had sustained her through the turbulent times that inevitably lay ahead.

It had given her something to cling on to as, gradually, she realised she was preparing to take a step into the dark.

She'd told herself how a biography was really only an oversize Case Study—longer, obviously, but essentially not that different, and psychotherapist Clara was of course already expert in that genre. And the decision to relocate to Paris she saw would easily satisfy the need for her to 'displace' herself which Zuniga himself identified as so central to the creative process. According to his theory, external displacements (in Clara's case, London to Paris) facilitate internal dislocations in the psyche of the individual artist that are crucial for activating creative energy. Clara had straight away seen parallels between Zuniga's idea of 'displacement,' his emphasis on the transformation of trauma into art, and the psychological idea of a 'self-in-exile' with which, as a modern-day psychotherapist, she was familiar. She'd determined excitedly to pursue all possible avenues to explore the linkages.

But Clara wasn't long in Paris before László showed up and started questioning what she meant by everything… 'trauma,' for example,—no two traumas were alike, surely—and he was objecting to her invoking the concept of 'exile' in this context. Clara didn't share László's misgivings but she was trying to respect them and, so far, she had retained a commitment to Zuniga's idea of 'displacement' while not being fully satisfied with it. 'Exile,' she admitted, had an extra dimension, a dimension of exclusion, and Clara felt something like it was needed to bring Zuniga's theory more into line with her own thinking. Privately, she continued to think 'exile;' László is too picky about words, and that's just him.

The notion of a 'self-in-exile' has an appeal to Clara yet it also has a repellent quality—a displaced internal self could be too close to the psychiatric configuration of the 'schizoid' personality, or more generally of dissociative states ... There's a thin line. And increasingly her work with Sadie has highlighted the many doubts she'd had about the limitations of psychiatric diagnoses—Creative is not necessarily schizoid, and dissociation is not necessarily pathological. László is right, words do matter. They have consequences. Names name. They categorise. These are obstacles Clara must negotiate if she is to write the book that will rescue Zuniga and salvage his theory from the rubbish heap, make it relevant for the present day. Thinking on many things has changed since Z's time.

19

Of course, all this 'being true to yourself' malarkey that Sadie's been grappling with begs the obvious question as to who you are and who and what is that 'self' to which you're trying to be true... It tends to be the main area where Clara's clients—creatives or otherwise—get messed up. Now Clara finds herself facing similar issues: an *étrangère* in Paris, a recently-singled woman, a would-be biographer, a biographer with no materials to work on, a writer with no writing to her name.

Stranded in the in-between, László offers.

Becoming a writer, Clara finds, is a tough transition. It involves a fundamental shift in identity, something she hadn't fully thought through. Then add on the issue of being True. And add on again when it's not just Clara's own self that remains elusive, her own life in limbo, but Zuniga's too: creating a life, a person on a page, it's all a bit daunting.

Clara had accessed Zuniga's actual published works, now long out of print, but she has piles of photocopies and transcripts from microfiches via the British Library. She'd studied *Trauma and Creativity* in detail, and read the others and his published papers more than once. She'd believed that if she could immerse herself sufficiently deeply in the work, she would penetrate through to the core of it and, from there, to the heart of the man. But nothing of the sort has happened. Instead, she's found blind alleys, ambiguities, contradictions, snippets that lead nowhere, nonsensical fragments. And worst of all, nothing at all of relevance in the Zuniga archive.

Freud himself was, of course, sceptical about biography, about even the possibility of biography, almost contemptuous. His starting point was the volcanic nature of the unconscious, that what is fundamental about the psyche remains inaccessible to the conscious mind, ever carefully guarded. Even prominent memories Freud saw not as directly reflecting experience, but as concealing it, as 'screens' block access to the rest of a room. Yet Freud had written Case Studies, regarded by some as important works of literature in their own right. Still, any writer of case studies would have access to a range of materials with which to weave their tales.

They wouldn't be trying to weave a story with so little to go on.

That is the territory of the novelist, Clara.

Clara looks once again through the photos she took on her phone in the Zuniga archive: just scraps, torn pieces of paper, pages ripped out of notebooks, fragments of photographs, scribbled faded and illegible notes, rusting paperclips, a couple of buttons off an old coat—apparently all that remains of the man.

20

Clara is no longer sure what it was about Zuniga that had pulled her towards him so quickly, what compelled her to want to know what lay at the secret heart or hearts of the man. There's a possessive aspect to any need to know, perhaps also a jealous edge, she's aware of that, but Clara had felt an immediate connection with Zuniga's work on creativity and a strange empathy for this unknown person.

Later again she felt for Zuniga the excluded, the victim; how easy to fall from favour in closed circles, how easy to become Other, outsider, *étranger*. Exile. A self-in-exile. Regardless of what László says, Clara is sticking with the view that Zuniga was obliged to inhabit a kind of Exile.

Clara presses the palm of her hand to her breastbone (a gesture Sadie often uses) as she thinks about what Zuniga must have gone through, cast out by the Father, ejected from the psychoanalytic 'family', his career in ruins. And by association, how all people carry within them the loss, the wound, the pain of abandonment that results from being cast out from the maternal body at the moment of birth. Zuniga's expulsion from the Society—from the maternal body of his professional organisation—must have reactivated that primal trauma. Clara has to remind herself to breathe as she tries to piece together the bits of history, as she seeks to impose some narrative form upon this unfortunate man's life that might help it make sense.

What lay behind his expulsion from the Society? Had it been the mere expression of his autonomy—him being true to himself, for instance—or was it theoretical differences, as with Jung's, that lay behind the clash with Freud, Zuniga's erasure from the record, his dismissal from history? There must have been deeper dynamics, surely; Zuniga's expulsion would link to other stories around the guarded boundaries of the Founding Father—the will to power, for example, Oedipal or sibling rivalries, sparring masculinities, and all set against the social/ political background of the rising tide of fascism in Europe. Yes, the political context would have had an impact, could at the very least have generated a struggle to gain control of the narrative. But even so, for there to be such a decisive rift in such a close relationship, and for history to be so complicit around the fact of erasure…it was puzzling.

The stuff of life, of history, László says.

Yet Zuniga had managed to transform the trauma of it all and gone on to write his theory and to position displacement at the core of creativity. The man deserved to be rescued from oblivion for this act and this act alone. An image of Sadie talking about her little collages of Paris flashes into Clara's mind and a quick visceral feeling of regret sinks inside her; the time Sadie brought her tentative works to the session—the first and only things that evidenced Sadie's creative spark since she came to Paris and Clara hadn't even asked to look at them.

PART 2

I am in an acute crisis about my work... and have already decided that I not merely can't but won't go on as I have been going on more or less ever since the 'Textes Pour Rien' and I must either get back to nothing again and the bottom of all the hills again like before Molloy or else call it a day...

Samuel Beckett, letter to Barbara Bray, 1958

21

Les Dormeurs 1

I go with Sadie to the expo Sébastien Lifshitz, *Inventaire Infini*, at the Beaubourg, wanting to investigate further her ambivalent interest in photography and to think further about what it is to be displaced into sleep and why she and I are often so afraid. Clara too knows what it is to be terrified of sleep.

In the photographs I see the babies and I wonder whether they are dead. And whether it is whether or if it is if, or if they are dead. Why are you in a photograph, baby, laying there alone with your eyes closed, as if you were dead?

You've thrown up your arms thrown open your palms you've splayed your legs at angles, all of which makes me wonder if you are dead.

Baby baby I know I know, beyond the crumpled edges of these stained old pictures, you undoubtedly now are dead.

Now here are some older folk, perhaps also dead. Lying in postures in pictures anonymous, folded, deftly naked in cases and, as with the babies, undoubtedly now dead.

Pictures taken through windows, through glass, through lenses; moving images clip purple sleepers, dreamers who have died or are dying in train carriages buses cars and look at them slumped up against windows and mirrors and up against each other tangles of people in transportations tangled up piled up like exiles like the refugees who died in that refrigerated lorry. People die of history in monstrous piles monstrous, pile upon pile of people they dig up mass graves in war zones they count the skulls the skulls the skulls piled up from greed the greed that makes people not matter. Now in some snaps we have holiday people who lie sleeping or dead, on deck chairs hotel beds on grass in sunshine on picnics, bodies spread-eagled with trust. And on the last wall of the gallery a nameless child is sleeping.

22

Les Dormeurs 2

The sleeper is under the watchful eye of the photographer and later is subject to the voyeurism of the viewer in an ever-available tale or tail like that of a serpent that coils round and round and is swallowed by its own mouth.

The subject no longer a subject but an object, a passive presence rendered vulnerable, deprived of agency and free will, a reified commodity sans everything; flesh pared away to the negative, scraped to the bone, an X-ray, the world inside out.

This is not a person. This is not a portrait. The photographs are images

are pictures that portray asymmetrical relationships

between those with some kind of power and those with none

as such they could render their subjects objects, slaves—captured frozen, *sans* everything, portrayed for the gaze.

Pictures can be exchanged for currency as slaves can. They can be considered as currency in and of themselves. They can generate value and more value as slaves can. They cannot rise up and away as slaves can and did and do and would again and should.

These pictures are objects that have value and the value derives in part from the unconscious shared skill of the sleeper as half-subject half-object and both and neither and possibly either way dead and in any event stolen, robbed.

We leave the gallery space in silence. We don't speak, Sadie and me. I leave her by the gaping blue throats of the Beaubourg on the *Piazza* and carry myself towards the Tuileries. On the way I stop and look in the window of the *traiteur* where Sadie buys her *gougères*. I see them piled up high and light like yellow-grey storm-clouds-in-waiting and I keep on walking.

In the Tuileries I am aiming to see the Louise Bourgeois hands, bronzed, in twos, threes, fours, with wrists holding, hands clasped together. Some of these hands she modelled from her own and those of her long-time helper, Jerry Gorovoy. The hands clasp their friendship, their struggles, transformed into art, their mutual dependence, their affection, embodied for ever, on show in public places shared out there for all people to share. Here it is. On the last plinth, alone and apart, the single small hand of a child.

I need to decide whether I should mention to Sadie about these hands. Or Clara. László will tell me it's not my business to tell him or them anything, they should be telling me and, anyway, he says, they already know about that infant's hand.

23

Clara is heading down the rue des Écoles on her way to the philosophy lecture on *Déplacement* by a visiting Professor from Norway. She's excited to see whether any of his thinking echoes or parallels her own, whether he'll make the connections she—via Zuniga—has done with creativity. Perhaps Zuniga will get a mention. Clara waits until she has walked past the statue of Montaigne before she crosses the street; she has to touch the shiny toe of his shoe before she crosses, it's a superstition, a thing people do to bring good luck. She closes her eyes and repeats *Zuniga Zuniga Zuniga* as she lays her bare hand on the great philosopher's cold bronze foot.

The Collège de France is a wonderful place, with free weekly lectures open to all. Clara will get there early as there are always queues. The *bibliothèque* houses all the works and many of the manuscripts of people who've been Professors there—renowned thinkers—like Barthes, Foucault, Yves Bonnefoy. Clara had hurried along there when she first got to Paris, believing Zuniga, though never a full Professor at the Collège,

had at one time been some kind of visiting scholar...
It turned out they did have some of his works on their
shelves, Clara was welcome to consult them, but when
the librarian checked the archive boxes in the reserve
she found nothing at all among the Zs. Kindly she had
offered to fetch Lacan as Clara was interested in psychoanalysis, there were a few Freud papers too, the librarian said, Clara was welcome to search among those...

But Clara declined. It was only Max Zuniga she wanted.
The lecture on *Déplacement* began promisingly enough
with a quote from 1950s *enfant terrible* Jean-Michel
Mension which appeared on a big Powerpoint screen—
the speaker read it aloud in English with an accent that,
with a jolt, reminded Clara of Johannes—*Journeys de-
form us*, he said, *which is good*. Clara jotted the phrase
down. It made her think of Louise Bourgeois and her
do, undo, redo. And about something Sadie had said
last week, about the need to reset herself after Sangatte, how she'd come to Paris for that purpose. The
Professor went on to talk about being in France, having
temporarily left his home in Norway, he was trying to
analyse, linguistically, the feeling of *dépaysement* he was
experiencing, a concept, he said, fully comprehensible
in the French language, but elusive in both English and
Norwegian. Clara remembered conversations with Johannes, when they were living in London, as she tried
to discover something of Johannes' experience, something beyond 'home-sickness'—*hjemlengsel*. Johannes
had talked about *utvisning*, but as far as Clara could tell
that did not mean the same thing at all, it was closer
she thought to 'expulsion,' to the kind of 'exile' László
talked about, the word he forbade her to use.

But in the end, to Clara's disappointment, the talk turned out to be not about geographical or psychical displacement, but more about 'displacement activity,' a subject Clara knew only too well, and it was too close for comfort. She'd found it impossible to maintain attention, had made hardly any notes, and left before the questions started.

24

After the lecture Clara felt low in spirits, and she began to realise how she'd been hiding this knowledge from herself, exactly the way many of her clients did. It had been difficult listening to that Norwegian voice. It had taken her to a place she didn't want to go.

She decided to walk back to her *atelier* on the rue Le Goff, but before even reaching the Boulevard her weariness weighed heavy, heavy like the sky was heavy, and grey, and dismal; the weather not conducive to enjoying a walk, or enjoying much at all. Clara's apparent dismissal of Sadie's collages niggled at her conscience. She should have asked to see them, at least asked something about them, what they meant to Sadie, how she'd felt making them. Something. Anything.

Clara stops at a café near the Sorbonne and takes a seat outside under the awning. It is cold but she prefers to stay out than to go inside which she knows will be cramped and overheated. The grumpy waiter is on, the officious one, he'll take ages to serve her because that is his way.

She thumbs through her notebook while she waits for the waiter. The notes in her journal are all about either Zuniga or Johannes, there's little else. It surprises her now to see how often she's drafted letters to Johannes, letters she would never finish let alone send, how her handwriting begins so neat and legible and deteriorates into a desperate unreadable scrawl. In places her pen has pierced the page.

Clara is gripped by the idea to call Johannes in Oslo. Suddenly she wants to share with him her little story of how foolish she's been, how naïvely she'd understood the French, how long it had taken to dawn on her what the lecture was really about… He'd laugh about that. He'd say, *Oh Clara, Clara*, and laugh some more at the foolish mistakes she makes. He'd be interested to hear something about the speaker, being a compatriot. Clara rummages for her phone in her bag, but the belligerent waiter arrives just as she puts her hand on it.

The waiter offers her a menu, a crumpled sheet of photocopied paper. Clara orders *un café allongé* but, a moment later, just as the waiter is moving on to the people at the next table, she changes her mind. *Non*, she says, *non, pas de café, plutôt un rosé, une demi-carafe de rosé*. He is on the point of leaving a second time when she adds an *omelette fines herbes* to her order. *Avec une petite salade verte*, she adds, after another short hesitation. *Merci monsieur*. The waiter turns brusquely and goes back inside. Clara recognises her own passive-aggressive impulse. She can tell he's going to bring her the expensive wine and/or otherwise overcharge her.

But at least Clara's minor aggressions towards the

waiter have released her to think a bit straighter and to decide it is not wise after all to contact Johannes. Not wise. Not now. Not ever.

She and Johannes, they'd been on entirely the wrong footing from the start, that's how it was and that was that, it was never going to work, there was no going back. She puts her phone back in her bag, zips it into the inside pocket to help her resist any new temptation to backtrack.

The waiter brings the *carafe* and a small glass. He lays down the cutlery swaddled in a paper napkin, and a small basket of bread. After he leaves Clara looks at the *addition* which he's tucked under the coaster. Yes, it is too much, but she'll let it rest. She has to practically shred the paper napkin to free the knife and fork.

25

I find myself sitting behind myself on the 63 bus, thirty-odd years suddenly gone. We stop at the lights at the Grand Palais where the new Miró is on. To my left the Eiffel Tower and, in front of me, there I am, beside myself.

Time reels in as the bus crosses the Seine with its barges and houseboats all lined up along the edge and in places three-deep and some with cars on board and every one different and it's all making me think the Styx the Styx and I don't know what she is thinking but at her age it would have been the Rubicon surely and not the Styx or I hope not.

The bus stops at Alma-Marceau and two people get off. I'd thought they were together but they're not and they go in two ways and I think of us as children cutting worms in half, each bit wriggling off in a different direction and I think of Robert Frost and his two roads diverging in the yellow wood and how she took the path less travelled by and why the wood was yellow. Then there's that stopping by woods in the snow, and the pony shakes the bells on its harness and you have to remind yourself to breathe.

I remember a dream from long ago: a baby is born and me pulling off my own head and then there I am trying and straining to sprout a new one by sheer force of will.

Now a sculpture by Louise Bourgeois I saw in Perth in Scotland, it must have been five years ago, the same day I saw her panel of hands (*10am is when you come to me*) on the wall as I came in the door and I did that shift thing when something takes you away from where you are and hell, it can be so hard to get back when you slip to that place where there's nothing, nothing between you and the universe.

The sculpture, *Cell XIV (Portrait)*, was made in 2000 when the artist was 80 years old. I want to be making art when I am 80 years old if ever I make it that far. The red, three-headed fabric sculpture, the blurb indicates, may represent different aspects of an individual, the multiplicities of human nature. The metal cage around it could be either haven or prison. That blurb doesn't go far enough so I rewrite it in my own three heads each taking a turn for starting up words that go round and round like the kookaburra song we sang in the Girl Guide camp and ate hot dogs.

Hysterical was made the following year, a naked upright female figure in pink towel-like fabric, prominent breasts, no arms, but she too has three heads, so talk about triplicitous, talk about reproducing yourself, talk about being split into bits beyond ambivalence; I ask you I ask you I ask you

Looking out now through the grimy window of the bus she and me we see plastic red and white latticed chairs lined neatly along the café terrace that goes on round the corner but it's early yet and no-one is there only us looking through and out at the empty waiting tables.

The bus turns left where the sign says Trocadéro and then we're passing a street market, a long long one with stall after stall of fish and meat and shoes and apples and cashmere. Then Iéna, that's our stop.

We get off the bus myself and I and I almost stay on because I am young enough and vain or old enough to want to hang onto something to make it last, young or old enough to want to keep watching myself in the window reflect or disappear but I step down in time and she steps up and we choose our paths and there we are each of us both of us beside ourselves and walking through Friday morning Paris.

I dictate some notes for Clara to make in the Z book, but I can see she's in a muddle, trying to keep things separate, trying to tease out this from that, no longer sure which page she's on. I donate her a splitting headache and leave it at that.

26

Clara wakes abruptly from a disturbed sleep. She reaches over to look at her clock. 4am. She's been dreaming about Johannes. Or was it Zuniga. Both. Neither. Some kind of shapeshifter bringing the two together, merging the two into one, like in *Persona*. Clara's insides tighten. Her notebook journal is on her bedside table. She switches on the lamp. Dreams are significant. Lately she hasn't been remembering any which she takes as a bad sign. She'll try to write this one down before it slips away.

Pursuing this Johannes/Zuniga person, in and out of dark empty rooms, some kind of derelict mansion—like in *Le Grand Meaulnes*—detritus and decay, old newspapers blowing as though in the wind, feels like some kind of hell and inescapable as. She's pursuing him/him from room to room, rooms all adjoining, dark, no light, smell of dark and mould. Then stumbling down some stairs, down and down, spiral stone staircase, walled in on both sides, like in a castle, circling down and down, Clara following, close behind, keeps catching sight of the tails of his coat—the coat could be anyone's or empty, the disappearing tails as the coat rounds bend after bend still going down... is it László, something's telling her it's László... Alone now, in a long dark gallery, windowless, a large mirror at the far end, mirror instead of a door, suddenly it's not a barrier, Clara's going right through it, the Clara in the mirror is reaching out its arms and pulling her into it and it folds itself closed behind her…

Clara takes a deep breath, puts her pen down.

Sadie won't be there until one o'clock; Clara decides to take the morning off, see if she can work through some of this agitation the dream has caused. She gets up, grinds the beans, sets the coffee pot on the stove, puts the oat-milk on to warm. She rolls up the blinds. Clara needs her morning ritual. Coffee, shower, breakfast, so much comfort in ritual, take refuge in the known. By 1pm she'll be back in charge and ready for Sadie. It's a while since she's felt like this. She'll go out and walk, get some fresh air.

Zuniga. Johannes. There's nothing even similar about them.

27

La Palette in the rue de Seine, almost at the river, is a lovely old café with large mirrors and paintings all around the walls, tomettes on the floor, varnished wood fixtures, live green plants. It's one of Clara's favourites and as she takes her seat at the far side she tells herself she is special and lucky to be here and she's checking off ticks in the positives list and being in the present. But even before her coffee and *pain au chocolat* arrive, the acute sense of disquiet from the dream comes back. The mirrors on the walls recall the *Orphée* underworld and Clara can't look at her multiple reflections. She'll go and sit outside on the terrace. She realises with some alarm that her preoccupation with Zuniga is tipping into an obsession. She's been thinking of little else. On the basis of nothing. Going round and round. And getting nowhere but back to the same place. Her heart thumps irregularly. Trapped. Like the sculptures in the cages.

The dream has shunted Zuniga into some new place. Johannes too. Now they're on horseback dragging Clara along behind them.

Oh Clara.

She'd thought she'd be a writer, a biographer, an independent scholar, autonomous, creative, committed… but probably she's ending up an obsessive loner.

An obsession is a cover for something, a pointer, a displacement. For a moment she wonders if this thought is just the result of that lecture she went to at the Collège, but she knows better than to explain such things away.

When her food arrives, she picks only at the edges.

Beside yourself, Clara. Isn't that what you wanted, déplacement?

She thinks back across the history of her interest in Zuniga—had it not started at the same time as her relationship with Johannes… in fact hadn't it been Johannes who introduced her to Z's work on creativity… the area of therapy she might specialise in… so many creative people get blocks… Johannes had happened across Zuniga in connection with a glass sculpture he was making, Zuniga's point being that the idea of mind, ever since Freud, had a sculptural quality, that sculpture was needed to express the nature of the beast... Yes, that's where Z had come in, it was where Johannes' artistic practice met her own as a psychotherapist... both engaged in mapping the spaces of the mind.

But then Zuniga became an issue when Clara and Johannes decided, some three years on, they'd have to go their separate ways. It wasn't what either of them wanted, but both agreed it was for the best, the only option, really.

The waiter arrives with the silver coffee pot, ready to refill Clara's cup but she hasn't touched the first one yet. She looks up at him, unable for a moment to make any sense of who he is or what he's doing hovering over her like that... He asks her if there is anything she would like him to bring. Clara shakes her head in a daze. The waiter turns to go and she's tempted to cancel Sadie's session altogether. She takes her phone out of her bag, then puts it back, ambivalent about everything. She puts a 10Euro note on the table and leaves the café, her coffee still untouched.

Clara walks up the Boulevard towards the Luxembourg gardens. Johannes had been packing up ready to go back to Oslo, boxing his books ready for shipping and there'd been an altercation about which of them owned the Zuniga *Trauma and Creativity*. They each of them had held, one onto either end of it, like two desperate kids. Johannes hadn't given way to Clara the way he usually did; this time he'd stood his ground and wouldn't let go and Clara had held on too even while she saw the utter ridiculousness of it. In the end Clara was the one to exercise the judgement of Solomon and let go before the book was ripped in two. Johannes took the book, wiped off the side where her hand had been, and zipped it into his case. She knew he'd never read it, not once she was gone from his life. And at that point Zuniga had changed from being an interest to a focus, a life-changing passion for Clara. A life.

Reading the book wasn't the issue though. There had been endless discussions with J. about transference and countertransference, and the precise meanings that Zuniga could have attached to the concepts, meanings that, as Johannes saw it, were very different back in the day and, in any case, were apt to slip and slide and could never be pinned down. As the weeks went by, and the day of separation grew nearer, the discussions became more heated leaving them both numb and exhausted.

It was at that point that Zuniga came to embody both Clara's big mistake—her doomed-to-failure relationship—as well as her possible means of self-repair for the future. She and Johannes went their separate ways—Clara to the archive in Paris to rescue Zuniga, Johannes back to his family in Oslo. It had been the putting into practice of a clear mutual agreement. Now an image flashes into Clara's mind: Passengers inadvertently swopping luggage on a station platform. How utterly disturbing to end up with someone else's baggage believing it to be your own.

The day she arrived in Paris, Clara had gone straight to Librairie Galignani on the rue de Rivoli and ordered a new copy of the book in the original French, hardly giving a thought to how much a new—now rare—hardbacked art book would eat into her limited budget and that she'd need considerable help with translation. No matter.

With the purchase, Zuniga morphed from passion, her reason for being in Paris, to her reason for being anywhere at all.

Now, when she arrives at her *atelier* in rue Le Goff, Clara takes the book down from the shelf. A postcard falls out, a Picasso of a woman crying she's been using as a bookmark. She glances at the back of the card, then props it against her lamp. She flicks through the pages she has marked with different coloured Post-Its, all things Zuniga she'd intended to follow up on in the archive. One by one she tears off the Post-Its, crumples them in her palm and throws them in the direction of the waste paper bin.

Clara understands only too well the meaning of the dream. No wonder she's been blocked trying to take the biography forward, blocked in trying to find anything worth having in the archive, blocked in making her fantasies real. Blocked in changing her life. She's been trying to wipe her own internal archive clean, just like someone long ago did with Zuniga. A strange case of repetition compulsion across boundaries and borders.

Shit happens, says László.

Clara lifts up her phone and leaves a message to cancel

Sadie. She lies down on her couch and pulls the mohair blanket up over her shivering body.

Oh, Clara.

28

i open my cupboard and there i am, there i am among all those things of mine, all those small things, objects i've gathered unto myself over all the years; i am there on the shelf in the cupboard of myself, the cupboard i left, which i left behind in the house, the house of myself, when i made my hurried departure.

i return now to open the great doors of memory, to see myself condensed in the mirrors of objects lined up on the shelf, a battalion of small things in clanking armour.

i open the cupboard and i face them now, and they face me, menacing with grimaces and needles, pitchforks and scalpels, wolves and derisions, their clamorous whispers ancient and ordinary, hiss-speak of snakes with forked tongues.

All the mirrored selves we are, storied among the stories.

29

Somewhere high up in the rue de L'Arbre Sec Sadie is sitting in her *petite chambre de bonne* looking out through the skylight across the rooftops of Paris. She likes to be this far up, looking out and over, towards far horizons.

To the south east she sees the coloured plastics of the Pompidou Centre and today she's imagining her work exhibited there. She'd been to the Brancusi Pavilion, she'd wandered along a little corridor she hadn't noticed before and seen some interesting graphic works by another Romanian artist, she'd made a note of his name but now can't find the scrap of paper she'd written it on, she'll have to go back to check. The works reminded her of Vasarely's more graphic ones, lots of colour and geometrical patterns that disturb your vision and invite you to enter new worlds; you could lose yourself in those colours and patterns, you could spin down into the vortex…

Or spiral up, László says.

The images reminded Sadie of the covers Vasarely made for a Gallimard series of psychological texts. She'd seen those exhibited not so long ago in the Pompidou Centre, an impressive set. She'd bought the Melanie Klein. She'd taken it to show Clara. Clara had overlooked the artwork on the cover and instead handed it back and said she wasn't sure she'd recommend Sadie reading Klein; some people found Klein…er…—Clara had searched for the right word—yes, disturbing… disturbing, she'd said, dismissing everything in a single word as she handed the book back. Sadie resolved there and then she was going to keep the book and read it from cover to cover.

Sitting this morning by her skylight Sadie has decided to abandon her foolish little collages; recently she's added a few photographs to her port-folio, a couple of charcoal sketches of Paris buildings, a water-colour abstract inspired by the Bauhaus, just a few fragments, not any good and not much to show for all her time in Paris, but at least they're something.

She dreams all the time of being able to work with freedom and abandon like she used to. She dreams of making something much bigger and better: variable expressions of her time in this city, individual pieces in different media, linked up with bits of text, a scrapbook approach, more dynamic than a single medium, less sedate than a collage. Overlays, she could print onto tracing paper... She's imagining how she could place such works around the walls—such as in that Brancusi corridor—they'd be readable, like a narrative, there'd be threads meandering through, weaving, looping, layers, disjunctures, connections, impossible opposites merging...

... Threads, you can tighten or slacken at will, as in smocking; you can under and over, weft and weave, as in tapestry; cross stitch, tie knots and make tangles so the thing becomes impossible to unravel; make plaits and twisted snakes and tails...

There was a word she'd come across one time, *supervening*, commonly used in mid 19th century medical texts... Sadie thinks of it now, what a good word it is, what a good idea it is, how it suggests all the layers, the palimpsest character of everything... *supervening*... imagine, to capture that in a photograph... the dynamic internal mobility of things, how nothing is static... how things subtend and supervene. Inspirations taking shapes via words.

For the first time since she's been in Paris, Sadie is beginning to see possibilities for new work even if she can't yet make it.

A scrapbook in which the significances of things stuck in at angles are long forgotten, so new meanings become ever possible, new combinations generate new energies...

If only she could get past Sangatte...

Or use it, says László.

Threads. *I do, I undo, I redo.* Louise Bourgeois made sewing work for her; she stitched pieces together, brought old cloth pieces alive with emotion, connected by the threads of trauma; she brought plain old clothes alive, harnessed with stitches the energies of repressed trauma to create works of art, mended the wounds with bandages, strong at the broken bits. Sadie surprises herself, thinking like this. She's starting to sound like Clara Delaney.

And Sangatte. László interrupts her train of thought. *What thread is that, Sadie?*

Sadie's face tightens. She wants to get past Sangatte. She really wants to leave it behind now. It's time to get over it, get over herself, stop dwelling on the past, let it go, move into the future, do something new, something positive.

Stitch some repairs at Sangatte.

Sadie knows she can't just abandon Sangatte. She'd tried that once and it didn't work.

30

Sadie gets up and goes to make herself a cup of tea. She rarely drinks tea but this morning it seems a cup of tea is called for. She makes it in the pot, which she warms first, because her gran swore by it, and because of what Clara tells her about the comforts of ritual.

She's fed-up grappling with her terrible mixed feelings about Sangatte. She's fed up with László keep nagging at her in that self-righteous way of his. She's fed up with Clara not being able to help her put the past behind her so she can get on with her life. Everyone's letting her down. Herself most of all. She can see people thinking—*why can't the girl just snap out of it and get on with living in the now.*

Because. She just can't. Something's got tangled. Something's got strangled. Something's closed up. Part of her's been left behind. She's afraid to even look into the dark place, the far side of the mirror, the other side of the lens.

The cup of tea does not change anything. This week she bought Lapsang Souchong, having read somewhere it was Beckett's preferred blend, dark and smokey. She'd been to see *Endgame* with her Academy year group and everyone was suddenly doing everything Beckett. The students were supposed to come up with ideas for stage sets for a new production but Sadie had found it impossible to think of anything, impossible to extricate herself from the play's inner world enough to be able to think at all; she'd gone to see it a second time—alone this time—to try to work out what exactly it was that was haunting her—Beckett's strange humour made the darkness all the more penetrating, and the characters, how they manifest such resignedness to futility… the very idea we're all struggling forwards to nothing, for nothing… it was acting like a brake on everything.

Sadie had mentioned it to Clara, how she'd been unseated by the play, how she couldn't shake off the feelings of unease. I'm not surprised, Clara had said. In Clara's view, Beckett's genius lay in his uncanny ability to access strange truths about the human condition from what she referred to as a 'schizoid' state of mind; Clara described it as being as if Beckett was able to step outside himself and be beside himself, and it was from that anomalous position that he created some of the greatest works of literature…. Mind you, Clara had added as an afterthought, in real life, what Beckett would have been seeking is the same as you and me, Sadie…. Safety. The self-in-exile is a precarious place, Clara said. It's all there. In Zuniga.

Sadie had come away from the session her unease doubled rather than soothed. It disturbed her to think of the things Clara hadn't said but which were there by implication. Did all creative endeavours take place on that precarious borderline she called 'schizoid'? Many creative people really had ended up losing their sanity. Only last week she'd been reading about Robert Walser who wrote great things but ended up in an asylum. And what about Robert Lowell. So many artists with uncertain mental health. Suicides. Plath. Woolf. So many promising young artists, dead at 27. Basquiat. Hendrix. Most recently Amy Winehouse. Sadie's not yet 27 but she nearly is. Is this why Sadie's blocked? Is compromising sanity the cost of creativity? Does being true to yourself mean turning yourself inside out to find out where the truth of you lies?

After the session, the idea that she wasn't merely suffering the after-effects of the Sangatte trauma, but that there might be something actually, inherently, psychologically, personality-wise, something actually *wrong* with her, *her*, Sadie, she found so disturbing she had to push it away to the very edges of consciousness and make a real effort to keep it from invading her. She had come away from the session seriously pondering whether she and Clara had any future and whether she herself should find something to do other than art. And today it wasn't helping to have László pick pick picking all the while at the edges of her thoughts. There are stories in there. Life. And Death. And Art. Beckett has penetrated, but the stage sets hardly matter. Sadie sits on under the skylight, her second cup of Lapsang Souchong gone cold.

As she gazes out over the misty autumn rooftops of this her chosen city, a revelation is forming in Sadie's mind. It begins from Beckett, and all those things Clara said and didn't say... What Sadie will later come to regard as her *revelation* arrives without forewarning and it arrives slowly but with insistence and an increasing intensity:

Everything, Sadie thinks, as she sits under the skylight, *everything*, she realises, *everything*, she sees with absolute clarity, *everything*, unquestionably, is *Story*.

Everything.

There's nothing outside the story. Nothing. Sadie knows this with certainty, a certainty she has never had about anything before.

The story is everything and everything is the story and it's all inter-connected.

Sadie sits on, trying to absorb these ideas that are transforming the fundamentals of how she sees the world. She feels strange, lost, dislocated, tiny; is this the 'splitting' Clara talks about? Is this the dissociation? Is this the madness taking her over, insanity in action? Is Sadie finally losing her mind?

Sadie, shrinking, smaller, insignificant, yet growing part of this much bigger thing, this way much grander thing, she's shrinking and shrinking and growing huger and huger, until there's nothing, nothing at all between Sadie Sarrazin and the massive infinity of the eternal universe.

Sadie has to remind herself to keep on breathing.

These thoughts materialise out of nothing, they arrive neither from wholly within herself, nor wholly from without; they take shape in some indeterminate boundary-less space in-between, a kind of third space that straddles internal and external, a space that is both, yet neither; it's difficult for Sadie to characterise what's happening any more precisely than that. What she is seeing is the collapsing of the inside/outside dichotomy.

Sadie realises, for all her education, she simply does not have the concepts with which to think about these thoughts that she's just thought.

Story. Stories. Everything.

Sadie calls to mind all the works of art she's seen lately—paintings, sculptures, sketches, photographs, collages, installations; as she sits in her *chambre* her mind scans a whole range of images from museums, books, films, graffiti, African art in tiny galleries on the rue Bonaparte and the rue de Seine, sculptures and statues in the Jardin de Luxembourg, the Tuileries, the black and white photographs in the Comptoir des Canettes… all kinds of art from all over the world, a long procession of images parades through her mind like an invading army; she watches each one as it passes and she sees that every single one, all of them, not just works of literature, but all the images too, all of them, are *Stories*.

31

And now Sadie feels the presence of László as she often does at times like this when her anchors shift, but she can't see him. He'd talked a lot about the stories he'd lived by. He'd said experience was storied even as it was being lived, even before it was laid down as memory in story book—fairy-tale—form… He'd gone further and said a person's very self is a collection of stories that we fashion to fit around ourselves like overcoats… Sadie hadn't understood at the time, but everything he said is all perfectly comprehensible to her now.

No story is innocent, László said, *however neutral it might look.*

Stories. Look at them, with their flimsy jackets, their trendy clothes, the clothes that cover their nakedness and fashion your desires. Stories capture things, they capture people and hold them in confines. They may look innocent, homely, attractive, desirable; but beware, László told her, the bad ones don't arrive marching in Jackboots. They arrive bearing smiles and promises of a better life. Look at them, all cosy and warm, all buttoned up in their overcoats.

László often talked of Gogol's *Overcoat*, the story of a lowly clerk who dreams of a magnificent new overcoat. On receiving an unexpected bonus, he manages to acquire the coat. All does not end well as the coat very soon is stolen. The clerk, unable to secure any official help, is returned to square-one level miseries and humiliations in which state he dies an untimely death. But after his death there are multiple reports of officials having their coats snatched, removed or stolen by a menacing ghostly figure.

Every detail in every story has its own story, László said.

Stories carry baggage, political baggage and cultural and social and historical baggage, family baggage, emotional baggage... And isn't this the reason Sadie can't face Sangatte... because it's part of a story—not just the story of a refugee crisis, exemplifying an ugly global political moment... but *her* story, a deeply personal emotional story, a story she'd prefer not to tell, a story she is not able to face up to, a story she hides from herself, that she'd like to be able to say ended differently but, in all truth, cannot…

The photographs she's stored on the encrypted disc are not just stories; they're storied and they're storied in stories that are too personally painful for Sadie to make into works of art.

Bottom line, concludes László. *Stories arrive with their coats on.*

Sadie's heart is beating fast, like it does when she's afraid, and she is afraid, afraid of what she is up against, not there in the outside world, but inside herself. She takes a deep breath, stands up, walks around her small room, she's pacing now, pacing up and down, trying to keep hold of something, and to let go of something, all at once. Something about stories, about how you can never be sure who the narrator is…

The clanging of the giant bells of St Eustache over by Les Halles interrupts Sadie's reverie. Midday. Sadie feels herself wrenched into the now as if from a deep sleep; she's having difficulty remembering what was on her mind only a few moments ago. She gets to her feet, disoriented, reaches for her coat. She'll go out and buy herself a *gougère fromage* from the *traiteur*, she'll eat it on the hoof, even though she knows proper *Parisiennes* do not eat outside while walking. Maybe she'll sit down under the arches in the Palais Royal.

The Real is real yet, at the same time, it is story.

László has lived through stories of Exile. Now he's exiled

in the stories of Paris. Living out the real exiled story of exile. He's been trying to tell this to Sadie in a way she'd understand, stuck as she is in her own white western story. Her own privileged story.

We all are stuck in story, she says, even you, László.

László shakes his head. *Not stuck*, he says.

You're the photographer, Sadie, László adds. *You're the storyteller. You choose what bits to capture with your dumb appareil.*

32

Not even realising she is skipping lunch Sadie heads to the Pompidou Centre and then straight for the Louise Bourgeois Cell *Precious Liquids* on the fifth floor in the permanent collection. She peers in through each of the doors—there are little ropes that prevent you from walking right inside. It is one of Bourgeois' Cells, this one like a giant barrel only it has straight sides, wood, and outside is inscribed, *art is a Guaranty of Sanity*, with that strange spelling and those misplaced capitals. Sadie wants to believe this. That art guarantees sanity. She so much wants to believe it. It seems so contrary to what Clara's been saying, but Sadie wants to believe it and hold it deep inside where her soul is. Inside the Cell is a metal-framed bed and some glass vials suspended in the air and, in the semi-darkness, and from any possible vantage point, you can see hanging up in there a dark item or items of clothing which may or may not be an overcoat or overcoats.

Lászlo shrugs with that *well, what did you expect* look.

Is Art relevant in troubled times? *That, my friend, depends on the Art and the nature of the Trouble and how well the Coat fits.*

Art. Stories. Overcoats.

According to What? In 1986 the Brooklyn Museum hosted According to What? It was at the height of the first wave of the AIDS crisis and Chinese artist Ai Wei Wei included a framed rubber firefighter's coat with a hole cut in and a condom fixed into the hole in the coat.

Patti Smith tells the story of a favourite overcoat that someone dear had given her. The coat got lost and it was such a bereavement; the dear person who had given it had also passed away. There was mourning, double mourning. Then a while later—months or years—I don't know how much the passage of time matters in this story—Patti comes across a photograph of herself wearing the coat and it is as if the coat had stopped by to say Hi.

Then, later again, she tells about wanting to spend the night in the Rothko Chapel. Having a sudden chill when covered only by her own thin blanket, she opens a cupboard and discovers a thick coat of Rothko's which keeps her warm until morning at which time her cover assumes once again the familiar form of her own thin blanket.

László says to any artist who will listen, you never know who your characters are, inside their overcoats, who they are to you, who they might be to others; the *personnages* resonate in different ways, behave differently in different company. They move out of your hands and into stories you know nothing about. The most important thing is that you have been true to yourself, that you have made work you love and that loves you.

PART 3

art is a Guaranty of Sanity

Louise Bourgeois, Precious Liquids, 1992

33

Is Sadie concerned, in her photography, with capturing or manufacturing essences, Clara would like to know. Or no essences at all? Just images? Can images be essences?

Sadie resents Clara making assumptions. Sadie never thinks *just* images, an image is never *just*, never *only*, in and of itself; it can't ever be, for as soon as there's a viewer, there are messages, telegraphing across the universe.

Nothing is not giving messages is a message often spoken.

Sadie takes photographs; she explains to Clara how she doesn't think in terms of essences. Essences might emerge, she believes, but they're not pre-existing; they're not *essential*, they depend on purpose and angle of vision. And chance, accident, serendipity.

Essences are situated, not essences as such, that's László's take on it.

Sadie likes photographs of photographs, reflections, echoes; she likes the way things reflect back on themselves likes snakes swallowing their tails; and refractions—Paris is so good for refractions, seeing through layer upon layer of glass, shift your viewpoint and you see something different, how the shadows shift and the colours change and shapes lose their outlines; and the way mirrors reverse things or make things up or make things have holes in when the silver is scratched off the back. She remembers as a child the discovery that the magic of a mirror is in the silver painted on the back, if you scratch that off, all you're left with is murky-looking glass.

Paris is a palimpsest, traces of layers from times ago remain despite repeated attempts at erasure... Sadie tells Clara of places in the city she's passed where there are holes in the walls, places commemorated by plaques for members of the *Résistance* shot on those spots during the Occupation... No, she's never tried to take photographs of those, she probably wouldn't ever.

The problem with being true to yourself, Sadie says to Clara, is what if there is no self to be true to... or what if there's more than one... how to address that person in the mirror... that alien, is it even a person?

Clara indicates with a slight movement of her head that Sadie should carry on.

Sometimes... often... Sadie stumbles through her words... sometimes I don't know where to find myself, I don't know where I stand... Then you tell me to be true to myself, and László as well, he's always saying to stop running away from myself...and... László says... and...

And? says Clara, a slight sharp edge to her voice, just what does László say?

... and László says selves are just stories anyway... so how can you be true to a story... how can a story be true to itself... And I don't want to end up, what was that word you said, schizoid...or cut my ear off... If it's Art or Sanity, I choose sanity.

Max Zuniga never implied that was a choice anyone had to make, Clara says in her school ma'am voice. I'm sorry if I gave you that impression.

Sadie sits up straighter, puts her knees together, tucks her feet under her chair. She puts her hand to her head and grips a handful of her closely cropped hair. Clara watches as Sadie breathes in deeply and blows out the breath with some force. The fifty minutes will soon be up.

You were saying, Sadie? Clara reminds her.

But it must be obvious from Sadie's changed demeanour that the emotional Sadie has given way again to the intellectualising one. Which is always a temptation when the going gets tough.

László says you can only ever see yourself from your current vantage point, Sadie is speaking in a didactic tone; and, hey, as time moves on, as new experiences are added to your lexicon, you're forever looking from new places, trying to catch up with yourself. Sadie pauses. It's what I mean, snakes and tails, Sadie adds, *there's no stepping away from the shadow of your past.* It was you who told me that, Clara.

34

In the following session, which comes a good ten days later—Sadie has cancelled twice in the interim and once simply failed to show up—Clara is anxious to pick up where they left off. She's been re-reading Zuniga and trying to be more real and distanced and not obsessional about it and not let Zuniga get all mixed up with her tangles with Johannes. People can and do write reasonable biographies in a scholarly and rational way and there's no reason why Clara shouldn't be one of those people. Plus, if Clara can keep Real and move forward with her biography work, she hopes thereby to guide Sadie out of the work-impasse Sadie is in.

Sadie offers no apologies for her absence but, evidently, she too is keen to take up where they'd left off. Being true to yourself, for an artist, it's not only a case of being true to you, Sadie is saying. When you're representing someone, writing about someone, or in the Point of View or the voice or persona of someone, being true still applies and the mantra becomes trust and stay true. Are you talking about the people at Sangatte? Clara asks.

But Sadie just continues her own thread. How is it possible to be true to someone else, she says. Artists use their subjects for their own ends, don't they. How's that ethical. Aren't artists and writers all cannibals. Feeding off the lives of others.

Sadie is very sure of herself, Clara reflects, after her little jail-break. Does she now mean therapists are cannibals?

You must know all this from your biography work though Clara, Sadie adds. I'm teaching my granny to suck eggs.

Not at all, Clara says. I'm always interested to hear what you think.

What's a writer to do when their characters would rather be philosophers than personnages... László quips. *What's a therapist to do... What's a client to do when the therapist...*

Characters waltz in and out of stories, as people move in and out of their own and others' lives: Sadie wants to capture this in her photographs, the process not the essence, movement not stasis, she wants to capture moments of change in ways that don't exploit the subject. She's not sure this is possible. This is the first time Sadie has ever replied directly to a question from Clara, albeit a question Clara asked her some ten days ago.

Sadie wants to show how it is that people step through doors and windows or under archways and step out the other side, altered.

It's the fact of change that indicates the existence of a story, she says, that generates essence, if essence is what you're after.

She wants to show what it is that alters when a person catches sight of their reflection in a mirror walking the opposite way to that in which they thought they were travelling.

Sadie pauses. Did she see Clara flinch just then? But no, Clara is just sitting there looking across at her like she always does. Sadie continues with her explanation. She wants to show how people—how we—exist only fleetingly for a moment a moment then a moment and a final unfocused moment as our mother leans into the pram to look at us, her face looms, larger, loses definition, and the 8mm cine film stops, the celluloid spins off the spool, crackles into the Real, and begins to unravel. The lights go up.

Clara nods almost imperceptibly. She seems preoccupied.

Sadie continues, the thoughts forming in her head faster than she can put them into words:

Personnages... Sadie says.

The French word captures it better than any English one can. The closest translation is characters but *personnages* says more than characters, they have a stronger symbolic dimension, a deeper interiority, they carry more weight. They may or may not be projections of their creator and, if they are, they're not ashamed to admit it.

Have you seen the *personnages* Louise Bourgeois made as stand-ins for people she missed when she moved from Paris to New York? They're made of wood, some are painted—I think I saw some in MOMA, sky blue and smooth and white—and look a bit like elongated torpedoes standing on end, or skyscrapers, standing singly or in small groups, not touching, separated by space.... Those simple bits of wood surely tell us something about the human condition... Sadie hesitates... has Clara stopped listening...

Sadie's desires floating unheard past Clara's ears, Sadie wonders whether it matters, whether it's enough that she's said what she's said, that she feels what is happening, is able to call it to mind.

Trying to explain her thoughts to Clara, her clumsy attempts to grope for the roots of them, Sadie grasps at some hope of her mojo returning. Her thoughts and feelings are still all jumbled and she can't distinguish one from the other in the mess of chaos of everything, the swamp she's been stuck in ever since Sangatte. But at least something feels like it's beginning to shift.

Sadie looks at her watch. Her fifty minutes was up ten minutes ago. How did Clara not notice that? Sadie gets up out of her seat, puts on her coat and goes to the door. As she leaves, Sadie turns to look at Clara. Clara is sitting on her cushions in her usual place under the window, a large vase of dusky blue hydrangeas on the table next to her. Clara looks like she's barely aware of Sadie leaving.

Bye, Sadie says, see you next time.

Clara doesn't respond.

Personnages, reflects Clara, only a dimly aware that Sadie is no longer in the room, *personnages*.

Personnages, Clara understands, materialise cloud-like, become tangible in the way of ectoplasm; they arrive wearing overcoats, they carry baggage; they take off their coats and they drop bits of baggage, they leave bits of themselves all over; an artist does well to keep up, never mind a psychotherapist, running around after them like a mobile concierge. What's Zuniga if not one of those *personnages* people create to have someone standing beside them.

What's a biography if not some kind of refuge? A life reframed for a purpose?

What Sadie said earlier, about the mirror, what it is that alters as a person catches sight of their own reflection in a mirror walking the opposite way to that in which they thought they were travelling… it's reminding Clara about that terrible dream, where she was chasing Zuniga/Johannes and the mirror reaches out and pulls her in.

On learning from the patient, László says in his Yoda voice. *Progress we shall have.*

35

At about this time several sculptures by Bruno Catalano appear in Paris, near the river. The figures are different but each is a man with more than half his torso missing; the figure is more than half fresh air and the only thing complete and intact is the large piece of baggage he's holding.

The figure Sadie is looking at now stands on the Left Bank at the corner where the Pont des Arts meets the *quai*. He's facing south, she's facing north, she's heading back to her *chambre de bonne* after this week's session with Clara; no-one can tell where the half-a-man with the baggage was heading before he stopped here by the Seine, his presence a mockery of the tourists who stare, looking straight through him via their lenses, the fool-happy lenses of their own displaced selves.

Sadie takes a photograph of the figure, knowing there's not much point, since whatever angle she chooses the figure will contain lumps of river and/or traffic, jagged spikes of *bouquinistes*' stalls, bits of buildings, slices of people walking by.

She heads out onto the bridge. She could take the *métro* or the bus but she prefers to walk back after her sessions with Clara. Today she stands still for a moment on the bridge and looks out over the slow grey river, then looks back at the suitcase the man is carrying, she takes a deep breath and carries on.

There is no dignity in the body, none in sleep; no dignity in being sans anything; no human dignity in being sans human anything, in having bits of yourself removed, your humanity removed, none in having to stuff all that into a bag and that's all you have, László says. *No dignity in being lost between.*

Crossing the river, Sadie always notices how her footsteps are soft and silent on the old wooden boards of the Pont des Arts. There's usually a man with an accordion, a few bars and he evokes the entire nostalgic Piaf Paris spirit tourists adore. No matter that it's a giant *cliché*. There's no sign of the accordion man today. Nor of the chestnut-seller who has his mobile brazier at the right bank end of the *Pont*. In the absence of these icons, Sadie's memory readily supplies the music of *La Vie en Rose* and the hot smell of chestnuts to fill the gaps in the stories.

Loss and lack and lack and loss create gaps and you end up like the Catalano men and half of you is missing and all that intacts you is the suitcase; you're immovably in your place via the baggage you hold.

Anchors to the Real, look for them in Art if you can't find them elsewhere, Sadie. Art is both the exile and the homecoming.

The bag's full of the missing bits of him, offers László.

This space inside is where my country was, there's sky there now, buildings or a river depending on how you swivel yourself
to look at me

Here let me show you where my lungs were
I'll open up my coat and show you where they took away a part of me
let me open up my coat and show you where were the missing parts of me, the transposed guts of me, the vitals you now see as skies/rivers/buildings
places I never wished to be

You look through me, you think you see me but you look through me you see things that belong to places and people other than me

My friend who stands beside me is similarly disemboldened by their loss of substance, the removal of body parts, organs, the failure of our soft tissue to keep up with the rest of us/you

Here we stand metastasised in photograph after photograph on a grey day in autumn on the edge of the Seine in Paris. We are the missing and the missed, anchored by the baggage that tethers us elsewhere

Like a person, a sculpture, a *personnage* carries who and what they are and the processes of their making and the *personnages* of their maker/s within the frame/s of their being and their medium/media of construction; they wear coats and embody their story/ies.

The medium or media through which a *personnage* expresses their trueness to themselves, the relation of the one to the other, is what sets Art apart. It's towards the essences and processes of the Real, the universal, the eternal—however elusive, however contradictory, however impossible—that Art is reaching.

You're being didactic, Sadie, says László.

Ta gueule, László, Sadie says. Art reaches towards the unreachable, requires displacement, necessitates exile ... this is what Clara and her Zuniga man say...

There's exile and Exile, László interrupts.

And homecoming and Homecoming, Sadie replies.

Another year and it's the Place des Vosges where there stands another man a partial man and if you draw close in you see there's a shadow that fills out the missing bits of him

The shadow's yours, my Sadie

Sadie allows her shadow to give back to the man some

substance, to restore an outline, fill the void with a shade of grey that overlaps the edges.

This one's washed up with his baggage in Paris again, this time in a crowded tourist spot, a little corner of the Arcade under whose vaulted ceilings other foreigners/ outsiders/ strangers/ Others are making their way in shade to sit in twos and little smiling groups sit down to sustenance they drink clear sparkling liquids from clear sparkling glasses

tall fine brittle thin-stemmed they promenade under the arches and, through the window in the corner where, for now unseen, waits half the Catalano man with his baggage

perhaps he will make them think of their own baggage, claiming peaceful corners in hotel rooms, how heavy it anchors them

perhaps it will make them think of this man's missing guts his removed internals his abandoned vitals

and what they are missing, those thin-stem glass transparent people who walk the arcades of the Place des Vosges muddling along with their own shadow parts

Sadie watches them licking ice creams, wet tongues like cows' flick out and in
pink tongues curl visible as reptiles catching flies.

What if, like the Catalano man, they had no guts to digest anything no insides to speak of no voices to speak, their organs removed with their countries made war zones or poverty zones for the profit of money-baggage-carrying profit-makers who lurk at the edges of countries where where where there's nothing but bloody baggage and the baggage is bloody

as László knows

your body's all wrong and you don't want to be where you are
you got there by accident and there's no possibility of movement your case is too heavy it's weighing you down

you know it doesn't have to be this way

be this way

the world looks through you, thinks it sees through you, you and your half-empty self, displaced and bits missing, and your baggage the only solid thing about you and god knows it's nothing to do with you, this baggage, this perpetual fucking baggage that you carry this weight that weighs you down;

exiled from elsewhere and nobody much cares which elsewhere

your stomach heaved so much you had to discard it, you had to leave it behind on a soil or a sea other than this one

you laid you down on the cutting bench

And you'll be getting your bags packed for a start our Sadie, the mother says, if you don't stop acting yourself.

You can stop that carry-on and stop it now or I'll be sending you packing.

Right, pack your bags and pack them now, that's it, that is it, I've had enough.

Then the mother goes and packs her own.

It is night. She has come into your room, the room you share with your sister, the attic room with the skylight. You sense her silent standing beside you. The mother has come into your room and she is wearing the red bobbly coat which you know is the best one. Your sister is sleeping. Your sister is always sleeping.

Tell your sister I'm sorry, the mother says.

She is standing beside your bed, in the space between the bed which is your bed and the bed where your sister is sleeping.

The red coat is talking, the best coat, the red one, with the bobbles, it's saying words but its words froeae in your chest, you try to breathe them back out but the lump in your chest stops you from getting air in or out and you're shrinking, punctured like the rubber ring you punctured for keeping you afloat, you stopped up the hole with a plaster but you couldn't avoid the Trouble and you thought never again would you be able to take air in or let it out but here it is again

You'll be packing your bags, the mother says, *if there's any more Trouble.*

Now the mother has packed her own bag and she's got the best coat on and the bag, the little blue suitcase she used to put your clothes in when they sent you to grandmother's house, it's there by the door, she's put it down there beside your bedroom door, the little blue case she took when she said she was going to Mary's but it turned out she didn't and nobody knew who Mary was and perhaps she wasn't anyone, there's the little blue case with its fasteners clicked shut standing there upended by your attic door and the handle of the little blue case is thick leather and worn and hardly blue any longer and it's pointing upwards ready to be lifted up off the floor like a baby or garbage.

Nobody knows it but you have your own bag half-packed under your bed, you've pushed it away way back at the back, back where the bed meets the wall, nobody would reach the sweeper in that far and that's why you've pushed it there beyond the reach of the sweeper and nobody knows a thing not a soul you haven't even told your sister and there it is half- packed, the case your aunty gave you when she got a new one when she went to the Costa del Somewhere she had to have everything new because it was going to be a new start she said a whole new start and old baggage doesn't fit a new start so she gave it to you and you told her you wanted to keep your treasure in and that was not wholly a lie. You have it now half packed under the bed pushed up its back against the wall away from the reach of the sweeper.

The mother is walking now towards the door, she's going to lift up the little blue case by the waiting handle.

She seems to hesitate, perhaps she is waiting for something, but there's nothing to wait for.

You are becoming adept at so many things, the slowing down of time, the stowing away of memory, at the putting of everything into slow motion into bits into slow motion monochrome frame by frame a transparent ribbon of bits.

The mother leans forward and lifts the suitcase with her black gloved hand. She turns and looks back into your room, into the dark where you are still lying down in bed half-propped up on an elbow, where your sister is still sleeping, you can hear her breathing but you yourself are no longer breathing.

You won't forget to tell your sister what I said now, will you, the mother says.

You shake your head. You have already forgotten. Your sister is sleeping. She is breathing the breathing of a sleeper. Your mother's footsteps tread one by one down the attic stairs. They track along the landing lino then one by one down the next flight, quieter, because there is carpet there, and a banister to hold onto.

36

How Sadie hates the nights. Having to sleep, having to come apart in sleep, black dogs questing for the dark questing in packs for the darkness that layers itself in sleep, how she hates the nights and having to sleep.

She sloughs her way toward morning barely grateful

how she detests the corporeal, better it was absent

how she detests that history is full of those poor souls who looked back in innocence and turned to salt or stone and got stuck in some kind of unforgiving stonified storified sleep eternal sleep

Could you move your baggage over there, the man says, you're not supposed to leave baggage unattended, Read the sign, the sign says Do not leave baggage unattended. The baggage is yours then keep it with you, it's your responsibility to keep it with you. At all times.

37

The scene is cosy with traffic—as it often is—as Sadie nears Châtelet. She's tempted to cross over and sit a while on the wide terrace outside the Café Bords de Seine, from there you can watch frame by frame the wild noisy chaos that happens here at this time of day. She'd love to capture something in stills of this *quotidien* energy of Paris but that's probably impossible; a film could do it, but she's not about to start making movies.

Sadie stops to watch the spectacle at Châtelet. Standing in the middle of the intersection, surrounded on all sides by impatient vehicles trying to get moving, blowing their horns and edging this way and that, there's a traffic cop in dark uniform with white gloves and a whistle—he looks barely twenty—he's ordering long lines of traffic with a strange bored efficiency, channelling them by turn into multiple directions. He gesticulates manically, insistently, repeatedly toot-toot-tooting loudly and with urgency on the whistle while managing to appear distanced from it all. Standing alone in the middle of all that moving traffic he could be carried off at any moment, but he carries on; so young, so alone, so determined, so vulnerable, Sadie watches the spectacle unfold as though the whole thing were choreographed.

Then, in the distance, getting louder, getting closer, a siren. SAMU. A medical emergency. The siren noise is piercing, the ambulance desperate to get through the traffic packed solid. The young cop alters his instructions and, like a miracle, like Moses parting the Red Sea, the traffic shifts *en bloc* to make room and, siren still blaring, the ambulance edges on through.

A lump forms in Sadie's throat. It's hard to swallow. This happens. Someone somewhere is in desperate need. A life is in danger. Someone from somewhere is coming to help. That is what people do, they help each other. It is heart-breaking, how people help each other. Sadie knows nothing and she knows everything. Something is crushing her chest and tears sting at her eyes.

These feelings immobilise her. She must stay Real, she repeats the word out loud with a capital R, as Clara advised, Real Real Real, stay with the Now, Sadie. Stay in the Real.

The memory that crouches against her *is* Real. It *is* now. This is what Sadie lives and re-lives and time and place are not relevant dimensions. *I do, I undo, I re-do*.

This *is* Sadie's Real. A repetition compulsion. This *is* Sadie's Now. Echoes repeating themselves with their cold hand.

Calmes toi. Come back to Now.

But Sadie is gone

like that day she got caught up with the *Gilet Jaunes*, it is like this time and again, Sadie transported away from Sadie; sees, hears things that aren't there, reacts to events that have not happened.

Sangatte.

This is Paris, Sadie, László is compelled to intervene.

Sangatte, Sadie feels the weight of the word inside her. What's in a word. A lot's in a word. Everything and nothing. The space around it. The basket it carries to market. The *vide grenier*. Sangatte. She holds it. Safe, she holds it. It's part of her now. It won't let her go. She won't let it go. She won't let her go. Won't can't won't. when when when Sadie Sadie when

The ground is shifting beneath her. She'd been about to cross the road but now she steps back from the kerb, turns to rest her hands on the closed green *bouquiniste* box on the wall, leans her head on her forearms. She stays still a few moments, steadying herself, grateful for the pandemonium of Châtelet going on around her, anchoring her to some kind of Real as the chains of the old tighten her captive.

Each time Sadie tries to talk about this to Clara, she fails; fails to find the words, fails to make the words she does find convey any meaning. She knows it's not just a case of vocabulary, of the right words not being there, or not being available; no, it's not just that. It's something more about how even to enter into her own thoughts, how to trust her perceptions, how to marry up her thoughts with her feelings, not having them going off in different directions. These feelings, they act as sentries, they make thinking impossible.

They overwhelm, immobilise her with panic, then, later, when she tries to remember, to tell how it was, there is nothing there, like something happened, only it didn't; it wasn't significant, only it was but now it's a blank, it's gone; it interrupted her life, then she carried on.

Clara says trauma is never lived in real time.

The silent scream, the Munch painting, that screaming figure on the bridge, like Sadie, standing on the Pont des Arts.

Like those towelling cloth heads Louise Bourgeois stitched together, stitched and mended, stitched up, the pink and white bandages wound round wound round the wound, wound round the squint holes left for eyes, the silent gaping mouths.

Paris alters the way Sadie sees, it changes the way the world is. Sadie can't deal with it and Clara's no help and all Sadie wants to do is to sleep but she's so afraid of sleep.

38

Sadie tells Clara about the revelation, about stories being everything, about there being nothing outside the story. Clara shuffles about on her cushions on the floor under the window. The blinds are half down because of the angle of the sun, so today Sadie sees Clara's face more clearly than usual when looking into the light.

Clara looks uncomfortable, physically and mentally, shuffling on her cushions and Sadie wonders what story of Clara's she's stumbled into.

That is something Sadie will never know. Such is the therapeutic relationship that one party remains private, one party is permitted to keep their overcoat on and stay warm, the other must strip naked and shiver. The distance must remain sacred.

The stories are all there, Sadie continues, but they're not all of equal weight. Some arrive in thick woolly overcoats, others are wearing only flimsy nightgowns...

Greatcoats, says László. *Dictators*.

The stories are all there, but not always all available... Sadie is searching for words with which to talk about silence, the silences she hears inside the stories, the gaping holes she carries with her, the holes that weigh so heavy.

Don't rush, Sadie. Stories as yet untold will wait in the wings, says László, *for their time, their place; it will come.*

And when the facts aren't there, or aren't available, it's time for speculation, you have to make things up? Clara interjects, she doesn't know she is talking on top of László. She doesn't know this conversation is about her issues with Zuniga.

Make things up. That's what art is. Sadie says. Art uses made-up things to tell deeper truths...

An artist can choose to hide the art, cover it up, store it away, decide not to let it tell the story or any story... László says.

Run away and say nothing. Save your skin.

Bury the tale and save your skin.

Swallow the tail, like a snake. Keep it inside you 'til you choke.

Shed the skin, like a snake. Leave it crumpled and brittle by the side of the road in the sure knowledge it will turn to dust.

Sadie tries to stop the Sangatte thoughts from circling her head like vultures. Clara sits on in her usual place, looking calmly across the room at Sadie.

And what of the Facts themselves? Sadie trying to track her own train of thought: Where do Facts come from? Aren't they too embedded in stories? Don't Facts also come with their overcoats on?

Facts are sacks; empty, they can't stand upright, says Pirandello.

Theories are overcoats too; facts put them on, to keep them warm and cosy, agrees László.

This is what happens when Sadie tries to think, her mind goes walkabout in all directions, as though to avoid itself but manages to keep intruding. This happens more and more in the sessions with Clara. Sadie can't keep focus. It's like at school. *Sadie can't keep on task. She has an over-active imagination. She lacks self-discipline. It's a pity she seeks to distract other pupils with her wild ideas.*

Now a wave of nausea passes through Sadie but the pressing of the corporeal brings her back into the room. She puts her hand to her chest, steadies her breathing, realises Clara has been talking to her, that she's still talking, in a flat but emphatic voice; Sadie hasn't a clue what she's been saying, how long she's been lost in reverie, in some other place.

Carry on, please, Sadie, Clara is saying. You stopped in the middle of a sentence. We lost you in the middle… Could you perhaps carry on ...

Clara's voice. No longer a request, this is a command.

Where did you go Sadie, where have you been?

Pussy cat pussy cat where have you been? I've been to London to see the Queen

As though from a long distance away Sadie hears herself gushing out words that speak themselves, that come from outside her volition.

All is story, masquerade, spectacle. What happened to True? Where's Real? Where do we put the *too real?* When Real gets too real you run and there's nothing left in its place, just a gap and a void and the guilt and the shame and the deep not knowing and that is the Silence…

And there can be Art…

Sadie hears her own voice trailing off. She's not sure if she's been speaking or not.

In front of her, the scene is blurred, behind a veil, then thick brocade curtains are being drawn back to reveal a small stage, a marionette theatre. There's music, other-worldy, a theremin, a whine, keeps fading… Sadie watches: across the stage moves a grotesque parade; all her doubts personified, a macabre procession, a strange troupe of actors with twisted body postures, grimaced faces, distorted masks, shredded costumes, *personnages* escaped from some circus of the underworld, their skewed limbs attached to wooden crosses in the air by tangled dusty strings…

There is and never can be anything worthwhile in any manifestation of Art as long as human beings are suffering and humanity itself is imperilled on the verge of planetary self-destruction. Some things are of crucial importance. Art is an irrelevance in a world as troubled as this.

Clara waits until Sadie has finished speaking. As I understand things, Clara says after a pause, speaking with a tone of unaccustomed humility, As I see it, those, Sadie, are the very sentiments—call them doubts if you like—that provide the motivation from which many artists make great works…the significance of bearing witness…

Sadie interrupts. She's standing up, she's pulling on her coat, stuffing a bundle of paper hankies into her satchel. Don't patronise me, Clara, don't fucking patronise me. I don't pay you to fucking patronise me.

László looks on from the sidelines as Sadie gathers up the broken puppets and, her arms overflowing with the macabre little figures, she leaves the room.

We think we understand each other, but we never do, he addresses Clara.

Clara won't bother to reply. She's tired of his Pirandellos.

Then she says, This is life, László. Not your frickin fantasy-land drama.

You don't need to tell me what is Life, lady, says László.

Johannes, Clara is going to phone Johannes. She really is going to phone Johannes this time.

But she won't, she'll resist, she must resist. In any case, she's deleted his number.

A desire to call Johannes is a sign the boundaries of the Real require reinforcements. Sadie has a knack of knocking holes in boundary walls.

39

The mind of the artist, says Zuinga, should not be judged by the criteria of minds not similarly in creative mode. Creativity, he says, is marked by the absence of thought controlled by reason. The phenomenon of creativity cannot be contained within rational discourse.

Clara stands up after she hears the door slam at the foot of the stairs as Sadie leaves the building. She rearranges the lilies in the vase in the corner of the room, raises the blind a little to let in some more light. Her limbs feel heavy.

Sadie Sarrazin has a lot to learn, including that she's not the only client. And not the only artist on the planet. And not the first ever to get stuck. Hemingway. Maya Angelou. Proust. Or to have schizoid tendencies. Beckett, semi-permanently enmired, most of his life.

And biographers. Writers and artists who came to Paris to escape the prisons of former lives only to find they confine themselves in walls of a different sort, says László.

Clara could make a major contribution to Creativity scholarship if she can manage—via Zuniga—to get to the roots of what it is that causes these blocks such as afflict Sadie, if she could say what exactly is needed to shift them… realign creativity and sanity… Clara has a hunch, not based on anything but intuition, that creative blocks are part and parcel… the nature of them is the clue to the intricate workings of Creativity itself. Did Zuniga get stuck? How did he rescue himself? He never talks personally in his books. Clara had hoped to find all that in the archive.

Clara is stuck but only by reason of lack of information. If she had the material, the primary source material, that was supposed to be here, in the archive here in Paris, if she had that she'd definitely be well into getting on with the job…

Clara

Now, after the dream, she's not sure if it is Clara herself who is stuck—stuck with Zuniga, or stuck with Johannes, or both, or neither. Stuck with herself. And now getting stuck with Sadie.

She could put on her coat, walk out into the morning, head along rue Monsieur le Prince, stop at the little Café Carrefour, order some *chocolat chaud*, exchange some small talk with the lady and the little dog who run the place; it would save her, something Real and as simple as that could save her. Such an air that place has, so *sympa*, so old-school Paris… The real the real the Real, beckons and recedes, distracts. But Clara can't leave her *atelier* because in ten minutes the next client will arrive and she needs to step back onto the stage of her own working life. Time to change places with yourself, Clara. Time to step into the mode of *an actor prepares*.

Dual existence is difficult, László says. *I know.*

Clara sits down. She runs a comb through her hair, re-applies her lip gloss. She has less than ten minutes to transform herself back into a therapist. She tells herself—as she keeps telling Sadie—get back into focus.

Clara's client does not show up. Neither does she ring or text to cancel. Clara determines to use the unexpected free time wisely, she will make some notes on trauma from recent thoughts.

The more she thinks about it—and much of this is arriving through her therapeutic work with Sadie—the more Clara realises that Trauma holds the key to the creative process. It goes to the heart of it, it's a *displacement*—and possibly, as trauma is not lived in real time, even a template for all displacements—as such, is it a precondition for Art?

This is not just Zuniga, and his 'transforming trauma into Art.' It's not just Louise Bourgeois and her return of the repressed. Neither is it Freud's 'sublimation.' This is insight arising directly from Clara's clinical work in the here and now, ideas emerging from the practice, and taking shape as theories, as Zuniga did. Crucially, Sadie's case has taught Clara that, if Trauma is the *key* to creativity, the key that can open the door, it is that very same key that closes the door, that locks it shut. If Clara can make a breakthrough into the depth psychology of these parallel processes, it will be of immense help to any artist suffering from a 'block' like Sadie is.

And you, Clara.

PART 4

Art is not about art...
Art is about life, and that sums it up

Louise Bourgeois

Zuniga. His theory is *Art*? Synergies between the Life and the Art.

Louise Bourgeois says, *I need my memories. They are my documents.*

You can't force these connections, Clara. László quips. *It doesn't work like that.*

Whose life? Clara's? Zuniga's?

All Clara's paths lead her to Zuniga.

How trauma resists narrative even as it tries to fix itself in narrative. Hence Repetition Compulsion. Bourgeois' *I do, I undo, I redo.*

Freud, in *Beyond the Pleasure Principle*, puts it like this: *The patient cannot remember the whole of what is repressed… and what he cannot remember may be precisely the essential part of it… He is obliged to repeat the repressed material as a contemporary experience instead of remembering it as something in the past.*

Trauma hauls us in and spits us out. Z—trauma, creates liminal space for creativity.

Looking at *vs.* looking through. A hymn, *A man who looks on glass, on it may stay his eye, or if he pleaseth through it pass…*

Looking out/ looking in. *It's not what you look at, it's what you see that counts.* Thoreau?

Each of us, László says, *part flesh, part shadow. Note that down, Clara. Lest we forget.*

Trauma—lived in cultural space.

Each of us, sleeping with ghosts.

Trauma not just an event that happened in the past, leaves its imprint on mind and body. Traumatised people, chronically unsafe, physically, mentally.

Humankind can't bear too much reality, T S Eliot.

Z considers creativity through prism. Trauma as prism. Breaking light. Lens. Refraction. Moving shadows and light. Off at a new angles. Cubism. Distortions of light reveal new truths.

Stained glass. Stained. The body of Christ. The blood of Christ. Boundary erasure. Soldering. Soldiering the window glass.

Reflection. Copy: Mirror, back to front, side to side, shifting. Moving, in water. Look at your reflection in the back of a shiny spoon and you've gone upside down. Reflect = consider, reconsider

Clara could shift focus, concentrate on the theory, creativity, the words, not the man ... How easy to separate the two? Would it be cruel to leave the man stranded a second time, a double abandonment?

You promised to rescue Zuniga: The genius, or the man? Or do you want the theory, the words to make your own?

For a brief moment Clara takes László seriously... then she goes on making notes which she's calling—neutrally—*Notes Towards a Case Study*. She did have a file marked 'Z' but she's changed its appellation. For years James Joyce referred to what would become *Finnegans Wake* as Work-in-Progress. It helps when you give things new names—rename and reframe—it's a kind of displacement. Names are talismanic. They summon in forces.

Donner un nom, c'est donner la vie.... Helène Cixous? *A name can fix. Congeal. Speak the wrong kind of power....*

Go to where the pain is. Write from the darkness.

As though a writer could choose where to go. As though they would even know where the pain begins. You can't see with your own eyes. The shadow never fits the person who's walking... László, disdainful.

It took Beckett many years of struggle in the wastelands before it dawned—a kind of epiphany fictionalised in *Krapp's Last Tape*—that the darkness he'd long battled to keep under wraps was the very place where he would—and did—find his most potent material. Standing at his mother's sick bed in Ireland, *suddenly I saw the whole thing, the vision at last ...* That day he conceived *Molloy*, a novel that begins in a mother's room. Clara ponders the nature of the shadow in Beckett's case: schizoid?

What is the meaning / what is the good of such a label, what is the point, László is shaking his head, as he often does with Clara.

Clara wants to *dissect* these creative breakthroughs. It's not enough to name them, or even describe them. She wants to be able, with Zuniga, to *unearth* them, *expose* their origins, *explain* them and, that way, break through herself to understanding the reverse phenomena of creative 'block.'

Clara, quoting Zuniga and remembering a recent session with Sadie, takes her red Sharpie and puts a ring around *trauma not lived in real time* makes it the centre of a spider diagram.

László says, *People don't see their own pain, they can't, not the pain that matters. They see something else somewhere else. They look in the wrong places. Even you, Clara*, he adds. *Necessarily. The deferral is endless.*

Clara listens. *No signpost to place where pain conceals itself,* she notes. She alters 'place' to the plural, but misspells it palaces. Freud was right: you can get insights from slips. She thinks about pain concealing itself grandiosely in palaces, in turrets, in fairy-tales hidden among finery-bedecked well-structured beautifully illustrated stories.

Like Sadie's stories; pain ever-present, always over there, always somewhere else. In her sessions, Sadie won't go to Sangatte. Or backwards from there.

Undoing the bandages reveals the wounds.

Exposure ever possible.

Louise Bourgeois concealed layers of wounds under those bandaged *personnages* with their gaping mouths, their multiple heads, some confined torso-less in cages…

Clara had talked to Sadie about the phenomenon of projection and how we put our pain out there when we can't tolerate it ourselves. Sadie's hand had gone straight to her chest as was her habitual gesture. Written on the body, stories are written on the body. Clara watched Sadie exact her breathing. In for three, out for three. The comfort of regularity. Ritual. The security of the predictable.

Repetition, with its ever-forked tongue/s.

The anxiety. The resistance. The anger. Sadie had been silent, then:

I don't see my panic as 'out there,' anywhere, Sadie's voice spat out. She hit herself flat on the chest with the palm of her hand. I feel it here, she said, here! She'd thumped her chest again and again, hard, several times.

41

Clara has not been finding it easy coping with Sadie's venom. There's something about Sadie that leads Clara to all that snake and tail stuff and gets them going round and round in circles and it seems she, Clara, always picks the wrong way out and she goes too far and

Sadie closes up and all that's left is the barren wasteland of the intellectual, the discussing of concepts as between colleagues, the kind of understanding that makes no sense and that a therapist would normally avoid altogether.

What had Clara been thinking, talking to Sadie about projection, of all things. Christ.

Sadie is not a girl who permits any rescue; she won't rescue herself, neither will she permit anyone else to rescue her, neither—and this is the worst thing, Clara notes, underlining her words in her notebook—neither will she permit Clara to pull herself back from any mistakes. Yes, with Sadie, Clara herself is getting stuck between intellectualising and relating. It's a space which might be good for creativity but it's not the space where anything works in the real damn world and certainly not in therapy.

42

Writing *about* trauma. Clara continues. *Notes Towards a Case Study*: Does writing a Case Study count as writing about trauma?

Writing about trauma is different from writing trauma, Clara notes the new thought in the margin. Sadie sits on the boundary. Sadie straddles a lot of boundaries.

As does Art.

The stories therapists tell. The overcoats they oblige their patients to wear.

Overcoat: Appellation, Diagnosis, Case Study. Stories fence trauma in. Keep it safe. Keep it warm. Button it up. Reframe. Retell.

Stories corral Sadie into unsafe boundaries, hold her there, she'll not let them go. Stories are stitching, repairing, mending, holding together, destabilising yet keeping her from falling apart.

Corral. Herds of wild horses in the TV Westerns Clara's dad watched on Saturday afternoons. The thundering of hooves, the *ping ping pew pew* firing of pistols; getting trampled by galloping horses and shot with pistols was weekend entertainment. Why don't the horses jump the fences, Daddy? escape from the corrals? What's to stop them running free?

Safety. Refuge. Containment. Confinement.

Perhaps horses don't want to be free, Clara's dad says, perhaps they're afraid of their own wildness. Now be quiet. I'm watching.

The comfort/ confinement of diagnosis/story. The point of the Case Study format where the protective walls of theory put the client's neurosis at a step removed. Render it manageable. Render it harmless. Make it safe.

Not only the client's neurosis, remarks László.

Clara seems to be coming at Z through so many reflections, refractions, images that shift in the light, disappear into the shadows.

That Cubism show she saw at the Pompidou Centre, it comes to mind. The Alexander Calder kinetic sculptures, so delicately balanced, so fine and beautiful, turning in their own way at the slightest current of air, the different parts move each in their own ways, yet all connected; and the colours, and the way they move the light, and the shifting shadows they make on the floor.

Like a family.

Recently, with Sadie, and Sadie explaining yet again why she can't possibly tackle any of the work she did at Sangatte, how she never intends to touch it, it will stay where it is on the encrypted disc until the programme becomes obsolete. Now she's added a new excuse, characterising her work as 'cannibalising the lives of others' (she means the migrants at the Jungle camp). Then she extrapolated and said all art works—particularly photography—*cannibalise* the lives of others and are therefore morally unsustainable; people should never be means to others' ends etc. etc., she had it all worked out and said it all off pat, leaving Clara silenced. Sadie wasn't just stuck, she was actually going backwards…

Backwards into battle. With you, Clara.

43

Louise Bourgeois faced it head on

Trauma

Or thought she did, says László.

time and again the traumas she'd stacked and re-stacked

in her memories

it doesn't matter if the claims an artist makes are factually correct or incorrect

facts get in the way of truths anyway

Facts can hide truths

for Bourgeois, trauma emerged, transformed, and re-materialised anew each time in each work of art

in a kind of shapeshifting repetition-compulsion *I do, I undo, I redo*

through which she harnessed her memories in giant spiders

laid them out on beds in recreated red rooms

confined them in Cells

sculpted them in metals

sewed them up in stitches

wound them up in bandages

stitched the torn parts, made repairs

reparations

all secrets will be ironed out, she said

she made figures headless heedless twisted dangling eternal on ropes and chains from ceilings

revolving

shaped and moulded, full of holes, scraped and scoured and painted

I do, I undo, I redo

though a repetition-compulsion she transformed trauma into Art and took control of the beginning the middle the end, the origins the process and the outcome

took control of the story

control that smoothed and soothed

the *personnages*

I do, I undo, I redo

Creativity the *passeur* who led the artist across the boundaries of trauma to new beginnings

the making of art has a curative effect, she said

Clara, a therapist can do little more than pick out the bits of shrapnel and put them somewhere else; after trauma, we seek comfort, stasis

all we want is to put on the same warm coat, step out into the same street, wearing the same shoes, sleep in the same sheets

screaming out for reversal

I do, I undo, I redo

44

There's been silence in the room for some minutes.

Sadie pulls her coat around her, it's cold in Clara's *atelier* today. Clara seems distracted by her own little speech about trauma. It sometimes feels like she's trying to educate Sadie. Then Sadie finds herself saying any old thing, speaking oddly, saying things she doesn't mean, or doesn't think she does. Clara knows different. Or thinks she does.

What does Clara mean, trauma is not lived in real time? Is it crowded out by Associations? Or hiding itself away in memory so fast as it's happening it simply slips away?

What Clara says sort of rings true but Sadie can't quite

grasp it. Clara is fond of quoting T S Eliot, *The historical sense involves a perception, not only of the pastness of the past, but of its presence*... the continued *presence* of the past, in the present.

The past is never dead, it's not even past, quotes László.

Sangatte, the winters were the worst. There's no use Clara keep asking about it. Sadie doesn't want to relive that and, even if she did, the memories are blurred; they've been blurred from the start—the events at the time they were happening were blurred, even then, it was impossible to make sense.

It is simply not possible to be or to stay ordinarily sane and perceiving when you're in the middle of such desperation, such utter *inhuman* degradation, so many people struggling hopelessly against hopelessness. It had tormented Sadie to be there, to be both on the inside and the outside, at the same time; to know she could leave, and could find somewhere to go, when others weren't and couldn't—that peculiar trapped feeling she had—the return of the childhood claustrophobia—the whole experience filled her with guilt, and shame from the privilege—yes, she had begun to see how her own path—painful though parts of it had been—was crisscrossed by numerous manifestations of privilege—rights and entitlements others didn't have, deep-set beliefs of her own worth that flowed, merely but with every certainty, from her accidental passport that came with rights of citizenship these desperately displaced people needed but didn't have and couldn't get.

Everything had got mixed up, Sadie, voluntarily displaced, voluntarily stranded among people who'd had no choice but to give up any sense of anchorage they might have had: whole families, children, little children... Ameena, there'd been Ameena, little Ameena... when Ameena suffered, Sadie suffered, through the nights and the days trying to keep little Ameena breathing, not sleeping, just watching, just waiting, and Sadie finding her own anchors cutting loose, not just to place but to values, to who she was, things she'd thought she believed in, humanity, humanity, it came to her then as so very vulnerable and at the same time so cruel, so very very cruel, and there was a part of her, yes a part, ashamed as she might be to admit it even to herself, there was a part of Sadie that could no longer connect, that stood empty and terrified on the outside and she knew would ever stand on the outside, an outsider looking in, unable to step closer, for fear, for fear, for her selfish fear for herself.

She'd stopped taking photographs. It was impossible to record the horror of it, impossible even to scratch the surface of the suffering, both out there and inside herself. She wasn't up to it. There was hope too, in the solidarity, friendship, sharing, the helping each other, but she'd reached the limits, limits Sadie didn't know where they came from and try as she might, could not wish away. You couldn't capture that confusion, those contradictions, in a photograph. Or Sadie couldn't. She wasn't up to it.

She could try again to talk through this with Clara but Clara is getting to her feet now, the fifty minutes is up. And she won't ask Clara next time because by then Sadie will have forgotten what the questions were, she'll have buried the demons once again, tucked them away safely back in their puppet boxes.

45

Now Clara is asking Sadie where 'Home' is. Clara can get quite insistent when she thinks she's on to something.

Sadie is reminded of a terrier who'd dig endlessly in molehills, dig dig digging and tearing at the turf with his incisors, then coming to seek her out with a pleading look, unable to close his mouth for the soil and the sods all stuck in his teeth and jamming his poor mouth wide open.

Now, again, those images of those Louise Bourgeois terry-cloth-bound bandaged unbodied heads, the mouths fixed open… the silent screams.

Sadie shrugs. She doesn't want to talk about home or even think about home.

She doesn't tell this to Clara but she half-likes the half-feeling that she half-belongs now in this her chosen city; how easy it is to walk either towards or away from yourself in Paris, depending. How she feels close yet distant. Which is a safe space a safe space. How for Sadie solitude, feelings of un-belonging, *déplacement*, being an Outsider, are what feels most safe.

Paris is good because you can 'belong' as an *étrangère*. Stranger is who you are. Stranger to yourself. Straddle the boundary. Stefan Zweig found 'home' in the very act of travel. He ended up taking his own life in Brazil. He fled because he couldn't stand the fascism that was taking over Europe. Sadie doesn't want to get entangled in discussions about that. Or about ambivalence. Home. Belonging. Because she knows it is all sure to lead back to Mr Zuniga the favoured one.

There's three of you in this therapy, says László. *Four, en fait.* Paris, the city where you can belong and remain an outsider both at the same time. Where you can belong as an outsider, take up your rightful place *as* a stranger, you don't even have to take your coat off and you can both belong and not belong as the feeling suits. This place even gives you the freedom to reach down into the safety sleep of exile which you haven't managed properly since Sangatte.

There's exile and Exile, reminds László.

Half and half

More and more it is half of everything

Half add half is not just one

It's somewhere else.

Half and between and waiting to materialise

Sarraute, *Pour un Oui, Pour un Non*

Winnicott's Transitional Space, Potential space, *The Place Where We Live*. Or could live if living would permit us to live: He says—*If we look at our lives we shall probably find that we spend most of our time neither in behaviour nor in contemplation, but somewhere else. I ask: where?*

It is Clara's 'palace'

The third space

It's Beckett, *I can't go on, I'll go on*

He could have shouted and could not, the start of it

And in the middle, between the half this half that, and in between and in the middle and neither here nor there nor one nor the other, there was the story

And at the end *They found her caressing his wild dead hair.*

46

And where is Home? Clara asks again, that look of satisfaction settling across her face.

The capital H does not go unnoticed. Therapists, Sadie reflects, are the only people more satisfied by questions than by answers. Whose insertions of capitals alter everything.

László frowns.

Sadie shrugs.

It's the response Clara was expecting. She looks more satisfied than ever.

Here's Olga Tokarczuk, writing in *Flights*: *Clearly I did not inherit whatever gene it is that makes it so that when you linger in a place you start to put down roots.... My energy derives from movement—from the shuddering of buses, the rumble of planes, trains' and ferries' rocking.*

More and more Sadie feels she's on a stage, the whole therapy-thing a performance. A ludicrous, stupid performance, it's impossible to draw a line between this life and this spectacle, this me and this performance of me, this me and that me ...

How right Beckett was. Sarraute. Pirandello. The most important things—the Real—they happen in the gaps and there are no words for what goes on in there. As the poets know, the gaps are a language in itself. The story's in the act of travel.

Sadie's eyes are drawn to the old angle-poise lamp that always stands on the corner of Clara's desk. It's probably from her student days. Today it's lighting up the pale wall behind the desk, lighting up nothing, just giving out its familiar moon-cone of light.

Then Sadie's in the spotlight, walking across an empty stage, it's dark, no props. The lights are gradually brightening, choosing their focus, closing in to position themselves to illuminate Sadie from angles she didn't know she had, fragmenting her by light and shadow, as in a Cubist painting.

It all has the feeling of farce, but frightening: Sadie watching Clara observing Sadie insinuating herself into Clara's train of thought, disquieting Clara and more so Sadie and yes, Cubism does fit.

A questioning look develops on Clara's face. She inclines her head slightly. Sadie hears Clara breathing. Sadie, suddenly not an ounce of energy left. She sighs, closes her eyes, sighs again.

We were talking about Home, Clara says eventually, capital H again.

Sadie, almost overwhelmed by the need to sleep. Like at Sangatte.

47

On her way back to her apartment in the rue du Bac from the *atelier* on rue Le Goff following her session with Sadie, Clara finds on the Place de L'Odéon a blue plastic lid from a Ventolin inhaler. She picks it up.

It makes her think of Johannes, like he could have just passed through this square a few moments ago and, carelessly, let the lid fall from his pocket.

Clara's heart lightens stupidly but only for a moment before a surge of tenderness and longing comes rushing to the surface, feelings she could never feel when Johannes was there. But now, the memories, how so often he had such a hard time breathing, how she'd hold him while he heaved and gasped and struggled to take in air; how terrified she'd be for him, how at those times she'd have done anything, given anything, to make his breath come easier.

Standing now in the pale autumn sun on the concourse of the grand Odéon theatre, Clara fingers the blue lid and thinks back to their early days when they'd take time out in NYC where they could be anonymous, nights they spent in the over-heated Brooklyn loft, spooned tight on Bula's pull-out; how Clara would lie awake to make sure Johannes was breathing, in and out, out and in, how she'd feel the deep aching pain of loving him and be so anxious and so grateful, desperate to make the most of every moment—even as she knew in those early days that the relationship could not last. And then harking even further back, to those childhood nights when she'd lie awake in her grandmother's house, listening for footsteps on the stairs. Always then and still now Clara so afraid of sleep—something she has in common with Sadie; the narrow bed, the fear of losing hold, of falling. She'd heard Louise Bourgeois talk about a fear of falling and she'd realised then all the things, all the terrible terrible things, a simple word like 'falling' means.

In New York, the sleeping Johannes beside her, Clara would lie and watch the thin curtains as they wafted gently at the open window, waiting for the light of morning until, outside, the sounds of the city waking, the rumble of the subway, the gurgling coo of the pigeons, the sounds of the early morning garbage collectors, and Clara waiting for safety to come drifting in with the sultry summer air.

She walks on now down the rue de l'Odéon.

There's a certain sadness that lingers around any decision. One decision and not the other decision and so much else excluded.

Clara's hand is clasped tight around the blue plastic lid in her pocket. She lets it go loose. She walks on faster and with purpose, looking straight ahead, *comme une Parisienne*.

Clara likes walking these streets in the 6th, that feeling of being able to touch the literary and artistic heritages of Paris, much of which went on in the 6th, being part of all that, it gives Clara energy and life. Paris is where she wanted to be; she shouldn't have to remind herself. This the street where Sylvia Beach had her anglophone bookshop, the original *Shakespeare and Co.*, from where in 1922 she published Joyce's *Ulysses* when no-one else would touch it. Her partner, Adrienne Monnier, had her French shop *La Maison des Amis des Livres* just across the street. And there, on the corner, the restaurant Méditerranée where Cocteau's paintings still decorate the walls.

Johannes liked Cocteau. He liked *Orphée*.

Clara remembers the dream.

Clara and Johannes, weren't they always tipping over opposite edges of something, skulking around underworlds, trying to anchor themselves in some other city on someone else's couch. Disappearing into mirror underworlds like Orphée.

Later, after New York, they'd have a bed of their own, then a bigger one then an even bigger one. And later again there'd be one bed each, then separate rooms as they tried to go their own separate ways. Now, it's separate houses, in separate cities, in separate countries, which is half-needed and half-breaks them. But isn't that what they intended, isn't that what they agreed. Split. Fracture. Fragment.

But not this fragmentation, not this broken glass.

Clara and Johannes each separately trying to gather up the pieces, index the scars and account for their scattered belongings: Is that my baggage or do you own it. Whose is whose. Who is who. Clara. Johannes. Someone else altogether.

Zuniga, says László.

Everyone searches for a way to be, not one of us really knows in which direction we're headed. There's so little understanding of what 'together' might mean when a person is striving for something other

or other than

There's been some kind of accident on the corner, a pile of broken glass has been swept into the gutter.

Clara puts the ear buds in. Barbara is singing: *Dis, quand reviendras tu…*

In her pocket, Clara's fingers close in, tight again around the blue plastic lid.

48

Serendipity being what it is, when Clara calls at Berkeley Books the following day Phyllis proudly shows her the new stained-glass panel that has replaced the one that was broken. Phyllis tells her the artist, Alison, used some pieces from the old broken window and incorporated them into the new one. This news to Clara is uplifting. So, broken glass can be made into something new and beautiful; it's a comforting thought, she tells Phyllis.

Glass smashed to smithereens, looks like precious jewels, says László.

I've just come across this, Phyllis says, scrolling down the screen on her computer. I was hoping I'd see you. Here, you may as well read it. It's only short.

Clara steps up to the counter and looks over Phyllis's shoulder at the laptop screen. It's a *Brainpickings* post on Rilke—his musings on Love, Freedom and Togetherness. It begins with a quote from Gibran. Phyllis swivels the screen so Clara can read it without glare from the window. I thought of you, Phyllis says, because I remembered you'd asked me if I had that book by Fromm...

Love one another but make not a bond of love: let it rather be a moving sea between the shores of your souls, Clara reads, a shudder of recognition runs through her. This isn't the first time this has happened in Berkeley Books; Clara has even been known to call the place Serendipity Central.

She reads on. Rilke considered this 'bipolar nature' of love, saying: *I hold this to be the highest task of a bond between two people: that each should stand guard over the solitude of the other.*

Clara knows only too well, personally as well as professionally, about these contradictory longings for intimacy and independence; she knows all about that need for personal space *vs.* those jostling needs for closeness when the other wants/ needs the opposite; how intimate relationships are see-saws, timings eternally wrong. She's watched over the years how relationships of so many people she knew fracture along this faultline.

Clara takes some comfort from Rilke; it may be paradoxical, she admits it does seem upside down, but it is only by giving enough space and autonomy to the other that a relationship survives. For most mortals, this goes against common sense, is asking the impossible.

Clara has been trying to counsel that stubborn Sadie along these very lines because—according to Zuniga—artists' relationships with their creations are not dissimilar. Sadie's ambivalent about so many things, that's why she can't get her work done, and she can't see past the ambivalence. She veers from one pole to the other, fails to occupy the creative space in which the opposites transform themselves, each in the presence of the other, to form a whole new space ... Sadie may have made it beyond the poles, but she's stuck in the in-between, flailing in an impasse, locked into the ambivalence itself, desperate for certainty, desperate for the escape key. Desperate for answers.

Extremes of ambivalence, Clara warns, immobilise; they fix you in Limbo, a Dante state in which we are lost, *our sole punishment / is without hope to live on desire...* That describes Sadie Sarrazin perfectly; desire she can't even access yet continually it boxes her in with blockages.

Sadie had interrupted Clara's observations, rudely, Clara thought. Just because you're living through this shit, Sadie said, doesn't mean I have to. Clara was taken aback by the apparent venom behind the words. But at least it indicated she was on to something.

László, observing from the side-lines, shakes his head. Such a fucking cynic.

49

Clara's interest in Rilke having been rekindled by Phyllis, she's been reading about how Rilke and psychoanalyst Lou Andreas-Salomé agreed that the only journey that mattered was the one within. The internal journey. Clara wonders if it might be possible somehow to glide over

You mean gloss over

glide over the external realities of a relationship in favour of a focus on the internals.

Mostly though Clara wonders if the two were strictly friends—Rilke being married to someone else—or were they lovers, or what category did their relationship fall into and is there even a category and did it start out Lou the analyst, Rilke the patient...

Salomé had what she called an *unfathomable marriage* with Nietzsche... and also it seems with Rilke... Where do truths lie in intimacy, and what happens in the hidden places; the stories are always more than one, and anyway they're apt to morph and shift...

And why do you even have to have a category for two people with feelings for each other... Johannes had asked that same question.

Your perspective, says László, *is not enough. Even for the time being.*

Somewhere deep down, Clara, you do know the truth of things. It's just that you keep trying to change the story, or find a way to alter the ending.

Clara agrees with Rilke, she's all for emphasising the importance of the internal journey. But the internal journey is not what the world sees. The world judges something else, it judges what it can see. The internals are assumed, and the externals cancel out the internals which are deemed irrelevant. Clara knows only too well it's impossible to wipe out the past, to erase the history of anything, to effect lasting repairs when foundations are askew.

She and Johannes have Form, they have Baggage. Did they have an *unfathomable marriage*, not that they had ever actually married, but perhaps they should have, in the circumstances. Perhaps that would have served in some degree to legitimise the union, fend off criticism. Marriage could of course have had the opposite effect, it could have been seen as a sham, a convenience, an attempt to sanctify the unsanctifiable.

50

László doesn't know where he stands on the issue of Clara's relationship with Johannes. He's inclined to leave it in the box marked Private but, at the same time, his antennae—as ever—are alert.

László also begs to differ on the issue of the 'true' journey being *within*, like he begs to differ on many things -Sadie or -Clara. *All* marriages are unfathomable. How can some things be *more true* than others. Why should interiors be more *authentic* than exteriors when it all depends on your angle of vision: ask the Cubists. Proust comes closest: the real voyage of discovery consists not in seeking new landscapes but in having new eyes. It all depends on your ways of looking and seeing which are not the same thing.

Take Sadie's stuff about stories. Take Clara's stuff about past traumas. Yes, László understands all that, he's not dismissing the validity of their perspectives, no, he can see through to the truths of what they say, of what they believe with a passion… But their truths and their faiths are—not personal, he's not going to dismiss them as merely personal, no—and he's not going to point out how they're circumscribed—which they are, but not only; he's not going to dismiss them when he says they're situated, contingent truths, No. But. László wouldn't know how to begin to explain to Sadie or Clara the full nature of his misgivings. He can see how some would find comfort in categories. But categories are not for him.

Beckett: *He could have shouted and could not…* This is life. Beckett's already told us how to write about life, to life about write.

To be or not to be. A cliché, for sure, and hence it's meaning too easily overlooked. Ambivalence. This or that. Either or. Splitting. How we each of us live in more than one world. Multiple worlds. Would Clara/ Zuniga see Shakespeare manifesting schizoid tendencies? What's the use of such boundary-less diagnoses beyond misplaced self-comfort, misplaced self-flagellation.

Clara talks about ambivalence, and Sadie knows ambivalence, and Shakespeare, and Beckett, they knew it too; *fuckssake, Clara!* Beckett made himself physically ill every time he went to Ireland to visit his mother, physically ill, vomit-ill, every single time.

When you've got bad stuff inside you it might be best to hive it off with a paring knife lest it destroy the rest of you. Beckett learned to hive it off into his writing. Louise Bourgeois transformed its energy in her art. Clara says Sadie's dark is what's blocking her. But there's such a thin dividing line between making use of the shadows and having them make use of you.

László feels ambivalence too, he lives it, an Exile in a foreign land where everyone knows he's *étranger*, yes, he feels it. He doesn't think or feel in categories, he's incapable. Dichotomies, incapable. Silences, inescapable. Ambivalence, sentries, ever present. Gold mines.

It's doubly difficult for László to criticise either Sadie or Clara—or, more precisely, to criticise and be heard—because he speaks from this position as Outsider: on the scale of Outsider-ness, if there were such a thing, László would find himself more Outsider-ed than either Sadie or Clara, for certain. Exile, and in Paris *sans domicile fixe*—SDF—yes, SDF it's a more respectful and humane designation that replaces the old *clochard*, but it's a designation nevertheless, a category László occupies through no choice on his part and one that has, to his mind, retained much of the unwieldy unwelcome—stigmatising—baggage that *clochard* used to carry. The discourses in which both *SDF* and *clochard* take shape have barely shifted.

Yes, as Sadie says, contemporary narratives are more open, more inclusive, more respectful, altogether more humane now and yes, László can see that. But they're still bounded, beginnings middles and ends in the correct order, still fundamentally categories; and people are only confined in categories for the conveniences of others—for governments, for the benefit of entire economic systems... As long as he can remember László has seen himself shunted into one category after another, a whole series of ongoing Othernesses he's been obliged to occupy, dragging with him the baggage of all the others, a baggage not his own, a history not of his choosing.

And ever will he remain

étranger.

In Paris, says Sadie, you can make *étranger* work for you. But László's not the only one who's trapped. He can see so clearly both Sadie and Clara are trapped as well, albeit not like him in a marginalised group of n'er-do-wells from whom nothing but the worst is expected. Sadie and Clara *believe* they are free, but their lives are controlled in so many ways from the moment of conception to the moment of death. And, in between, their thinking, their desires, their aspirations, their internal selves are straight-jacketed by who and what they are, the fact of their citizenship/s. Yes, Sadie and Clara, each in her own way, is critical of the dominant patterns of thought they bring under their various lenses for scrutiny, they both are questioning their privilege, each actively trying to shift the terrain on which they stand which, if László thinks about it too much, induces in him a terrible mixture of anger and pity. Their eyes and ears, for all their great intentions, remain half-shut. They are bound to fail.

Take the discussions Clara and Sadie keep having about Exile, for example, like they know what they're talking about, like it's nothing more than a word, neutral, some word that Clara likes to play with; Clara sees Displacement as some Zuniga-ish facet of the creative process, like Exile is a game, like the word means the same to everyone, like it means the same for ever, wherever. That's the trouble with words, they fool you into thinking you know what they mean and you could be a million miles off the mark.

Not every word translates, either.

Exile, it flips too easily off their complacent tongues like it means exactly whatever they want it to mean, like Humpty Dumpty: *'When I use a word,' Humpty Dumpty said, in rather a scornful tone, 'it means just what I choose it to mean—neither more nor less...'*

László's tired of calling them out, they don't listen, they can't listen, they're so fixed in their ways of seeing and hearing they're incapable of stepping outside the safe little worlds of their tired vocabularies. Every time, they assume that Exile means the same to him as it does to them and it doesn't it doesn't it doesn't and you'd think Sadie would have some kind of inkling having spent all that time at Sangatte, but she hasn't... No wonder she's blocked about that episode.

Exile, *száműzetés*, *exilé*, outcast, expatriate, the state of being banished from one's country Go away Go away Stay away

Exile: László understands something different, understands it better than people who haven't lived through it, he is still living through it, it's not just a word, it's a story, and it's not just a story, it's a human story, and it's not just a story of people, it's a whole collection of stories that belong to this person, to this person and that person and that other person over there and it's not just Laszlo's story, not just a single story or a personal story; it's not just a state of mind; it's real, it's painful, it's ongoing, it means you're being wrenched apart limb from limb again and again on a daily basis, it means you are living with your guts exposed...

All this shit Clara talks about the truest journey being internal, she hides behind her bookshelves, her Freud couch, her Zuniga, she stays safe in her little category box and talks about Exile. She says she's going to write it out but she doesn't and she doesn't because she can't because that kind of exile required by a writer sometimes is impossible. You can't just choose it or wish it.

Shit Clara, the truest fucking journey, this is all such shit.

Has anyone ever looked at you with hatred or, worse, with pity in their eyes and you know, you know that they actually can't see you, they see your category, Migrant, Exile, *SDF*, and you're supposed to be fuckin grateful when they throw you a couple of *sous*.

Oh the gravity of being here. László doesn't have the words to explain. Maybe there are no words, no words unless you can have words that bleed real blood when their arteries are slit open.

51

The window of my apartment in the rue des Canettes looks out over a small courtyard and all around me there are many similar windows: windows of other apartments, other streets, other cities, other lives.

I sit at my table writing, occasionally looking up, looking out, waiting for a day when I see someone over opposite, before the window of their life, looking out, like me, looking through the window of mine. In these moments, when I'm waiting, I examine my own reflection that appears in the mirror of the glass beyond the glass; I am in the display case, I swell in the once clear water of the river. Until then, I wait.

Writers, writer Nuruddin Farah tells us in a masterclass, must know how to wait, the worst thing a writer can do is try.

Farah tells László how he wrote his way through Exile while he was waiting. László shakes his head, says there's Waiting and waiting, like there's Exile and exile. László knows where he stands. László has two of everything. Doubling up, doubling over, echoes, reflections, shadows. László knows about doubles, and waiting.

Waiting and listening, the sounds of the city: the rumble of the *métro* at Mabillon. The sirens of the *pompiers* and the traffic shifts over to one side of the road. The shrill whistle of the traffic cop as he gesticulates wild and impatient by the boulevard St Germain/ St Michel intersection where the road's up; the great bell of St Sulpice chimes the turning of the hour.

As always at lunchtime on a Wednesday, László is making his way to the soup kitchen opposite the Apple Store in the rue Clément just round from the covered Marché St Germain. There's a queue outside the Nespresso shop as he passes. László likes good coffee, but he can't understand Nespresso, for the life of him, he can't get his head around the need for such a thing.

He looks around, sees people coming together in twos and threes in so many places, in the cafés, on the terraces, the *patisserie*, small groups milling around inside the *marché*, coming together around Food; people homing in like bluebottles, hornets, ant armies, clouds of locusts, swarms in a feeding frenzy, it's all so horribly primitive; none of these people are starving, none of these people will ever starve.

So it is, with his usual Wednesday heavy heart, that László pushes open the door of the soup kitchen and steps into the warmth. The smell of warm bread, onions frying. He washes his hands, puts on his apron, ties it up at the back, covers his hair with the blue cloth they wear when serving out the soup, washes his hands a second time. László is directed by Mauricio to the grill counter. They don't usually put him there, as he eats only plant-based. Mauricio asks him if he minds. László says no, it's ok, he can manage, he's happy to be where he is needed most. In a short while, they'll open the door to let the hungry people in.

Wednesdays are tough days, for all the obvious reasons, but particularly tough this week. Monday, it had been László's birthday and he'd made the mistake of telling Sadie, then allowing her to give him a birthday 'treat,' which, in itself had been disorienting. Sadie had been given some tickets—or so she said, László suspects she actually shelled out cash for them, and they must have cost a lot which is why he'd felt obliged to accept. Anyway, the tickets were to hear the Monteverdi Vespers in the Chapel at Versailles. Versailles. He would have loved the music. But Versailles. The place teeming with armed guards and privilege, post-revolutionary privilege. That had been Monday, it had been a terrible day, and he hadn't seen Sadie since.

Why's he thinking of Versailles when he's scooping out lentil soup to homeless people in a soup kitchen.

László.

52

I'd like to write mornings, spend afternoons with you, most evenings, some nights.

And here, in the Luxembourg garden, the cosmos flowers you loved, rising their pink heads tall above the newly clipped hedge. Yellow pansies line up in beds for the winter, earthy spaces between. Leaves are piled up in their cages. A few men play chess at small tables amid the uniform arrangement of the trees of heaven. The green tin chairs are almost all stacked.

On the court, a tennis ball thuds back and forth, back and forth; skill, style, spirit, the deep groans of the players' efforts, the cries of *faute!* I watch from the small grove of almost leafless horse chestnut trees, the Tour de Montparnasse rises in the distance. A player wipes the sweat from his brow with his tee-shirt, bends down to pick up the ball the colour of a *gilet jaune*. He breathes deep, leans back, raises his racket, gathers up strength to serve again. And smack. There it goes.

The windows of the *Orangerie* are open, letting in the air, the breeze almost warm. Children on half-term holiday scuffle through the fallen leaves, their pleasure in the living rustles of les *feuilles mortes*. The older men *jouent à la pétanque*; younger men, at basketball, the coach hollers from the sidelines.

The smell of earth after rain. The high excited sounds of children, the rhythmic thud and thwack of the tennis ball, the traffic on the *boulevard*; the quiet of the café tables, now almost empty, as dusk begins to draw us in. And there go the ponies on their final circuit of the afternoon, their little riders lean in holding tight onto the fronts of their saddles, tired hopeful parents walk alongside to prop them up; small people at the start of everything.

Now, here's the thing, Johannes: if you could manage to get to Paris by 1pm tomorrow, the new Ken Loach is opening at the Odéon, *Sorry We Missed You*, it's about the terrible conditions in which so many delivery drivers work, and how it affects their lives…. Do you think that could be possible?

Clara closes her fingers around the blue plastic lid she keeps in her pocket. She won't send the message. There's no point.

She presses the delete button, watches the eager plea disappear letter by letter.

Dis, quand reviendras tu…

A new low sunlight is touching the tops of the lime trees. Clara's heart beats its uncertain beats. She'll get back to her apartment and take a beta blocker; alone in the city, she shouldn't take chances with her irregular heart.

53

We ran our marriage from the high trapeze
   all around us monkeys were swinging

our breaths were shallow with altitude

we passed petals and stones on the snow

and shadows moving at angles we didn't know

we stayed in the swing as the shadows glanced slant
   and twisted

and the ropes wore thin

our voices were lost in the din of the Big Top

collapsing,

the sky falling in

Now we conduct our mourning from the high trapeze

from here we orchestrate memories,

our feet on the batons, our hands on the ropes

our paths follow predictable patterns

in arcs and vast swings.

Sometimes, as in life, our arcs cross, your feet on your
   baton, my feet on mine,

your hands on your ropes, my hands on mine, we
   swing past in time.

Sometimes our arcs intersect but only with hindsight,
   or predicted in future like stars that align

in the here, in the now, the ropes tangle and tighten
   around our small neck

and we sleep badly in the knowledge of

54

Yes, Sadie and László did go to hear the Monteverdi Vespers at the Chapel, Château de Versailles, in peacetime.

They take the Métro 10 then the RER to the Palace. It's winter now and icy wind and rain hit their faces as they go through the gates and begin to cross the plaza—*le cour d'honneur* of the Palace is huge. Straight away they're struggling to walk against the wind across the uneven cobbles.

It's not clear where they have to go. There are very few signs, some are ambiguous, some have blown over. On the plaza people are hunched up trying to walk crouched together under umbrellas that keep blowing inside out. László only has that threadbare jacket. They manage to locate the Chapel at the far side but it is shrouded in a giant blue *bâche*, the building is all cordoned off with metal barriers that have gone askew, the securing tapes are broken and the massive tarp is coming adrift and flapping so loud it sounds like a surveillance helicopter.

László, Sadie sees, is doing much the same as she is, trying not to show how he feels. He must be freezing. She wishes she hadn't persuaded him to come. She's been selfish. She hadn't counted on there being triggers, for her or for him, not in this place.

László's eyes are looking towards the uniformed guards lined up around the chapel. Each one has a huge firearm, positioned at the ready.

People are looking up to where, on the roof of the Chapel, a massive stone statue is swaying, it's moving in the wind, it looks like it could fall. Sadie nudges László and points up to what is happening.

Instead of being a Saint and solid and reliable, the statue is moving backwards and forwards as though it is drunk or wants to be away from the place altogether, like it has given up on sainthood and wants now just to crash to the earth and shatter in pieces and possibly kill people. A small crowd is gathering to watch, despite the howling wind and rain, people are standing around and gazing upwards, waiting for the drama about to happen.

Sadie feels László shuffle beside her. He seems uncomfortable. There's nothing to be afraid of if they keep well back. Some of the guards are actually standing at the foot of the wall directly below where the statue is swaying. Others are further out to prevent the public approaching the danger zone. László indicates that he wants to move away, but Sadie catches hold of his sleeve and pulls him back, they might as well wait here as anywhere until the Chapel opens for the Vespers, if indeed it is going to open.

But the guards are guards and they're brusque and they're gesturing for people to move back and then they're ordering them Go away Go away Stay Away. People are asking for help and where should they go and is the Chapel even open: we came to hear the Vespers, but the chapel looks closed, is it going to open, can you tell us please where is the door… But the guards are guards and they are brusque and they don't reply to questions, and they don't look at anyone, they keep their eyes away, and they keep shouting in monotones and waving their arms and telling people Go away Go away Stay Away

Sadie pulls László by the sleeve and gestures to lead him to where the guards have got people lining up well away from the Chapel. László wrenches his arm free from Sadie's grasp. She knows he's thinking that kind of fascistic fuckery is coming way too close and he cannot stand it. She knows those guards should have been nicer, they could have been smiling and nicer, even in this weather, even with those guns, even with that danger, it doesn't cost anything to be kind.

But the guards are an arm of the state and an arm of the state is an arm of the state whatever country you are in. The sentry men have large black boots like robot boots and they have limited words like robot words: Stand over there Stand over there, they repeat, expressionless, Go away Go away Stay Away

Sadie is torn between the impulse to do what she's told and wanting to stick with László who's turned and is already moving away in the other direction. It's like the people who are waiting for the sacred Vespers in the thrashing wind and icy rain are a species apart; it's like, for a moment, they aren't *Homo sapiens* at all; it's like they have wandered into an un-specied Hell.

Hell is the place where people lose discard or take leave of their humanity, where people take leave of themselves, where Them and Us are carapaces, burnt out empty but for the power of force, of reconstituted law and order, of chaos, of lies, of Hell, the territory of Enemies. Hell is where power hides in their holsters and stands in their boots and chokes in their locked-up throats.

But there is a sad irony, and it's not lost on the patient sacred-Vespers-waiters, not lost on the Stand-Over-There-Go-Away-people lined up in the icy wind and rain waiting to be admitted to the Chapel where the statue of the Saint on the roof is swaying, swaying, and may at any moment topple, where the statue could at any moment be knocked over and down by the blasting wind.

Sadie walks fast across the *cour d'honneur* to catch up with László who is already disappearing out through the main gate.

The irony, had the sad angry Saint fallen, the irony lies

in how it would have smash-landed right at the black-boot feet of the sentries, how the patiently waiting Stand-Over-There we-do-as-we're-told murmuration of people would have shrieked and rushed forward as one to push the guards out of harm's way.

55

In Paris, Clara says, I like to live out of cupboards. That is something you and I have in common, I think. Sadie.

Sadie doesn't like those statements that ride along as though they are innocent questions.

Sadie shrugs.

She doesn't want to pursue this conversation. She doesn't see herself as even a tiny bit like Clara Delaney.

I don't like cupboards. I actually mostly hang stuff on the backs of doors, Sadie says in a bored voice. I had to make space in my *chambre de bonne* for my desk, well my table I mean, and now I've got no room for anything. I'm supposed to be preparing a dissertation. What I actually need is an *atelier*, like this one, a studio…

Studio? Clara interrupts. You mean study.

No, I mean studio, Sadie is emphatic. I mean *atelier*. László tells me I need a studio like the one you've got here. He reckons I need it more than you. Sadie shifts in her seat, sits up straighter.

She is not aware of having spoken ambiguously.

Clara is sitting on the floor at the other side of the room, her back against the wall under the window, her legs stretched out in front of her. The angle of the light makes it difficult for Sadie to judge the expression on Clara's face. This is not unusual.

Clara's *atelier* in the rue Le Goff in the 5th is high up and looks out over the Sorbonne, the Panthéon, and across the rooftops of the Quartier Latin. Sadie suspects she chose it—though Clara has never admitted it—because rue Le Goff is the street Freud lived in for the year 1885 or thereabouts that he spent in Paris. Clara doesn't seem to know where Zuniga lived.

No way would Clara ever consider giving up her *atelier*. Clara shrugs. She's becoming less confident in dealing with Sadie's envy. Today it's making her angry.

You'd be more inspired, Sadie, she ventures, if you got a place in, say, rue Férou, where Man Ray had one of his *ateliers*. And isn't it that little street where part of Rimbaud's *Bateau Ivre* is written out along the wall…

You think I'm only inspired by dead men? Sadie interrupts, laughing dismissively. Like you are, she adds, getting to her feet.

Sadie had noticed Clara eyeing the clock. Why does she have to be so sly but make it so obvious. Why can't she just say, Sadie, your time's up, like they call in the pedalos on the lake at Gérardmer: Come in Number Seven, Come in, Sadie Sarrazin, your time's up.

56

Clara is walking up the rue du Temple, heading to the mahJ—*le musée d'art et d'histoire de Judaïsme*. It's only 10am but a short queue has already formed. You have to pass through strict security, have your body scanned, submit your baggage for X-Ray, as at an airport now. This is unusual, this level of vigilance, when there's no immediate reason for alert; it's been like this ever since the tragedy at Bataclan, and it makes Clara think of the horrors that happened throughout Occupied France, throughout much of Europe, to the Jewish people, the horrors of the Holocaust, lest we forget. Clara's mood is a sombre one as she climbs the stairs and enters the expo: *Sigmund Freud, Du regard à l'écoute*. She's been looking forward to this, if 'looking forward' is the right way of expressing it.

She walks up the stairs where, at the top, a few people are gathered in front of a TV on which is playing a black and white film—some crackly snippets of old ciné film footage from Freud's life that have been cobbled together into an amateur movie. She stands to listen. The footage is narrated by Freud's daughter Anna, herself a prominent analyst, and now a white-haired old lady, *la grand-mere avec les cheveux blancs.*

It's 1931 and here we are in Vienna, the place of Freud's birth; he's an old man of seventy-five now. This is the year following his mother's death, and it will be only eight years until his own death, from cancer, during his exile in London. Nazism in 1931 is already showing its ugly face but, for now, Freud looks content enough sitting in his garden, surrounded by family, petting his old Chow, Jofi. It is said that the dog accompanied him everywhere, was even present in his consulting room when he was seeing patients.

Clara takes the brand-new notebook from her bag. It's the special one she'd been saving for her Zuniga work but she's decided after all to just use it for any old thing. She'd ordered it before she even left London and it came by post from an artisanal producer in the Basque country, the area where Zuniga was born, near Gernika—the little town destroyed by the Nazis in 1937 and now better known as *Guernica* after Picasso's painting depicting the horrors of the Spanish Civil War, the horrors of all wars. To think, this painting was made in Paris. In the *atelier* in the rue des Grands Augustins. Clara has walked past it many times, looking, imagining. This is what Paris does to you. It makes you feel part of the glory.

There is such warmth in the way Clara holds the little notebook, real warmth in the way she opens it and prepares to makes her notes. Clara likes ritual, she likes to forge these little intimate connections. On the inside cover she'd written Clara Delaney and, later, the address of her *atelier*. Centred on the title page she'd written *Max Zuniga, A Life*. She'll stick something over that another day. She could tear the page out, but it'd show, there'd be that jagged bit and it would spoil things.

Today she's interested to discover whether there is any mention of Zuniga in this exposition of Freud's life and work. Zuniga died in 1939, the same year as Freud, and this is the 80th anniversary of their deaths. Clara feels good to be bringing Zuniga and Freud back together, even if only in her vision. Who knows what might emerge from their reunion...

On the film, scenes from 1932. Clara makes notes, enjoys that feeling, the surge of confidence, the sense of purpose, as her Muji pen (newly acquired) marks the page. Here's a clip of Freud with his archaeologist friend, Clara didn't catch the name. Freud maintained a lifelong interest in archaeology—geology too—and the uncovering of ancient artefacts, whether from in the ground or from the depths of the unconscious.

Clara reflects how those ancient things, dug up and brought from far-away places, now have such different meanings from those they carried in Freud's time and which were different again from their significances in their original environments. Clara pictures the collection of artefacts that stand like eccentric little sentries on Freud's desk—what artist Louise Bourgeois referred to with some disdain as his 'toys' while at the same time expressing an enduring respect for the artefacts Freud discovered in the depths of the unconscious. Clara makes rapid notes, enjoying the criss-crossing of associations.

All these things Freud looked at daily as he sat at his desk, their provenances, their stories, written and rewritten, their truths and their worth reappraised anew in the light of successive takes on colonialism as the norm... How structures of dominance and inequality have become embedded, embodied in even these little figures, the smallest of objects...

And yes...the psychological complexes unearthed by

the early psychoanalysts from their archaeological excavations of the unconscious, became similarly embedded in ideas and theories about the structure of the mind, they too must have reflected dominant implicit values and ideologies... Feminists—Juliet Mitchell—their work around gender politics in the history of psychoanalysis comes to mind. Clara notes she needs to keep an eye out for that in Zuniga. She'll re-read his case studies with a feminist pair of eyes. A valid reason for not passing on him altogether, not yet. And for not yet getting started on the writing.

Having begun to jot notes down in the former dedicated notebook, Clara feels, as she stands in the museum holding it in her hands, a curious sense of power, a new energy, a sense of having finally begun on the project that she came to Paris for but that she feared had almost defeated her; she's come so close several times to abandoning Zuniga. Today, in the Freud expo, Clara has a sense of elation. She has started work.

57

On the old film footage, some clips now from 1934-37, Freud still in Vienna—he's not yet fled, though by 1933 his writings are being openly burned by the Nazis in Berlin. For now—and it chills Clara to see this—he is reclining in the garden, with Martha, his wife, and her sister Minna, and there's Marie Bonaparte, being busy. It must be September, because they're celebrating the Freuds' Golden Wedding. It's a garden party, with presents and flowers, granddaughter Sophie is playing in the grass; this scene looks for all the world like an idyllic family gathering, though we know now, of course, that Nazism had already taken a firm hold and that neither Freud, nor any member of his family, nor indeed any Jewish person, was to be safe from relentless persecution until the Nazi state was finally defeated in the Second World War.

In 1938 Nazi Germany would annex Austria, and Freud's apartment would be requisitioned by the Gestapo, but for now it is 1937 and in the next clip here we are in the Waiting Room at Berggaße 19; there are flowers in vases and the walls are covered with pictures and photographs. This is Freud's consulting room and the place where the early meetings of the *Wednesday Psychological Society* (which would later become the *Viennese Psychoanalytic Society*) would have been held. Clara quickly switches her phone on, wants to try to capture the spirit of Berggaße in a couple of snapshots, though she knows a picture of a picture from old ciné film will inevitably be blurry, but she tries anyway. In the early 20s Zuniga would, as a member of the inner circle, have frequented that place, would have sat and walked and talked in that apartment, in that very room. Clara wishes the film would slow down, so she could get up close and examine the frames in detail; she likes to imagine Zuniga there, confident and powerful, recognised, respected, listened-to, influential, before his puzzling fall from grace and all that he valued was torn away.

Clara checks the shots she's taken from the film, they're not clear and the light is bad, but she'll save them anyway. She presses 'save.'

In her mind's eye she places Zuniga in the consulting room, but she can't put his features together to make a face. Neither can she make him sit down in either of the chairs, nor in Freud's own chair. She definitely can't make him sit on the couch, she won't even try. It seems the best she can do is view Zuniga's blurred shadowy figure from behind as he peruses the books on the shelves of Freud's library. Would Zuniga's own works be on those shelves? If she could access photographs of Freud's library, Clara could use her phone to zoom in and examine each of the titles along the shelves...

That's not obsessional. Whether Freud had Zuniga's books on his shelves is a matter of public interest.

Late summer in Vienna, 1937, Clara writes, finding it a little difficult to get back to her task, 1937, only one year before Freud—by then a sick man—would have to make his escape into exile, to London via Paris, an escape that was made possible by the aid of his disciples, particularly Marie Bonaparte; daughter Anna was arrested in Vienna, though later released, she too went into exile.

1938. In the final clips of the film Freud is exiled in London, with friends and family, by now obviously very sick, looks drawn and worried. Zuniga living in Paris. He too has only a short time to live.

There must be more papers somewhere, it's odd that there is so much missing from the Zuniga archive. It's all very strange, the paucity of records, his expulsion from the Society, the apparent erasure of the record that might cast some light on why...

This further confirmation of the lack of visibility of Zuniga in the Freud record re-fuels Clara's determination to get on with the biography. She's wasted enough time hovering. The man deserves recognition and she can—she will—make that happen.

58

Clara moves on to the room where materials concerning Freud's work on Dreams are gathered. She stops on the threshold as the memory of the Zuniga/ Johannes dream comes back to her, the two men merged like in Bergman's *Persona*. Clara really doesn't want to think about this now. She doesn't want to go back to that dream, not back to that darkness and confusion, not when she's only just started feeling a bit more upbeat about her work. She steps on into the next room, her attention caught by some of Freud's thoughts on Paris she sees on the wall, a quotation from 1900, Clara copies it down:

Pendant bien des années, je ne rêvais que de Paris, et le bonheur extrême que je ressentis en posant pour la première fois le pied sur les pavés, me sembla garantir la réalisation de mes autres désirs.

"For many years, I dreamed only of Paris, and the extreme happiness I felt when I first set foot on the cobblestones seemed to guarantee the fulfilment of my other desires…"

It expresses the exact sentiment Clara shares. It's good to remind herself that Freud was among the band of

Paris devotees, though he never spent more than a few months at a time here, and his enthusiasm came largely on the tails of his admiration of Charcot at the Salpêtrière hospital, just as hers came on the back of Zuniga.

There are times when Clara feels so powerfully within her the spirit of this city, feels it stirring alive inside her, it can be overwhelming but, even then, it never satisfies. Instead, Paris fills her with a strange inchoate longing, a need for belonging, a longing to be here, to *be* here, even as she walks these streets, even as she *is* here, even as the soles of her shoes beat beat beat their steady step against the *trottoirs*, that terrible gaping gasping need she has *to be here* presses continually at her temples, as if she's demanding more of the city than the city is willing or able to give.

Paris is witholding, it fuels her desire at the same time as it thwarts it, it tugs at her, it stops her in its tracks and reminds her, taunts her, Clara Delaney, *vous êtes une étrangère.* The city beguiles her like a lover delighting in his own absence.

Oh Johannes

Tu me manques.

59

Clara becomes increasingly agitated as she wanders through the remaining rooms in the Freud expo. She's losing direction and is no longer moving systematically through the spaces. Gone is that good feeling she had earlier, that feeling she was on a path, a path of potential, of systematic conquerings. That hateful memory of the dream she managed to push away has now been replaced with distressing images of the exiled Freud—the great man looking so ill and desperate—which has now pinned itself up behind her eyes.

Freud, for all his greatness, was human. Just human.

Sick, sad, exiled.

Dying.

Vulnerable. Like the rest of us.

Human.

60

And even in the Dream section of the exposition, she finds no sign of Zuniga.

Freud, vulnerable. Zuniga, absent.

Reality: piecemeal, sharded, fragmented, angled.

Clara thinks of Picasso's *Weeping Woman*, that face of shattered glass.

Everything Clara sees in the remainder of the show confirms this jumble of unsettling thoughts and feelings. The pictures that Freud had hanging in his rooms, they're all disturbing; many are images with which she is familiar, but today she's looking at the images with new eyes and the familiar is carrying layers more sinister than she has noticed before. The ordinary has become uncanny and it disorients her.

Clara is losing her place in the story, no longer sure what she wants from it. She is making increasingly brief and messy notes in the new notebook. Venturing into the Uncanny. Going through mirrors, like Orphée, hesitating on the threshold, crossing into the Underworld of the dream.

The paintings that Freud would have looked at daily. They're depressing.

Edvard MUNCH, Le Cri / The Scream/ earliest version made 1893 when Munch, almost a contemporary of Freud's, was 30. Clara has seen this before, in various forms, in Oslo. With Johannes. She puts her hand to her face and covers her mouth as she feels the scream enter her own body and well up inside her. How easily her boundaries slide, how easily they dissolve.

She walks on past the other pictures as though in a trance, hardly registering what she is seeing, making only the briefest of notes.

Max KLINGER, b1857, drowning man, before head disappears under water. German, contemporary of F's. Water = unconscious. Madness = disappearing into the ucs. Drowning.

Not waving but drowning. Clara remembers that Stevie

Smith poem, people think it's funny but it isn't funny at all.

Arnold BÖKLIN, b1827, relief, papier mâché, head of Medusa, hair of writhing snakes. Clara stares at the note she's made. Her handwriting says *hair of writing snakes*. They'd told her in London, writing's not easy, it doesn't just flow like that, easy, simple, you know, Clara... She understands that now. The Caravaggio *Head of Medusa* she saw at the Uffizi. With Johannes. How hard it is to negotiate the possibilities of venom.

Émil SIGNOL, b1804, painting: *Folie de la Fiancée de Lammermoor* depicts—as in Walter Scott novel—mad/ terrified pale woman in white nightdress, bloodstained, crouching in fireplace, dark unprotected space. Clara goes cold; that terrified face, those stains, that hunched up posture, what vile thing has happened to that woman, to any woman, every woman... Clara's boundaries struggle to contain the pain.

Grief and loss, every place.

Calmes toi, Clara, calmes toi

Freud lived and worked among these disturbing images of madness and pain. Yes, Clara sees the 'stories' Sadie talks about clear enough, how they take you beyond your boundaries, how they take you further than it is safe to go, how you have no control over the endings. And she's had enough. Clara has had enough. She's ceased taking photographs, she's ceased taking notes, and she no longer has the energy to think through any of it and she just wants to go home.

In the knowledge of: Zuniga apparently erased altogether from the record. His profession—and hers—has a very shabby edge.

61

Outside breathing in the open-air Clara feels herself reconnecting, her boundaries re-establishing themselves. She stops at the first café she comes to and takes a seat just inside the covered terrace; it's chilly so she'll keep her coat on, but she removes her gloves and, when the waiter arrives, orders a small *rosé*.

If Clara had been hoping for any new insights or leads into the life of Max Zuniga in the Freud expo, they have not materialised. Zuniga's absence, when he'd been at one time so prominent in psychoanalytic circles, is inexplicable, except as some grand repression. It's as though Max Zuniga, psychoanalyst, one-time collaborator with Freud, had never existed.

Sitting in the café waiting for her drink, Clara can't help but marvel at the terrible deep irony of how Freud the Father of Psychoanalysis, the man who brought us the reality of unconscious motivation and all the necessary workings of repression, appears to have obliterated—or presided over the obliteration of—all trace of a former colleague with whom disagreements (presumably) arose. Is that what happened? It appears to Clara that repression can function, not only at a personal level, but at the institutional level of a whole international movement.

In the café Clara's drink arrives and she begins sipping it straight away. She nibbles at some peanuts from the small dish the waiter has put on her table. She takes the notebook from her bag and jots down a few more thoughts. Repression—individual, social, institutional, elephant in the room. Perhaps this will become the Zuniga notebook after all. Clara's realisations seem significant, historically important. Hannah Arendt's work on how democracies slide into dictatorships reminds itself to her.

Thinking back too, from her present vantage point, she casts an empathetic—and critical eye—over the succession of images of women she's seen in Freud, today on the walls, but more widely implicit in his work. Yes, more committed feminists than Clara, have sought to tease out the normalised misogyny implicit in the work, from the innovations Freud made in terms of explorations into the unconscious and the treatment of neuroses. The ongoing need for such critical commentary has never appeared to Clara in such a stark form before.

Time has passed and many things now must be rewritten, given new places in new stories.

Everything, Clara, is of its time, of its place. Reality shifts as you do, as we all do. László reminds her. *Zuniga too.*

Palimpsests. Stories. You're on Sadie-territory, he adds.

Clara doesn't always hear László or listen to him when she does hear him, but his words are not lost. This time Clara's preoccupied by the idea that Freud—the man who told us time and again what a palimpsest of a world it is we live in, the man who convinced us of the futility, the absolute futility, of anyone ever trying to wipe any slate wholly clean—yet he appears to have presided over the erasure of Zuniga.

Time indeed for new stories. The new story Clara will tell is not the story of Zuniga but the story of the absence of Zuniga. The man is an absent presence in a much bigger story. Clara jots all this down.

The absence of the man and his work from the record of the other man and his work such as she has seen today energises Clara. She resolves here and now that she'll track Zuniga down, she'll do anything and everything that needs to be done to reinstate him in his proper place in history, and she'll get for his theory of creativity the recognition it, and he, deserves. She will do this without becoming obsessive, of course.

The waiter brings the *addition* and instead of paying up and leaving, Clara orders a further *demi-carafe de rosé*.

62

Sadie has happened along to the mahJ and the Freud expo at Clara's recommendation. Clara probably has hopes that Sadie will, via the visit, develop better understandings, insights, and an altogether more positive attitude towards her therapy via some direct acquaintance with Freud.

But Sadie has a different idea. The bits dealing with Freud's life and his theories and his vast dubious collection of antiques and little artefacts fetched up from heaven-knows-where, his spectacles, his notebooks, his medical bag, Sadie can't manage to drum up much enthusiasm for any of those. When it comes to the art works though, Sadie's ears prick up, especially the section on Surrealism. She's interested in that.

It's fascinating to discover in more detail the crossover, the mutual recognition, in the 20s and 30s between these two disciplines, Psychoanalysis and Surrealism, how they fed into and off each other, a real cross-fertilisation; Sadie feels the old stirrings inside her, the awakening of desire.

She's looking intently at *L'Origine du Monde*, a painting by Gustave Corbet, bought by psychoanalyst Jacques Lacan in 1955. The painting depicts a close up of a woman's genital area and abdomen. Sadie's hands go to her own abdomen in the way a pregnant woman's hands will spread out over the skin to caress and to guard.

The picture tells the story of the creative force that arises in the female body. It makes Sadie think of the explorations into the fecund female form made by Louise Bourgeois—sculptures, drawings and paintings, and many things stitched—the ambivalences they express, the envies they invoke, the identifications, the ambiguities, the angers, the power, the fraught beginnings and ends of everything. Sadie finds the painting intensely beautiful. She is so privileged to have seen it, so privileged to carry something of the creative force inside herself.

Distracted now, Sadie lays a bet Lázsló would not be

wowed by the obvious dream-scapes of some of these Surrealist works. He'd find them too superficial, László himself being a bit surreal.

Irreal? Yes, there's a difference.

László would be on the side with Freud, sceptical about surrealism and its claims to directly express unconscious material.

You don't find the surreal only in dreams, or paintings, my Sadie. It's in there, in the heart of you, like I am.

63

I often sit in the same café in the 6th where it is said Perec sat for three days watching and recording each and every one of the ordinary things that went on in the Place St Sulpice: he gathered together the elements of a picture, not of a city with its history and monuments and all its magnificence, but a Paris of the ordinary, of the people who passed by and through, and the dogs, the traffic, the sounds and the smells and the sirens and the huge gushing fountain and the great clanging bells of St Sulpice, and the whole *ambience* of everything seen and unseen, heard and unheard and what a long long list it all makes, making visible the trailing purple innards of Paris.

I sit in the same café in the late afternoon and nurse a *chocolat chaud* and try, like Perec did, to watch and absorb, to ponder on things, to hope, and through an engagement with the *quotidien*, to penetrate the veil, the cloud, the crusted stuck facade of the image; like Djuna Barnes, like Éluard, and Beckett who sat in this same place, to pierce and peel and discard the personas that people make and remake to present to the world, personas that like armours harden into fact and in the end require hammers and chisels to dislodge.

I have not yet succeeded in this or any other enterprise, *Perécien* or otherwise, but I continue to carry my pen in my mouth like a dog with its bone and I'll sit on here on the terrace at the Café de la Mairie until the cows come home.

64

Clara wants Sadie to go to see Bergman's *Persona* with her. It's on for two days next week at the little cinema St André des Arts in the 6th where Clara has a season ticket.

Sadie is in two minds about going anywhere with Clara, it's not as if they're friends or anything. Clara had been very strict at the start about boundaries and how important they are, especially in therapeutic relationships. In the early days she'd talked a lot of jargon about the ground rules—Sadie hadn't understood a word. But, later, curiosity had got the better of her and Sadie had looked it all up on line; she'd found out about *transference* being crucial and, innocently enough, she'd asked Clara whether it—whatever 'it' was—was working properly for them.

Clara had interrupted—rudely, in Sadie's view—and

had become quite heated; she'd effectively silenced Sadie with some muddled explanation that felt to Sadie more like a put-down and she felt unable to question further. It reminded her of her mother, some things were simply 'not Sadie's business' and that was the end of it. Now Clara, using humiliation to silence...

So it's a strange thing now for Sadie to be invited to a social event, for the two of them to be planning a pally pally to the cinema. As far as Sadie understands, any meeting of therapist and client outside the therapy room would be a transgression of the correct and proper 'transference' boundaries. But there hadn't been time that day to raise the question again, let alone go into details; Sadie had just left it with Clara that she wasn't sure about the cinema trip, saying she'd think about it and would let Clara know next time.

65

That day, unusually, Sadie takes the *métro* back to her *chambre de bonne* after her session with Clara. She's not in the mood for walking, nor in the frame of mind for mulling over things that came up in the session. Today she's tired and walks to the *métro* via the Luxembourg gardens just as they're closing, the *gardien*'s whistle warns the gates will be locked in five minutes. Sadie goes down into the *métro* at Odéon, boards Line 4 for Châtelet.

Contrary to her intention, as the *métro* rattles northwards, Sadie can't help but turn over in her mind recent issues that have arisen with Clara. They'd been talking about trauma on and off for weeks but today things had perhaps come to a head, and not just because Clara had invited her to the film.

Clara says traumatic events, once they've happened, however long ago, are not over and done with, not past and gone, but continue to live on—if no longer in accessible memory or the conscious mind, then certainly in the unconscious, as well as in the body. The mind—and Clara had cited Freud here—Clara likened trauma to a palimpsest, where you could scrape and scrape away at the surface but full erasure was ultimately impossible. She cited as evidence Sadie's ongoing 'free-floating anxiety,' her frequent and debilitating panic attacks that arrive apparently out of nowhere; these were, Clara said, evidence of the ways in which past traumas continue to resonate and to manifest themselves in the here and now. Old patterns, Clara said, are apt to repeat themselves and to go on repeating themselves again and again and again…

Freud said… Zuniga said… Sadie had found it too difficult to keep on listening. Reading between the lines, she'd concluded Sangatte was locked inside her, inside her mind and her body, and she would never be free of whatever resonant deeper trauma it was that provided the energy to tear her apart from the inside and put a complete block on her creative work.

Sadie brought to mind Louise Bourgeois' art, her *I do, I undo, I redo*, and for the first time the things Clara said had begun to make some sense to her. She could see patterns emerging in her life, if she was honest, if she told herself a certain kind of story, if she examined her experiences in a certain way. Yes, she could understand in her thinking brain what might be going on, but the knowledge didn't immediately make her *feel* any better. On the contrary, the more Sadie thought in terms of the language supplied by Clara, the more anguish was stirred up inside her.

And Clara had gone on to say something even more worrying; she said it was possible for a person to get *stuck* in the 'dark helplessness of trauma.' That was how she put it. *The dark helplessness of trauma*. Like having one foot nailed to the floor, she'd said, by way of illustration.

Sadie registered what Clara said and immediately applied the words—the diagnosis—to herself.

So, Clara thought Sadie was stuck.

In the dark helplessness of trauma.

So that's what Clara thought was wrong with her. That is why she can't move forward with her work. With anything.

Sadie couldn't have explained how or why, but the thought of that diagnosis, that category, the realisation of how accurately it applied to her, caused a fresh wave of panic to well up in her chest, almost stopping her from breathing. The idea that there was something *really wrong with her*, Sadie couldn't stand it. If there truly was something wrong, a definable wrong, a diagnosable wrong, a category wrong, then she might never get well... never ever get well... She might never recover from this eternal affliction that was blighting her life…

The light from the window behind Clara had reduced her to a silhouette, Sadie saw only a black shadow whose mouth was moving in the manner of a marionette…

Clara didn't say where she thought the trauma had come from…where it came from…what it was…what was it…where did it come from… On her way back on the *métro*, these thoughts echo echo echo inside Sadie's head along with the rhythm of the train…

These are the last thoughts Sadie wants to confront in the dark underground tunnels of the Paris *métro* but she can't silence them, can't put them out of her mind, they're starting to stifle her…

The train, she realises, now with an acute sense of claustrophobia, is deep under the earth in the place where they bury people—the Catacombs—this train, full to capacity, is crowding her in with no space no space no space… She can't push away the feeling. It overwhelms her, consumes her, it's making her sweat, she's far too hot, she's got no air, she can barely breathe, her heart is racing and jumping beats. She's going to be sick. She's going to pass out. She has to get out and into the open air.

The train jolts to a stop, the doors open and Sadie stumbles through the crush to get out and up to the surface where she can breathe the air. Gare de L'Est—she's gone several stops beyond Châtelet where she'd intended to get off. It's rush hour now and people are crowded all along the platform ready to push their way onto a train that is already full. Grasping her tote bag close against her chest, Sadie forces her way through the throng only just managing to exit the train as the doors slide shut behind her.

She needs to get up out of the underground to the open air. That terrible feeling Clara talked about, that *being stuck in dark helplessness*, it has taken tight hold of Sadie and is squeezing her throat and crushing her chest and making her heart beat outside her body.

Up in the street she stops and she breathes, she sits down on a law wall next to where someone sleeping rough has left a makeshift bed, a few filthy blankets, half concealed behind a collapsing cardboard wall.

Sadie is trying to breathe her panic away by inhaling the cool evening air slowly and steadily, in through the nose, out through the mouth, to a count of three. Between her cheek and her gum, she carefully places one of the dissolving tablets the *médecin traitant* had prescribed for acute attacks like this. Sitting on the low wall outside the station, just breathing, Sadie takes some small sips from her water bottle, waits for the pill to have its effect.

66

It takes some minutes for the acute panic to subside, then Sadie manages to hail a cab. She can't afford to take cabs, but this is an emergency. She keeps a twenty euro note folded up in the card pocket of her purse for emergencies like this. At that moment it seems to Sadie that her money is better spent paying cabs to take her to safety than paying Clara to be the agent of greater undoing.

Back at her *chambre* Sadie lies down with great relief on her bed. Another day, another anxiety attack, full-on panic in the *métro* only barely averted; what's wrong with her what's wrong, why can't she just be like normal people and do normal things and not feel like this. All she wants is sleep, and sleep and never wake up...

You're afraid of sleep, Sadie...

She can't go on like this, she's coming to pieces, unravelling, she can't do ordinary normal things any more, not without falling apart.

Sadie lies down on her side, pulls her knees to her chest and holds them. She's not really supposed to, but she takes another pill. She lets go of the pressure on her legs, tries consciously to let the tensions recede, the inner conflicts dissolve...

What is freaking her out most of all at this moment are the things Clara said today—Clara has a horrible habit of just throwing out remarks, apparently with no idea of the consequences, the cruel impact her words can cause...

Sadie breathes slowly and deeply trying so hard to stay on top of this demon.

Today Clara, on top of the dark helplessness thing, had let float the idea that Sadie was, not an accidental victim of trauma, but the *willing agent of her own destruction*. Clara implied that Sadie wants, or is choosing, to remain *fragile and stuck*, that she *doesn't really want to let go* of any trauma at all… She wants to keep it. Hang onto it. *Protect it* from Clara! The memory of this exchange in the session causes a whole new wave of nausea to well into Sadie's stomach and throat. She retches, staggers across to the sink and throws up.

Clara didn't say those actual words, Sadie.

No, she did not use those words, but she hinted, Sadie is sure that's what Clara believed lay at the root of Sadie's troubles, that's what she was saying, between the lines, in that horrible obtuse *I-know-better-than-you* way of hers.

Sadie goes back to bed and lies down looking up at the ceiling, up at the cracks in the plaster that branch out like tributary systems, like arteries and veins full of blood travelling to and from the heart, the entire nerve systems that carry the pain and the messages of pain...

Sadie finds it unthinkable that she could or would actively *choose* to *hang onto* anything about her present painful mental state or any of the traumas of the past. What would be her motivation for such a stupid self-destructive thing? Why would she have sought therapy if she'd wanted to remain in the grip of neurosis and psychic pain? In the kind of brave moment you have when you're alone, Sadie decides to confront Clara head-on with her suspicions, her indignation, her disappointment. These thoughts passing through her head, the second tablet takes effect and Sadie falls into a deep sleep.

67

In the event, Sadie tries to broach the topic with Clara in a more tentative way. Clara remains calm, and merely comments in a neutral voice that all she meant was that there can be something 'safe about a symptom, a diagnosis, something comforting about that kind of confinement...' Then Clara goes on to extend the thought to an idea of Zuniga's about how 'self-sabotage' can stand in the way of getting where one wants to be...

To Sadie's thinking, Clara had obviously never experienced acute anxiety or a panic attack or she couldn't believe such a thing. Anxiety is the opposite of comforting. The sufferer would give anything to be free of the continual threat of panic. Clara shrugs when Sadie says as much; then, after a brief pause, she says in a closing-of-discussion kind of way, *It's your therapy Sadie, what symptoms I may or may not personally have experienced is not what's at issue in this room.*

Once again, Sadie feels the sting of the put-down. She wants to retaliate, but the energy has drained from her.

The film, *Persona*, what's it about? Sadie hears herself asking, compliant, her voice thin, far away, unfamiliar. Dutiful daughter.

Oh, I wouldn't want to give anything away, Clara replies, I promised you, no spoilers.

Yes, but how will I know if it's my kind of thing?

It's about what we've been discussing, Clara says with that finality to her voice again. About trauma. And boundaries. 'Transference' if you want the technical term. It will be good for you to see it. It will be good for both of us. Yes, I think we'll both find it interesting. And useful.

68

They'd ended up going to the 18h15 screening on the Friday at the little indie cinema in the rue St André des Arts. They met outside the box office where people were already queuing, but probably not for *Persona*, as Clara remarked as she handed Sadie her ticket. They made their way up the stairs to Screen 2. Going up, Sadie experienced a strange sensation, a sinking feeling, a kind of desire, a queer mixture with an edge of panic which came from knowing she was out with Clara and that Clara was following up the stairs so close behind her.

They took their seats—had it been up to Sadie, she'd have chosen an aisle seat, but Clara evidently preferred the centre of the row which placed them square-on to the screen. They sat down and Clara explained a little about the plot and the characters while they waited for the lights to go down.

Sadie struggled to listen. She was finding sitting this close to her therapist—or was Clara now her former therapist?—whatever, she found it disconcerting and preoccupying—their upper arms through their coats were touching and, though the touch was through layers of cloth, it seemed to Sadie exaggerated as though they were skin to naked skin. In the darkness, Sadie was aware of Clara's breathing, and the faint wafts of her scent—the same rosy smell there always was in the consulting room—and Clara seemed genuinely engrossed in what she was saying and this fact seemed to Sadie interminably strange.

The film, Clara said, was about two women, a former actress and her nurse/carer. The actress had been incapacitated by having suddenly gone mute and now could barely move—Clara characterised this as a *hysterical reaction to trauma*, in this case to having encountered certain images from the Vietnam War...

At this point, at the mention of *hysterical*, Sadie had begun to feel queasy and she deeply regretted not speaking up earlier about preferring a seat at the end of the row. She waited, only half listening to Clara, vigilant to see if anyone should come and sit between herself and the aisle escape route. The issues raised by the film, Clara was saying, were relevant to Sadie—very relevant, she stressed, leaning in so close that the rosy scent was too strong and Sadie could almost feel wisps of Clara's hair touching her face—Sadie, she said, had been similarly traumatised, directly by personal experience, and indirectly—vicariously—by having witnessed the trauma of others at Sangatte, people she'd tried to help but ultimately had been unable to rescue...

Clara had never addressed Sadie like this before, never as directly, never had she so simply summed up her idea of what Sadie's problem—the *origin* of her *trauma*— was. It wasn't accurate but that was hardly Clara's fault. An acute feeling of discomfort hit Sadie in the stomach and she felt herself shrink inside her coat. She was too warm, she wanted to take the coat off, but the film was about to begin and taking off her coat would be too disruptive, it would mean she'd probably have to bump up against Clara in the struggle to wrestle her arms free from the sleeves... She was trapped in her coat. She was trapped in her story. It was all impossible. Sadie sat back in her seat and tried to relax. She had kept her coat on but had never felt more naked.

Did Clara have any idea how difficult it was for Sadie simply just to sit back, relax and enjoy—not only now, in the cinema, but in so many ordinary situations? How long was it since Sadie had been able to do so many of the ordinary of things people took for granted, did without thinking.

Wafts of Clara's scent continue to reach Sadie: rosewater, mild and fresh and clean and feminine. Exactly what you'd expect Clara to smell like. A bit olde worlde. A bit overpowering. Almost like a grandmother, the smell of that old fashioned rouge a grandmother might wear. And those semi-crumpled linen clothes. Those soft soft leather shoes from the Natural Shoe Shop, soft and tender as gloves... The lights go down, Clara turns in to look at Sadie and smiles, Okay? she asks and, for a moment, her hand rests lightly on Sadie's forearm. Sadie nods and together they turn their heads to face the screen. The film begins with darkness; then two bright lights appear, they increase in intensity, a portion of the leader flashes by and there is a sense of a projector starting to run.

Sadie is momentarily distracted from her inner discomfort by the way the film begins. Suddenly she's interested, not in the hysteria or the trauma or the weird stuff about identity that Clara's fixated on, but in the form and the structure of the movie. She has a sense it could help her move forward with her own work. If there's going to be an aesthetic of visual self-reflection in this film, it could be up Sadie's street. For a few moments, sitting there next to Clara in the darkened cinema, listening to the soundtrack—a meditative melancholy piece by Bach, an adagio for strings—Sadie is greeted by a renewed sense of hope—a dawning of excitement—about her work; she hasn't felt 'beside herself' in any positive way like this in a long time. The early part of the film passes in something of a haze as Sadie floats along on these new sensations. Cinema is a powerful medium, she should go more often.

But the good feeling fades as Sadie is pulled more and more into the world of the film, no longer just watching from afar on a screen but being fully present in those scenes where what is being depicted by Bergman is the profoundest sense of personal psychological agony she has ever seen on a screen. These are characters, *personnages*, whose masks are slipping, whose boundaries are dissolving, whose inner selves are spilling out and getting tangled up with each other's guts… Two women, the one who talks is screaming *I'm not you* at the one who doesn't talk, and they both look terrified and they both look more and more like each other, then their faces merge and there is only one ugly distorted tormented face that belongs to both of them and neither...

Sadie covers her face with her hands and is racked by deep uncontrollable sobbing. Next to her, Clara is standing up, she's taking Sadie's hand, she's helping her up. Sadie clutches onto Clara and allows herself to be led blind with weeping from the auditorium.

69

Clara has to wonder whether it had been her intention—unconscious of course—to bring things to a head like this. Everything feels so strangely veiled.

She's taken Sadie, drained pale and trembling, back to the *atelier* and put her onto the pull-out with a hot water bottle and the mohair cover. Sadie is sleeping now and Clara is sitting in the chair trying to work out how she's managed to preside over things going so badly wrong.

She knows better than to speak about this in the passive voice because this of course isn't the first time she's messed up like this. It's not the first time she's managed the boundaries so badly that identities have come adrift from their moorings. All that shit she'd gone through with Johannes... She'd sworn she'd learn from that... She thought she'd learned from that... But the compulsion she'd felt to go to *Persona*, how innocent it had seemed to invite Sadie along... What a fool she'd been, what a bloody blinkered fool.

Clara gets up and goes to close the tall shutters against

the night. She makes herself a chamomile *tisane* and sits down again. As she puts down her cup on the little table some liquid splashes out and Clara realises how badly her hand is shaking. It's a stupid place to sit anyway. She gets up again, wipes the wet up with her sleeve and goes to sit at the desk instead. The mug makes a wet ring on the desk. She stares at it, hearing only the sound of Sadie's steady breathing. Clara turns on the angle-poise and stares at the big bright moon circle of light it makes on the wall as the rest of the room is swallowed in darkness.

Look how a single light both defies and defines the darkness…

Deep breaths, Clara.

Time to undo the bandages that cover the wounds that hold together the wounded.

70

Clara has been lecturing Sadie all this time about transforming her trauma, never once thinking about her own. She's been quoting Zuniga like a soothsayer, in the absence of any real knowledge of who he really was, what he stood for, never questioning his wisdom. She's been hauling Sadie's demons out of their hiding places and exposing them to the sunlight, all the while holding her own darkness at bay. Talk about denial. She looks across at Sadie still sleeping steadily on the pull-out. Sadie, so young, so talented, so at the start of everything.

Clara, what have you done?

Yet Sadie's also fearless. Despite all her terrors, torments, anxieties, she's fearless. Sadie might not know it, but she's already well on the way to becoming her own person. Unlike Clara. Who is twice as old and not half way there.

Oh Clara.

Even after the *Persona* debacle, Sadie can sleep. Even carrying the Sangatte trauma inside her, she can sleep. Even being as stuck as she is with her creative work, she can sleep. Even afraid though she often is of sleep, even up against those panic attacks, she manages, she pulls herself through, she carries on. Sadie can sleep.

Clara cannot sleep. So often, it's Clara, the person behind the therapist who makes mistakes, Clara who can't sleep.

And now she can't even drink the tea. She pushes the tea aside, gets up and pours a large Armagnac into a big bowl of a glass, sits down and takes a few sips.

It would not be unheard of for envy to raise its head in the transference.

The thought makes Clara go cold all over.

She has in recent times felt gouged by the claws of Sadie's envy, shrunk away from Sadie's evident desire to draw blood—her covetousness over the *atelier*; her preference for László's crack-pot ideas over Clara's interpretations—tantamount to saying he's a better therapist, more worth listening to... And Sadie's—mocking?—refusal to take any of Zuniga's ideas seriously, saying he didn't understand the first thing about aesthetics and creativity, yes, indirectly mocking Clara's efforts at getting the biography started... undermining her... sabotage... Yes, Clara has felt the barbs of Sadie's envy.

She takes a few more sips of the Armagnac.

There's another story, Clara.

Clara has belittled Sadie. The time Sadie brought those little stitched-and-stuck collages to the session, Clara hadn't even looked at them; her conscience had pricked at her long afterwards but still she didn't mention the apparent return of Sadie's creative mojo... just greeted Sadie's efforts with silence.

Then, *Persona*. Taking her to *Persona*, of all films... Bergman.

Clara Delaney is not immune to the acting out of envy.

She's been too preoccupied with Zuniga...

Obsessed.

Obsessions cloud judgement. They put a person in no fit state. But even so there is no excuse for messing up in the way she has. She'd let her desperation about Zuniga eclipse everything and the worst of it, she hasn't even made any headway with that project anyway.

Clara drains her glass and pours herself another. Envy can have two outcomes: it can provoke a will to emulate and even to excel. Or it can bring on a desire to destroy. Either. Both.

Clara looks across at Sadie still sleeping soundly on the couch. It is not inconceivable that Clara Delaney wanted to destroy Sadie Sarrazin when she invited her to the screening of *Persona*. The screaming of *Persona*. Pray God she has not succeeded. Clara had given up her supervisor in London when she gave up being a therapist and came to Paris to write… She now wishes to God that she hadn't.

Time to undo the bandages that cover the wounds that hold together the wounded.

71

It is 3am. Sadie has gone and Clara has put herself to bed on the pull-out—the place still warm where Sadie had lain. Clara is reeling from Armagnac and turmoil. Sadie had woken an hour ago, said she was fine, no problem, no really no problem, just wanted to get back to her *chambre*. She'd smiled weakly and it had broken Clara's heart to see Sadie's resilience beginning to crack, to witness how brave Sadie was struggling to be, Clara had had to look away.

Of course, Clara knows Sadie is not fine, she can't be, but she'd had to let it go. It would have to be sorted out another day. If there was another day. Sadie put up some resistance but, in the end, accepted Clara's offer to call an Uber to take her back to the rue de L'Arbre Sec, she'd turned down Clara's offer to stay over at the *atelier*; she wanted to get back to get on with things, she said, the deadline for her Scholarship submission thing was closing in and she wanted to get her head sorted out.

Clara knew Sadie was letting her off the hook, for now anyway, knew that she herself should have proffered a sincere apology; but she didn't and she hadn't and the fact is she couldn't, she couldn't formulate the right words in her head let alone get them out of her mouth in the right order, and not just because of the Armagnac. Her relationship with Sadie was as doomed as hers with Johannes had been… Things had, once again, flipped the wrong way round.

Not suddenly, Clara.

So Sadie had left in the Uber. But just as she was about to leave, she'd remembered something—Oh I almost forgot, Sadie said, I had something for you. It was to say Thank You, for the film, and everything… Just a minute, I've got it here. Sadie rummaged about in her satchel and produced several slightly crumpled sheets of A4, stapled together at the corner and folded in two. She straightened them out with the flat of her hand. It's an article about Max Zuniga, she said. Well, it's not *about* him but it mentions him. I came across it in La Galcante when I was looking through the Surrealism box. Sadie handed Clara the pages. I told the man you were writing about Zuniga and he photocopied it for you. He said he probably could find other stuff in the press archive if you cared to stop by…

The Uber had sounded its horn out in the street and Sadie grabbed her coat and ran off down the stairs leaving Clara holding the crumpled pages. That was Sadie all over. Getting stuff crumpled. Getting there first.

Sadie gone, Clara fetches her glasses and, in a haze of alcohol and weariness, sits down on the pull-out to look at the article.

The piece, from a 1939 copy of *Match*, is an Obituary: a well-known actress, Josette Jamet, had apparently taken her own life in Paris on being informed of the death of Max Zuniga. The article raises the issue—though avoids any conclusion—that Zuniga may himself have taken his own life the week before. The piece suggests that the pair—the former prominent psychoanalyst and his equally prominent patient—had conducted a long-term intimate relationship outwith the therapy—and outwith the basic rules of therapy—and it eventually took its toll on them both.

Clara has to stop reading. She rests the sheets of paper on her lap, closes her eyes and steadies her breath the best she can, trying to relax the tension that has rigidified her body and is making her hands shake so. She stands up. She goes to the window.

Zuniga, it seems—and poor Josette, poor poor Josette—had paid the ultimate price for transgressing boundaries. At the time they lived, Clara knows, less significance than now was accorded to transference issues but, even so, the article strongly suggests that it was Zuniga's relationship with Josette that lay behind his break with Freud and his expulsion from the Society.

Johannes. Johannes. Johannes. Breathe, Clara, breathe. She gets up and drains the last of the bottle of Armagnac into her glass. She lies back on the pillows and breathes out a long breath. The room is starting to spin. Clara closes her eyes. As she falls into sleep the pages drop from her hand onto the floor. She has neither locked the door nor turned off the lights. She drifts in and out of sleep, her mind circling round and over what happened with Sadie, what happened with Johannes, the underlying demons that must have drawn her to Zuniga; what should have happened, what should not have happened; Clara Clara *Oh Clara*, look at you lying there, the epicentre of chaos.

72

It's still dark when Clara opens her eyes. She's thirsty. She reaches for her clock, it's not even seven, she's had barely three hours' rest but she won't get back to sleep, not now, not with this knot in her guts, everything has magnified itself during the brief torment of sleep. She gets up, drinks water, goes to put the coffee on. She doesn't make it to the hotplate before her stomach is retching and she has to run to the bathroom.

The battle lurches on inside Clara. The instinct to run, to leave it all behind, she's felt this before, she's done this before. The impulse to hide, to cover things up, smooth things over, carry on, carry on, she's felt that before too. The desperation to do anything, anything, whatever it takes, to make this horrible thing go away.

You tried those strategies, Clara. They didn't work then. They won't work now.

Clara shuffles back to bed, she has to lie down.

The time has come to undo the bandages that cover the wounds that hold together the wounded.

Whatever lame excuses she dreams up, whatever cowardly schemes she can muster to duck the blame, Clara knows she can't avoid taking responsibility for her transgressions, not this time.

Transgressions. Of boundaries. Of professional practice. Of ethics. With Johannes. Now Sadie. She has to face up to the consequences. Make reparations. If she doesn't, there will be repetitions, and repetitions, endless.

It scares her more than anything to think even one step ahead. To have to face this self-sabotage, this terrible will to destroy that erupts from deep inside her.

She'd all but destroyed Johannes. Now Sadie is the target.

Perhaps, Clara, you have a will to destroy yourself. A surging need to rid yourself of a traumatised part of yourself, the vulnerable part, the dangerous part of Clara Delaney.

She can't think like this anymore. She'll go mad. She's not strong enough to get through this, she knows it, not on her own. And there's no-one she can lean on.

She hasn't been looking closely enough at the mirrors therapists and clients hold up to each other's distorted faces.

As in *Persona*...

73

And yet, perhaps there can be hope, another story, one that could allow Clara's mood to take a different turn. There are a couple of famous cases—she's thinking of Beckett and Bion—where transgressions of the transference in therapy had apparently 'worked' to bring beneficial outcomes for both patient and analyst. Perhaps something similar can happen in her case. Clara pours herself a second cup of coffee and goes to fetch the Beckett biography.

Beckett, she confirms, was in analysis with Bion in London in the mid 1930s when analyst invited patient to a lecture given by Jung at the Tavistock. Jung had spoken of harnessing energies from one's symptoms and complexes and channelling them into productive and creative pursuits... This apparently had been revelatory—it had opened a whole new dimension in Beckett's understanding of his own psyche, his central artistic dilemma, and his creative blocks. It is said that his attendance at Jung's lecture marked a decisive shift in both Beckett's analysis and his writing. Afterwards, he was able to complete Murphy, a novel in which he explored the psychic schisms—Zuniga's schizoid states? his self-in-exile?—as places where creative impulses reside, working along the blurred and mutable boundary between 'sanity' and 'madness.' This was the point at which Beckett knew that his unique creative force could be harnessed from his own peculiar internal areas of darkness. It was said that Bion too benefitted from his close encounters with Beckett as they transgressed therapeutic boundaries together...

Clara is calming down a little with these thoughts. The idea of Beckett's success and Bion's apparent success must complicate considerably any simple assumption that the transference is sacred and must always be protected... Perhaps she's over-reacted to the *Persona* fiasco. Perhaps there's nothing to worry about *vis à vis* Johannes. Perhaps Sadie's fine, like she said she was...

It's so long since Clara has heard anything from Johannes.

Oh Clara, Clara, Clara. László is compelled to intervene. *This kind of thinking has a name, and well you know it.*

PART 5

Rocking to infinity the red skein it will never be interrupted, abandoned or cut. There is one eternal thread and it is you

Louise Bourgeois, 2003, 2004

74

For Sadie's part, she is not going to think about Clara. Clara clearly has issues and they're nothing to do with Sadie. That's what the student counsellor at the Academy has said. Sadie should disengage and persevere with her own creative work.

Today Sadie is in a Life Class and it's difficult as she doesn't like life drawing which makes her not very good at it. Where the tutor goes on and on about strength and form, all Sadie sees is vulnerability and fragility. Sadie is the only person she's ever heard of who'd stood in front of Michelangelo's *David* and wept, not for the beauty of the great work, but because she was unable to see anything beyond the profound and terrible fragility of his masculinity, of his very humanity.

Her tutor tells her to capture the fragility then, draw it, go on, draw it, he goads. Sadie suspects the tutor is mocking her insistence on the fragility of dignity and the dignity of fragility. He probably never thinks about snakes swallowing tails. Draw it then, he repeats. Other students clamour for the tutor's attention but he seems to want to monitor the reluctant off-beam marks that Sadie is making.

Sadie thinks of Munch's *Puberty*: a young girl, naked, is sitting on the edge of a bedstead, her skinny shoulders hunched. The model today reminds Sadie of that girl. How anxious she looks, how fragile, how scared.

An image of herself, sitting hunched on Clara's couch flashes into Sadie's mind and disappears.

Sadie could never paint the Munch, not in a million years; it would destroy her completely to step inside the soul of that girl enough to paint her. Sadie is having enough trouble hanging onto her own soul.

Another image of herself now, more recent, occupies her vision; Sadie lying under the mohair blanket on Clara's pull-out, Clara bending over her, bending down close, the sickly rose smell of that scent, her face too close but Sadie can't move, she's rigid, riveted, pretending to be deep in sleep. *Persona*, the faces of the carer and the cared-for, merging, the mute and the vocal, merging

I am not you.

Getting the connection and the distance in life drawing is an impossible dual task.

Sadie shakes her head to try to rid herself of the images invading her, as if she could scatter the disliked bits of her internal being like a poppy shakes its seeds. She looks again at the model, focuses, knows beyond a doubt she's seeing something other than this girl who is sitting there. Without any real awareness of what she is doing, Sadie removes her drawing sheet from the easel, puts it into her port-folio, ties up the ribbons; she drops her charcoals into her apron pocket, and excuses herself from the class, complaining of a headache. She hears the tutor let out a loud sigh as she collects her coat from the peg and opens the door. As she leaves, the tutor begins in his loud didactic voice to instruct the class on the next stage of the studio work. Putting on her coat on the other side of the door Sadie listens in for a moment.

How do we know when a piece of work is finished? he's asking.

Sadie pictures him prowling among the easels, his hands in fists thrust deep into his pockets. No-one replies. It's a difficult question. There are no easy answers. Then someone ventures, 'It all depends…' The tutor interrupts. 'It all depends…' he echoes. 'Depends on what?' That interruption, that mocking tone. Silence again. 'On what?' he repeats. 'On what does finishing a work of art depend?'

Suddenly Sadie knows the answer. Or she knows *her* answer. She's finished putting on her coat and now she's heading back to her *chambre de bonne* so she can finish today's life drawing. *Sans* model. *Sans* tutor. Sadie knows the answer.

75

Sadie walks quickly, she wants to call in at the Louvre shop on the way back. It's difficult to get into the Museum when you're in a hurry, there are always such terrible queues snaking round the barriers that are set up by the big glass pyramid on the plaza to contain the crowds and monitor the numbers going in and out. There's lots of guards, big security, since lives were tragically lost at Bataclan.

Sadie knows a quick way in, it works best if you're only

going to the boutique, which she is. She hurries down through the tunnel on the far side of the road that separates the Palais du Louvre from the Tuileries gardens. In the shop it takes her no time at all to locate what she wants. She's had to pay 24Euros which is more than two days' food, but she has no regrets. What she's going to make feels important. The old familiar excitement is stirring inside her and she likes that. In ten minutes, Sadie is back at her *chambre*, her precious cargo sticking up out of her backpack like a beacon.

The important item Sadie has carried back to her room from the Louvre boutique is a large print of the Munch *Puberty* painting. She pins it up it on the wall so the light will fall onto it from her skylight. She's hoping to photograph it using natural light. She hopes there will be enough coming through the little skylight. She'll wait until the sun comes round to that side, but autumn sun is unpredictable and might not be high enough. She sets up her Polaroid on its tripod. She wants to do this properly, not just a quick digital picture on her iPhone; she wants objects, not images. She may have to wait until tomorrow for the light to be right. Or the next day. No matter. It will be worth it.

If it takes time, it takes time, László nods. *Time takes time.*

Sadie will go out and buy a *gougère* while she's waiting for the light to move. Perhaps she could branch out for a bottle of plonk. Celebrate. It's so long since she's been in art-positive mode. She can do the strict budget thing next week as her rent's not due 'til the end of the month. It's strangely liberating to be so firmly on the wrong side of Clara. To have the upper hand.

Sadie arrives back at her room at exactly the right time. The late afternoon sun is slanting in through the skylight and bronzing a section of wall by where she's hung the Munch. She has no time to lose—she has a whole series of shots to fit into a tight time window before the low sun sinks too low. First, though, she uncorks the St.Emilion she bought in Monoprix—she hadn't gone for the cheap option as she really does have something to celebrate—she uncorks the bottle and leaves the wine on the table to breathe.

Sadie works quickly. First she repositions the print correctly. Then she photographs the Munch with the Polaroid, pulls the print from the camera and, without even waiting to see it materialise, she lays it on the desk and moves on to the next. For the second shot, she drapes an old coat loosely over the naked girl in the picture and nails it into place, takes another shot. Parts of the image will be missing and parts will be fuzzy as can happen with Polaroids. That's the challenge with this camera, you won't know until later. It's full of surprises. And fuzziness is not a bad thing always. Next Sadie lays the coat almost like a shroud, lets the nails be visible. In this way she takes a series of Polaroids with the coat positioned so as to reveal progressively more of the girl in the painting. The final photograph is that of the naked girl much as Munch painted her with the coat a crumpled heap discarded on the floor.

Sadie scans the polaroid prints into her laptop, keeping their edges visible. She uses Photoshop to adjust the scope and the edging and finally to remove the naked girl entirely so in the very final picture all that is left is the bare bed with no-one sitting on it and the crumpled coat on the floor like a recently shed snake skin. Last, she makes a picture of the coat folded tidy in a suitcase on the bed, as through about to depart on another journey. She thinks of the Catalano men by the Seine, their suitcases full of missing body parts, according to László. The main part of her work complete, Sadie picks up the coat, shakes it out and hangs it on the back of her bathroom door.

It's been dark for hours by the time Sadie has finished making and printing and scanning and putting the final touches to the series of photographs. She realises she hasn't even touched the wine. She prints her finished pictures out onto A4 sheets and sticks them up along the wall in a sequence with masking tape. She imagines them along the far wall at Chez Georges. She'll write the text for them tomorrow. She'll take the scans on a flash drive to the print shop in the morning and get some decent full-size ones made. A3 from the already expanded Polaroids will be grainy and uncertain and that's what she's aiming for. As long as she—and anyone looking—can make out the coat, the shifting form and function of the coat, and the naked shivering girl.

Sadie jams the cork back into the wine bottle and lies down on the bed, fully clothed, not even bothering to do her teeth. She looks up at the moon through the skylight. You can never see stars in Paris, there's too much light. But the moon is good. Sadie lies on her bed feeling pleasantly possessed. It's a thousand years since she's felt as good as this.

76

The following morning when Sadie wakes it is way past ten and she's missed her *rendezvous* with Clara. Sadie's rarely slept this late in living memory.

Clara's never going to believe she has an actual genuine reason for failing to show up—that's how Clara will phrase it, as Sadie *failing*. Things between them have been unbearably fraught since *Persona*. Sadie's been trying to act like she's brushed it off, but it seems Clara neither accepts nor wants that. Honesty has gone under the table. Sadie feels for Clara who is evidently taking it badly and wants to dissect it with scalpels and surgical tweezers, while Sadie just wishes Clara would make up her mind how a line can best be drawn under it. Sadie, after all, is paying for this damn therapy, and today she's thinking about how to end the whole thing without feeling even more guilty and getting into more tussles with Clara.

She tries to phone but it goes straight through to answerphone which of course it would if Clara is waiting there in the *atelier* which she will be. Sadie pictures her sitting waiting and the image does not make her feel good. She leaves a message, apologising for missing the session. She's in the middle of saying she'd stayed up too late *working* when the answerphone cuts her off. She makes herself a coffee and wanders over to look at the work she hung on the wall last night. It feels liberating to have missed the session with Clara and to have this new work to look at. Looking closely at it, Sadie can say, yes, she's actually pretty pleased with it.

The very fact of the work is a sign she's coming through that terrible impasse she's been stuck in. It began at Sangatte, the stuckness, if not the *trauma*; Clara always says she doubts that Sangatte was the start of the trauma, the things you think are beginnings very rarely are, many triggers can get set up along the way. The very fact of the work being made, here and now, whether it's good or bad—though she does happen to rather like it—is a big step forward for Sadie. She can't wait to see Clara's face when she tells her she's managed to harness the energy of the *dark helplessness of trauma* and used it to make new work... It's like she's followed a Zuniga template. Clara is going to be well impressed. Sadie makes herself another coffee, takes it back to bed with her laptop and starts to write the blurb that will go alongside her Life Drawing submission.

Life Class, Sans Model by Sadie Sarrazin

My work (*Sadie Sarrazin, nude/s with/without coat/s, 2020*), Sadie types, addresses the question of how it is possible to tell when a piece of creative work is complete—this is an important question all artists face and which we have been asked to address in the *Life Drawing* class.

To my mind, Sadie continues, taking a sip of her coffee, all works of art are, at their core, *stories*. Paintings, photographs, sculpture, they're basically all stories. All things, all images, have stories embedded within them... it's the task of the artist to draw out the stories... they do this by means of hints, symbols, suggestions in what is depicted and the means/ methods/ materials by which the ideas/ sentiments are depicted... the art will work at its best when it sets up resonant associations in the viewer... this means there is a real sense in which a work of art is never 'finished' but there is an optimal time when the artist should let go...

With stories, beginnings and endings are highly significant, while middles are scenes of shifting purpose... I've made a series of prints of my topic which can line up in various ways to make a story or stories... I've also attempted, in the way I constructed each print/image, to indicate, or lead the viewer into the *depth* of the stories; each image can function as a kind of palimpsest of where the story has been/ leaves its traces, at the same time as it depicts where it is at this moment...

Sadie is interrupted by a knock on the door and in walks László. He looks worse for wear this morning. Sadie suspects he is sleeping rough somewhere down near the river but he'd never admit it. She's given up trying to prise information out of him, it just humiliates, so she's learned to take him as he comes. She presses 'save' on her laptop and gets up to make him a coffee. She'd planned to call in at the library at the Fondation Custodia to look up a few references for her submission, but that can wait until László's gone.

While Sadie's making the coffee, László wanders to the wall and is looking at her new work that is still taped up. Sadie watches from the other side of the room to see his reaction; his body language doesn't give anything away, but it never does. László accepts the steaming coffee Sadie hands him without saying anything. He must like the work, because otherwise he'd have said something critical. He turns to look at Sadie as though inviting her to tell him something about the new work.

It's that I'm sort of saying something, trying to say something, maybe like that all art is stories and stories arrive wearing overcoats... like you said, Gogol... wearing their own coats, I mean, Sadie says, like they're going somewhere or coming in from somewhere and they know where they're going or coming from... like and the artist has to trust... and to follow... And now I just have to, like, fit it into words... translate from the pictures... I'm supposed to say when an artist knows a piece is finished...

You know a piece is finished when it takes its coat off, László interrupts, turning now towards her. *I see that's what you're saying here.*

László, ever the wise one. They laugh.

I can never see anything as clearly as you do, Sadie says as she re-opens the laptop and types out what László just said. Now, the next bit... help me with the next bit... I have to say stuff about influences... whose shoulders am I standing on, László? I mean, apart from yours!... What am I deriving from where...

Whose shoulders? Well Munch, obviously, László says, turning once more to look at the pieces on the wall. *And every other artist who ever lived...And every pubescent girl who ever lived and shivered naked on the edge of a cold brass bed...*

My work should speak for itself you mean?

László nods. *You can't reference everyone. You'd be on for ever, compiling lists. Lists of not just artists. Anyway, it's not important. The artist doesn't complete the story. We each of us—makers, viewers, writers, readers—we all cast the characters, fashion the plot, excavate the endings for ourselves... Mind if I have a shower?* he says, finishing his coffee.

Go ahead, Sadie says.

Sadie won't go to the Fondation Custodia to look up references after all. Lázsló helps himself to a second coffee and sits down on the floor under Sadie's new work, both hands warming around the cup. Sadie throws him a clean towel, presses 'save' on her laptop and gets ready to print out her commentary. She's referenced only Edvard Munch and Kathy Acker. And, at the last moment, a citation to Max Zuniga.

László is happily singing away in the shower as Sadie leaves her *chambre* and closes the door behind her.

77

Waiting in her atelier, Clara hears the answerphone click on, then Sadie's voice leaving a message, apologising for missing the session. She hears Sadie starting to explain that she's 'doing a Zuniga,' has started to make some new work out of the *dark helplessness of trauma...* Clara gets up and switches the answerphone off. She is not in the mood to be entertained. Sadie may not be aware that she's taking the piss, but the aggression behind Sadie's words is not lost on Clara, the mockery, the contempt in her tone, and it wounds her; it shouldn't wound her, not in the circumstances it shouldn't, but it does.

Clara must find a way to move forward.

Undo the bandages that cover the wounds that hold together the wounded.

The Zuniga biography is a non-starter, Clara finally has to admit that to herself. Perhaps it never was a runner, never could have been, given what she now knows about the reasons behind his downfall. It's too exposing. It'd bring too much shame. All those issues unresolved, all those gaping holes. And not just on herself. On Johannes too.

Oh Clara.

The idea that she'd thought it reasonable, feasible, desirable, to rescue Max Zuniga, was foolish and arrogant. Clara has misread so much, been blind to her own motivations. There was nothing there to rescue, Clara, there was no-one. It's Clara Delaney who's all this time been in need of rescue.

László nods agreement.

78

Walking along rue Vaugirard on her way to Red Wheelbarrow Books and Sadie walks by the blue-fronted *La Maison de Poupée* with its windows wrapped around two corners and the ancient cracked-limb lace-dressed charades of china-faced ladies taking tea behind the glass. She stops to look in the window. There's something about dolls, their eerie macabre faces, these miniature *personnages*, that shifts your centre of gravity. They capture your gaze, they absorb everything you pour into them, they cause you to stumble, they won't let you pass.

The depth of the scene through the *vitrine*, the layers of light and shadow, the shifting reflections; yes Sadie, that's you, a transparent vision of you through which the stage world of spectacle takes shape, you among the shifting layers of reflections, moving at different paces, moving in three dimensions, moving from the centre to the side, to exit stage left, the dolls taking their tea on an endless loop of dolls taking tea…

Sadie, almost overwhelmed by the possibility of new work in-the-making, grabs at László's sleeve for stability and almost steps into the road. She's not ready for the new. She has stories to finish. But there's that disoriented feeling new brings with it, a floating kind of lostness, a fragmentation, an emptiness that fills you, that fills every corner of you… carrying the same baggage, it bites you with the same incisors, takes hold of you just the same as when despair descends and you can't work at all. Sadie wishes she could find a way of telling this to Clara, of making her understand that the creative process, and the absence of it, have the exact same roots…

Right now, Sadie must avoid stranding her reflection among the soft-bodied *poupées* and the stiff marionettes with their wooden wedge-mouth stares that peer at her from beyond the plate glass *vitrine*, watch her like they want to include her in their peculiar conversations. She doesn't want to hear what they're saying. She has hold of László's sleeve but he is pulling away from her, trying to move forward. László has one eye on the far side of rue de Vaugirard to where, outside the *Sénat*, armed guards are standing sentry, apparently looking over in László's direction. Sadie feels László stiffen. She shouldn't have come this way, not this way, past the armed guards, not with László. How stupid and thoughtless. How he ever comes back to her, stays loyal, helps her, guides her, Sadie has no idea.

He's been talking about leaving, about having something elsewhere he has to attend to. Sadie hadn't taken it seriously, couldn't imagine where László could be if it wasn't in Paris. But he's hurrying now. He's caught Sadie's wrist and he's pulling her along, they're running, now right opposite where the armed guards are standing. Sadie stumbles on after László. He's yanking at her arm. She's going to trip up. She doesn't want to be pulled like this. She wants to be mistress of her own life. She came to Paris to be mistress of her own life. She wrenches her arm free from László's grip and stands stock still. László hesitates a brief moment, looks back, then he keeps on going, he breaks into a run, leaving Sadie standing alone outside the green press kiosk at the corner of rue de Vaugirard, the armed guards motionless and emotionless on the other side.

Sadie watches László's back disappear into the crowd now exiting the Luxembourg gardens. The *gardien* blows the closing whistle earlier and earlier now, as the nights draw in.

László's gone, he's left her, like he did at Versailles.

Like Sadie left Sangatte…

79

Dolls, they absorb everything. From tears and need and tenderness, to our broken rage. They become us, then they leave us, angular, bereft, discarded and despised in corners.

There's a hierarchy. Aware of favourites, and the guilt that goes alongside choices, the shame that attends our inability to care, our bleak desires for personal improvement, or for nothingness, our wilful refusals to muster.

The fixed expressions of hope on their smooth porcelain faces. Rose-cheeked rosebud-lipped they wait for the world to start happening. Their eyes close automatically when you lay them down.

You can open their eyes with your fingers. You can hold them staring open. They are looking out. You want them to see you.

You squeeze their soft cloth bodies till your fingers meet and their internal organs could be squashed to destruction as when next door's dog killed the rat that time and there wasn't so much as a toothmark.

You twist their arms round on the elastic in their sockets till their stupid hands are facing the wrong way. You wrench a look between their legs splayed open. There is nothing there, only cloth and staining. They smirk. They are always smirking.

They allow their clothes to be pulled off and on, on and off. They take orders, but do nothing. Sit up, lie down, sit over there. They never object to their makeshift lives lived in makeshift beds in random rooms.

Makeshift, we are left in corners
Splayed with waiting, disaster, disorder
Abandoned to abandonment
One eye open
The other closed.

80

Today is *Toussaint*—All Saints. Clara is in her studio in the rue Le Goff, she's taking a few days off and has just finished clearing up some paperwork and now she's planning to go and spend some time with Agnès Varda up in the cemetery at Montparnasse, see how many chrysanthemums have been left, maybe she'll sit on that bench under the conifer Agnès planted, a *parapluie* for Jacques Démy, Clara needs this time out, hoping she'll be able to think through what to do about this whole awful situation she has landed herself in. Sadie is not the only one destabilised by the *Persona* episode, but she seems to be surfacing from it much better than Clara.

Clara resolved to give up on the biography project but she's finding it hard to abandon Zuniga altogether even though she knows the whole idea of 'rescue' now is a non-starter. She's been trying to think through the impulse, the *compulsion* to rescue. She's making self-analytic notes on her laptop but mistypes *rescue* as *refuge*. She stares down at the screen, she looks at the keyboard, she can't see how she could have made that mistake. The slippage she sees causes her breathing to stop. She goes for the delete button. Then goes to type in the correct word. To her absolute horror it is *refuse* and not rescue that now appears on the screen. She claps the lid of the laptop shut without even pressing 'save.'

She needs to get out. She's been too long in her own company. She'll get ready and go to Montparnasse as planned.

Refuge. Resting places are quiet and still and are places of contemplation which is what she needs. *Rescue*. Clara has so many times found solace in such places. *Refuse*. What is it she's refusing? *Refuse*. Garbage.

Clara has a purpose and she is going to Montparnasse and she will take with her a flask of hot coffee because it's cold, it's cold out there and a cemetery can be colder even than the ambient, especially French *cimetières*, all those forbidding grey slabs and stone, rarely any grass, and the plastic flowers, they alone make the world look stuck in eternal winter. Yes, Clara will take with her the flask with the hot coffee to offset all things cold and drab. She'll head straight for Jacques Demy's bench that Agnès put there under the tree. She'll sit there until she feels better.

But where's the flask? Where did she put it, the green

one she bought in Décathlon? Clara's eyes scan the room but the flask is nowhere visible. The longer it remains not visible, the more imperative it becomes that Clara finds it; no way, absolutely No Way can she go to a cemetery in this cold without some means of warming herself from the inside.

Clara. Clara.

She repeats her name out loud. She says it like Johannes said it when he wanted to make her know something she already knew but had forgotten she knew. The tones he used, the tones they'd used, the tones that said things beyond the words, the tones that spoke the opposite of the words, the tones that made the cloud they'd carried around, the cloud that made the bubble they'd lived in… We can't go on living in a bubble like this, my Clara…

> *This is the man all tattered and torn*
> *That kissed the maiden all forlorn*
> *That milked the cow with the crumpled horn*
> *That tossed the dog that worried the cat*
> *That killed the rat that ate the malt*
> *That lay in the house that Jack built*

Clara had agreed, no, they couldn't, they wouldn't, they won't go on living in the house that Jack built. Then she'd punched the wall, again and again, she'd punched at the wall and Johannes had had to pull her away.

It had all crowded in, the two of them prising themselves apart and neither could find any smooth way out, any proper way out. The exit, it happened, it became real enough, in the end, but it left them broken.

Clara. Clara. Always half way there. *Half way Clara.*

She can't remember where she put the flask, she can't say if she has even seen it since the day she bought it. That she can't locate it, and that she can't do without it now feels like a great gaping hole has opened up inside her.

Johannes. Zuniga.

Zuniga. Johannes.

> *This is the man all tattered and torn*
> *That kissed the maiden all forlorn*

Clara sits down on the edge of the bed in the house that Jack built. She closes her eyes, concentrates hard, tries to steady her breathing, tries to calm her stumbling heart.

Many minutes pass, how many she doesn't know. Perhaps it's hours. Perhaps it's dark outside, she can't tell. She doesn't want to open her eyes.

Clara gets up from the bed and feels her way around the walls, her eyes still shut she is making for the *coin cuisine* to fetch a drink. She's almost at the sink. Her hands are shaking. She stops and rests her arm against the cupboard to steady herself. Suddenly she knows where the flask is; it's in there, the flask is in this cupboard, she remembers now. Clara opens her eyes and opens the door and yes, it's there, still in its box. She closes the door and goes to the tap to run the water. You always have to run the water before you drink it here because it lies in the old lead pipes of certain *immeubles* in Paris and the toxins might affect your brain. She'd been going to buy one of those Brita filters.

Clara's not taking any chrysanthemums to Agnès Varda for Toussaint after all. It's an early night for Clara. She looks at her phone. A message from Sadie. Cancelling again for tomorrow. She says she's working, her dissertation submission stuff; could that be possible, the state she's in? At least she's thought to text and has not just abandoned Clara without saying a word like she's been doing of late.

Clara sits on the edge of her bed, looks at her Instagram on the IPad, sees Patti Smith is, at that moment, making her way from Vienna, Austria to Cambridge, England. Clara wonders if Patti visited Berggaße 19, what she thinks of Freud.

Instagram. Patti Smith. Memories. Social media. Paris. All refuges of sorts. When a refuge becomes a prison. A place of *refusal*. A palace of *recluse*.

Clara pulls back the mohair cover and gets onto the pull-out. She switches on her bedside lamp, checks her glass of water is on the little table. She wants to think through these troubles but there's something she's not catching. It's one of those things that the more you try to grasp it, the further it slips away.

Oh Clara

And her hand is all swollen from fighting something.

81

On All Saints Day in her tight little *chambre de bonne* at the very top of the apartment building in the rue de L'Arbre Sec, see Sadie Sarrazin, newly emboldened, spending the morning writing the first draft of her 1500-word *Introduction* to her Academy submission— the first section (plus draft synopsis, work plan, etc.) was due in last week and she hasn't made it and now in her desperation to catch up she fears getting further towards nowhere.

She's been eating chocolate brazils but now she should get off her seat and take her camera—she's enjoying the new Polaroid the Academy gave her, it's making her think twice about everything, she'd got a bit stuck in digital... Anyway, today it's *Toussaint* and a day for remembering the dead so perhaps she should visit some cemetery and peruse some famous graves and photograph them at angles with the Polaroid and capture a bleaker—more melancholy, more thoughtful—Paris which no-one else much bothers about.

Not everyone dead has a grave, Sadie.

László is always interrupting. Sometimes though Sadie prefers her own train of thought. People have a habit here of romanticising cemeteries and Sadie would like to find a way to counter that. It'd be hard, though, such is the well-established iconography of the Père Lachaises and the Montparnasses of Paris. Today could be a good day for making dreary images... Sadie looks up out of her skylight. Yes, it's grey, thin, wintery, cold, rainy, and altogether dismal out there. She's really not tempted to stay in struggling with the dissertation Intro. The task is doubly difficult because she has yet to pull together a plan for a final piece and she is still stalling about what she actually wants it to say.

Sangatte, László reminds her from wherever he is, *Tell them about that, Sadie.*

Sangatte, the Sword of Damocles that hangs over Sadie's head, held in place by a single hair from a horse's tail, both her undoing and her means of redemption...

László, it occurs to Sadie now, to speak the way he speaks, must surely be carrying the burden of some Sangatte of his own... she'd been too preoccupied with her own burdens to notice; she'd allowed László to preoccupy himself with her burdens as though his shoulders could and should bear the weight for the two of them. And she'd failed to take any account at all of the possibility that Clara, too, is undoubtedly grappling with her own demons...

Sadie, Sadie.

82

One day in November she and László go to the Vilmos Zsigmond expo at the Institut hongrois, close to St Sulpice. The visit takes forever and Sadie becomes impatient. László wants to examine each photograph in detail, Sadie watches him peering up close to every one and a knot keeps gripping the insides of her; it's as though he's forgotten she's there. But through the silence she picks up on his mood—she's churning; with László her boundaries don't function—she can feel absent, irrelevant, drained, alone, exhausted.

Chapelle Saint-Roche, Eger, Hongrie, 1956

A tiny country church, two windows, a bell, exterior peeling plaster; the shadow of a crucifix on the outside wall shifts with the light of the daytime hour, an unwitting sundial, disappears in the dark. Sadie stares at the shadow of the cross, imagines it moving as it is in the nature of shadows to alter their position, their shape, their size, according to the run of things and the direction of the sun.

A small country churchyard, the gravestones falling over, tipping over at angles, a child would believe they were being unearthed from below, by the dead, unearthed from the Underworld; but the tipping is caused merely by nature, by worms, by the shiftings of soils, the brute strength of roots. Here they are in the photograph, the gravestones, lives captured in their stories, our stories, arrested in the process of being unearthed and unearthly, stranded now behind glass that clouds over when you breathe. Sadie stands back, continues to look from a distance, aware of her heart beating.

László moves forward to take her place close to the photograph. His voice shakes. Sadie hasn't encountered him like this before. The grandfather, he says, put the child to hide in a tiny chapel, just like this one, at Eger, this one in the photograph.

There's a child playing; yes, right here, in the photograph. László reaches forward to touch the glass with his finger, reaches out to the child behind the glass. The heat of his fingertip leaves a whorled pattern on the glass.

Standing next to him, Sadie feels the warmth of him, the wonderful alive warmth of him, the rough cloth of his jacket just touching her shoulder. The sleeves are fraying at the cuffs.

Why a child is playing among the toppling gravestones at the little church at Eger, miles from anywhere, László cannot say. Neither can he say where the parents were, nor how churches that once were sanctuaries become disused and faiths fragmented. He had and has no idea what becomes of roots or exiles beyond some slim facts of survival.

Memories are stories and stories are fashioned for reasons. Used, misused, misplaced, stolen. Written. Rewritten. Erased. The past returns and speaks to us in signs. It possesses the present, makes stories prone to multiple endings.

Here it is again:

I do. I undo. I redo.

Like at Sangatte, Sadie wants photographs to answer questions and they can't and they won't and they never will. She wants Art to reassure her and it can't and it won't and it never will. Ever since a child, she's wanted stories sewn up with happy endings, some kind of comforting closure.

August Sander's black-and-white photo portraits: the curation of that Edinburgh show *People of the 20th Century*, its extraordinary juxtapositions—one, a young Nazi soldier, in uniform, proud and, next to it, a photograph of a Jewish family, just being ordinary, a small group of people, standing in a doorway. Sadie had looked at them for a long time, gazing from one to the other until, as now in the Insitut hongrois, she'd turned away, broken, lost, lost in the lives of unknown others, exhausted; the answers she searched for, more elusive than ever.

Stories, personal, global. Photographs. Memories, now, then, now.

I do, I undo, I redo.

Bear witness.

Resist linear versions of history.

Uncertainty is okay.

But where are the answers? What, what if there are no answers?

The important things are the questions, not the answers, László intrudes on Sadie's train of thought.

Your work—our work—is important because it asks the questions, László adds. *That's what art does. Raises questions.*

I can't work, says Sadie. *I have no work.*

You have. You can, László says. *You are. You will.*

Artists work without knowing it, says Agnès Varda.

83

Voyage: the Bateau à New York, 1957

People were leaving, the lucky ones; in a narrow window of time, the lucky ones were leaving. There they are, being sick on the sea, sick all through the wild Atlantic storms, made ill by the crossing and the events that led to their hurried departure.

László, leaning in towards the photograph, puts his hand to his throat. Sadie knows that gesture. It's to stop your heart from stopping.

The photograph shows children arriving in New York with tags around their necks with numbers, like parcels, their eyes wide with something.

Help me, someone, yes, I am, I'm grateful to have made it.

We're in Paris now, Sadie says, we're safe, in Paris. She reaches out to touch the sleeve of László's careworn jacket.

Don't be a fool, László says, snatching his arm away. *There's no such thing as safe.*

84

As they descend the stairs towards the Exit at the Institut hongrois, strains of the Monteverdi Vespers drift out through the open door of the lecture room reminding Sadie of their—no, her—failed attempt at Versailles. What was she hoping for, coercing László to come to the Vespers to the point of lying about the tickets... How stupid, self-centred, how patronising she'd been. What was she thinking of? She wasn't. She wasn't thinking.

Sadie and László step out into the late afternoon light and cross the road from the Institut onto the Place Saint Sulpice. They sit on a bench and watch cascades of water gushing out from the mouths of the masked urns round the giant stone fountain. They don't speak. There doesn't seem any need for words. László is sad. He never talks about what happened, how he ended up in Paris, why he never goes home, wherever 'home' is. But neither does Clara. Neither does Sadie.

What happened mattered, and doesn't matter.

We belong here now.

As soon as past becomes past, it's transformed into something else, it morphs. It exists and doesn't exist. It's gone and it's here. It's one and the same, in another space.

We're from here now.

Listening to the incessant gushing of water, Sadie has a strong sense that, in so many ways, she occupies the same edge-lands as László; they have so little in common, but for that one important thing, the space where they live, the gap, the absence of Home.

It's cold on the square and Sadie buttons up her coat. Look at László though, all he ever has is that worn-out tweed jacket, it's ancient, threadbare in places. Someone has stitched leather patches on the elbows but even they are worn thin. Sadie takes off her scarf and puts it round László's neck and ties it. László lets her do it without moving. He's sitting up straight and looking directly ahead.

They're both of them on a borderline, a blurry line, a thin line, the line of the tear the cut the rip the score that separates the Real from the unreal, the dark edge-lands of the creative life. It's a land where anything might happen, where things could rip or tip or slip any which way, a schizoid state—as Clara would have it—of suspended animation; two people, between two worlds, inner and outer, here and there, now and then, Sadie and László.

Like Beckett's unnameable narrator, they carry on, though there may be nothing to carry on for.

Sadie looks at László next to her on the bench. He is lost in some deep reverie, staring at the eternal movement of water through the fountain. She touches his forearm lightly, feels the roughness of his sleeve through her gloved hand.

The exchange of bare essentials, half-fabricated, erased, no matter.

The story's the same, it just morphs into its different frames, depending on its conditions of emergence.

We're all engaged in masquerades.

In Spectacle.

The whole History of Art; it tells over and over the bleak chequered history of humanity, the flawed glory of the human condition.

Sadie's battling these demons, these barriers, they're preoccupying her. If she can't conquer these doubts and produce some actual work she'll have nothing to show for her time in Paris. She's supposed to be all passionate about the significance of Art, the crucial relevance of photography… But how can you write about something you no longer believe in.

Or that no longer believes in you.

Sangatte is as absent and as present as it has ever been, Sadie's experience there a pit she can't climb out of, casting its persistent shadow. An absent presence that blocks everything.

Sadie has been trying to get through this with Clara but it's going nowhere. Clara's fixated on past traumas but seems unable to unravel Sadie's. And more and more Clara seems distracted, battling demons of her own. Things between them have been even worse since *Persona*.

Sadie wants to tell all this to László, but sitting in the square of St Sulpice that day, it seems that László's silence is the kind of silence that asks not to be broken—a silence, she fears, that cannot be broken. There are some silences that, if broken, it's too much, it changes too many things.

The silence of someone leaving.

85

6pm and the great bells of St Sulpice are calling the faithful to *Messe*.

As though by some unspoken agreement, Sadie and László rise from the bench at the same time, they walk together across the Square and up the steps and into the *église*. They had not planned to attend the service, but somehow, in the moment, it became the right thing, the silently agreed thing, the only thing. Inside, sombre music from the organ sounds discordant. Sadie doesn't know what it is, can't even guess the composer. She catches hold of László's sleeve as they step into the Baptistry.

Liszt, László whispers through his teeth. *Ad nos, ad salutarem undam.*

What? Sadie says.

The music. I thought you wanted to know what it is.

It's uncanny, this connection with László, how he tunes into the way she thinks. He doesn't need to speak. Just to be there. Be there and not there. László, so close, so far away.

Inside the church, the all-penetrating loudness of the organ reverberates, the combinations of notes and tones sounding together at so many levels. They say this is the biggest organ in Paris.

People are moving about quietly and with exaggerated respect, picking up service sheets and prayerbooks; small groups bend their heads in towards each other to talk in low voices. People take their seats in silence, lean forward to pray, sit back, remove their coats, fold them onto the seat next to them. Sadie accepts two hymnals from a curate; a woman in a buttoned-up coat hands her a service sheet.

Sadie follows László down the central aisle. She feels the vibration of the organ in her feet as though it is coming up through the old flagstone floor, some of the stones, old gravestones, engraved with ancient lettering.

Whose bones are these we tread upon as we pass along our way…

The seats in the nave are filling up. Is this some kind of religious holiday they have stumbled into or is the congregation always this size. The congregation is increased, of course, with Notre Dame closed since the fire.

Sadie wants to whisper to László the single important fact she knows about this place, namely that the Marquis de Sade was baptised here. Only a few moments ago there had seemed such a gasping need for them to share something light-hearted… But now it's different. Sadie wants to be silent, reverential, feels pulled to be at one with this place, very much aware that, whatever her views, her beliefs, her doubts, and disbeliefs about Religion, in this place she is in the presence of the Sacred.

The multiple vibrations of the organ resonate—every cell of Sadie's body is thrumming with its tones. She sees herself as though looking in at herself from the outside… *a man who looks on glass / on it may stay his eye/ or if he pleaseth through it pass / and then the heavens espy…*

Sadie in slow motion, time collapsing.

She looks upwards into the roof space, a feeling of moving beyond, of becoming lighter, of being lifted, higher, higher, on the discordant notes that are rising now to a crescendo. Sadie's anchors are loosed, her bearings scattered. Light as air, transparent as glass, her boundaries dissolved, up and up and up she goes, Sadie, a tiny speck and getting tinier until there is nothing, nothing at all between her and this vast and endless miraculous universe.

Moments later Sadie, disoriented, is back on earth, still walking down the aisle, her feet once again on the solid stone floor. Silent tears have spilled onto her cheeks. László is still walking in front of her, he pauses to genuflect on his right knee. From behind she sees his arm move the sign of the cross over his chest. Then he is shuffling sideways along one of the rows and sitting down. He undoes the scarf Sadie had tied round his neck, hands it back to her without looking at her. Sadie wipes her wet face on the scarf, sits down next to László on his left-hand side. László leans forward and falls onto his knees in an attitude of prayer. The boundaries of Sadie's world have shifted.

Sadie's grandmother used to tell her she was not alone, that she was held in prayer. How often has Sadie turned over that thought in her mind and never managed until now to grasp what it could mean.

Sadie stands up, she sidles back along the row and makes her way to the little Chapel of the Holy Angels where the restored Delacroix murals are. She wants to look at the one on the ceiling, Saint Michael vanquishing the demon. But straight away she sees the demon in the painting has not yet been pierced by the spear of the Saint. That is yet to happen. The snake at the foot of the stone continues to slither. The triumph of good over evil is yet unfinished business.

Sadie lights a candle for her grandmother. *Thank you for the love you gave me, for teaching me to battle demons. I lost faith in myself, I went wrong, I neglected my gift. But I'll put it right, I promise. Lux æterna keep you, my dearest Nan.*

Sadie returns to her seat as the Cantor is taking his place. Her eyes are drawn past him to the apse, to the dominating statue of the Blessèd Virgin by Pigalle—Mary standing on top of a rock holding the baby Jesus in her arms. Sadie stares, not at the Virgin, but at the hateful snake at the Virgin's feet, the evil thing about to curl up her legs. The sight of it makes Sadie so fearful, it's irrational, she knows but, in that moment, she is flooded with remorse for all the wrong turnings she has made, all the people she's let down or betrayed. She stares at the hateful serpent trying to dominate everything.

Sadie gets back to her seat just as the Priest and the servers begin to advance down the aisle. A strong smell of frankincense comes from the censer the Priest is swinging.

These ancient rituals, this massive beautiful cold stone edifice to a god Sadie can't conceive of. The way this place makes echoes and echoes of echoes of everything; the fragmented colours in the stained-glass windows; the shifting light and the shadows; the multi-layered music of the organ that shakes the walls and shakes the soul; the incense that catches in your throat, the flickering candles that make tears sting at the backs of your eyes. All so big, unknowable, incomprehensible.

Next to Sadie on the wooden pew László is still leaning forward, his forearms resting on the back of the seat in front, his head on his arms, his eyes still closed. She realises with the force of a punch how alone and desolate László is.

This is what they share. Sadie sits down, steadies her breathing, tries to calm her thumping heart.

Aloneness, desolation, yes, but you Sadie are in a different position from which to live out these things. You have choices. You are blessed with a different past. You are blessed with a privileged heritage. You are the Academy of Art and Design Scholar. You have Clara. You have money to pay her. You had a grandmother who held you in prayer. You have all those things.

You have László.

What does László have? Only his own determination.

What did the refugees and migrants at Sangatte have.

Only their own determination; their humanity which cannot be taken away.

The organ music fades and the church falls silent, only the sound of people shuffling a little, a few muffled coughs. The members of the procession are taking their places, the Mass is beginning and Sadie feels the weight of something old and new and terrible.

As though he follows her train of thought, László sits back, turns and lays his hand on Sadie's forearm. He looks round into her face and smiles. Reciting a poem from memory, he whispers to her:

In the church of Saint-Sulpice

the Virgin holds her baby to her chest

as she stands on the round earth,

appearing to be unaware

of the serpent she is crushing with one foot...

Crushing? Sadie says, Crushing? She's interrupting, speaking much too loud. Are you saying the Virgin has her foot on the snake?

How hasn't Sadie noticed that herself. It makes a whole different story to the one she'd imagined.

Did you say *Crushing*? Sadie repeats.

László nods.

Sadie leans round to try to see the statue again, but her line of sight is wrong.

According to Billy Collins, László says.

It's not what you look at, it's what you see that matters, László adds. One of his favourite sayings.

86

Exposition, 2019 : Hommage aux Écrivains de la Grande Guerre, La Mairie du Sixième, Place St Sulpice, Paris 75006

Thick grey-black cover of glazed clay, dulled; pitted as from shrapnel; coloured as coal or charcoal, cinders, clinker, as burned, gone porous. *Sur le sujet des crimes allemandes. Noir. Noir* for real thick *noir* non-fiction. Straight black spine shines sharp as anthracite, stitched with careful soft red thread. *Allez Allez (fait Françoise MUNDET après Joseph Bédler, 1915)*

Standing on the shelf above the charcoal-pitted-black, a dark blue night sky criss-crossed with searchlight beams of battle and some twinkling stars. Some stars are red. Some sky is black. (*par Rose-Marie DATH après Daniel-Vincent, La Bataille de l'Air, 1915*)

Et après ça, les morts, "Les Croix de Bois," les belles belles belles, les croix de bois, (par Christiane LAMON après Roland Dorgelès) shimmery shading almost greens and blues on aluminium, and crosses, so many crosses, made of wood.... *How beautiful are the feet of those that preach the gospel of peace...*

Little tiny diaries, little tiny writing tiny tiny words crammed in like there's no space no tomorrow. Page after little crumpled page. Illustrations. How the trenched soldiers took the trouble to show and to tell and to make, make such twisted ugly stories become such beautiful objects, how they may have found solace in making and marking, in transforming the bleak with their creative spirit. How we find solace now and recreate it in reading, looking, loving.

And Blaise Cendrars, *J'ai tué*.

Art doesn't need to be beautiful, whispers Sadie. She's starting to sound like László. Art just needs to be itself.

Truthful, says László, *Art needs to be true to itself.*

87

On Sadie's recommendation, Clara too goes to the *Hommage* expo at the Mairie in the 6th. She makes rapid notes in her Zuniga notebook, the contents of which no longer aspire to relate exclusively to matters Zuniga but she hasn't crossed out the name on the cover because that would make the notebook look ugly. She walks around the expo and discovers that, inside these beautiful covers, the pages of the exhibited books are blank, the words all missing. Sadie hadn't mentioned the middles being absent. Being the artist, perhaps she'd focussed on the covers, on the books as objects, perhaps the innards didn't matter to her. But innards matter to Clara.

The words that were inside are gone, if ever they were there. The words they were are swallowed whole, the covers stand alone and ended, enclosing empty. They have no vitals, no guts, no organs, no insides; bereft, these covers are sentries, confined behind glass, guarding nothing

There's an immense sadness emanating from these beautiful creations. These empty books, like Clara's intended Zuniga biography, their contents immaterial.

Perhaps some pages are destined never to be written, pages from stories that have not yet managed to pull themselves together enough into the present, to force themselves into the Real, the remainers, the hangers on, the as-yet-unnecessary, undiscovered, the eternal waiters in the sidelines.

Clara looks at the grey-black clay cover pitted with shrapnel, she looks again at the deep blue starry night sky criss-crossed with the searchlight beams of battle, she looks through the glass and sees her own face reflected, the face of the therapist that hovers in the glass transparent and beyond, the Cendrars, *J'ai tué, J'ai tué,* and she knows she could never capture a life in words, not Zuniga's life, not any life, not even her own.

Lives are stories that can only ever be told in ever-shifting ways of their own and they hold their ways secret, necessarily secret; there are no keys because there are no doors. As Freud said, that which is precious and true is carefully guarded and will ever remain so. It keeps its overcoat on.

Clara looks again through the glass at the beautiful covers with their blank pages and absent contents and she knows these really are *hommages*, not just to the victims and survivors of wars, but to us all, to the lives we live, to the stories we live by, the ever-morphing stories of struggle we live by. To the mistakes we humanly make.

By adjusting your angle of vision, Clara, you reshape yourself, make yourself appear or disappear. By moving slightly, you cause the glass to reflect or refract. Clara, there but not there, real but intangible, present but absent, visible but invisible.

Art changes us. Beyond the words are the missing words. What say you now, Clara?

88

Today I am walking to the Shoah Museum, it will be the third time I have visited the Holocaust Memorial in Paris.

I am walking from my studio in the 6th to rue Geoffroy l'Asnier in the 4th. A lot of shop people in Paris are washing their windows this morning, it's good to look into a clean *vitrine*.

A clear window makes it that much easier to look through to yourself and through yourself and out the other side, to the objects beyond the glass displayed for you with care and with hope to engage your desiring.

But oh here comes the rain to splash the windows up, the cold of it will cloud the glass from the inside with a film of steam.

Oh, it's hail now, ice pellets, and on the rue des Quatre Vents the workers in hard hats up high on the scaffold are carrying on, yelling across levels and making all the sounds of that building being re-built and fixed and mended.

Then, on the pavement in front of me, a man disappears down into the sewer; he's pulling behind him a thick plastic pipe.

I am on my way to the Shoah Museum. This will be the third time I have visited. It's harrowing there but there remain lessons to learn and today I am going to listen again to the remarkable testimony of survivor Vivette Baharlia who speaks her pain and her hope like a poem.

There is a possibility that the museum may be closed because of this virus that is scaring people and threatening to kill so many of us or this is what we are being told. There will be clampdowns they say.

Now the man in the sewer is yelling up to his friend who is guarding the big iron lid. Does he know that his voice echoes and echoes and carries and echoes all round those filthy sewer walls and up and up from the bowels and up and out into the street. The street will suspect a madman yelling from some deep private hell.

The man who is guarding the lid on the street peers down at his friend, oblivious; he feeds more of the pipe down down into the black hole. It must be a relief for him to be the one on the top, the one who stays on the outside, silent,
silent and breathing but then after the silence
what

People are still walking about in viral Paris though not as many as usual.

I'm walking all the way along the Boulevard. I'm walking quite slowly. Oh look, a patch of violets; spring, always special after the long cold winter. At the end of here I will cross the river. The violets are almost completely concealed among periwinkles and under the tree they push up through thick leaf mould with their determined life; at the border they find their way through the iron bars of the fence and tumble down towards the pavement.

I pass beside the little Cluny garden, the daffodils, the spurges, the scent of sweet daphne stir in me a certain longing to leave the city, return to the countryside. I wonder if my writing is almost done, if my time in Paris is spent, if I'm all topped up and done with Paris, whether, like László, I'll be moving on.

Some of the petals of the pink and white blossom are already starting to float away and fly yet I feel like I've hardly seen them, like they've hardly spent any time here and now they're leaving us.

I cross the rue St Jacques which tumbles me into someone else's memories. How easily another's memories become your own, as though by osmosis or magic, how easily the story transforms the Real.

People disappear in ones and twos down into the *bouche* of the *métro*, so full of trust.

The Seine is flooded. It is no longer possible to say the Seine is not flooded and to speak the truth. Noisy lorries spouting diesel fumes line up by the Pont St Louis for the ongoing repairs at Notre Dame.

I'd been on the bridge that day in April, there'd been upset at home and I was walking walking when I happened to look across the river to the Hôtel Dieu and I saw smoke rising up behind it and realised a fire had started. I did not at first think it could be Notre Dame. People on the bridge beside me were likewise staring in incomprehension at the billowing smoke and then we saw flames then we heard sirens, but the traffic all along the *quais* and across the river was thick and the *pompiers* took a long time to get through—no-one realised there could be a catastrophe unfolding. It was impossible to think of Notre Dame being destroyed by fire, but that was what was happening. Thick clouds of smoke continued and worsened, grey then green from the burning zinc and lead, travelling with the wind westward along the river.

Today cars and taxis lose patience and blast their horns to get by as the trucks manoeuvre to line up to park for the repair work. It all takes time, minute by minute, stolen, removed, and effort, but it's essential to rebuild when important things have been taken away.

I do, I undo, I redo.

That sounds like the mantra of God, says László, *the history of creation.*

The Seine has so much water there are no longer any walkways along the edges. The river is thick green-grey like the smoke from the fire or the colour of that soup made with puy lentils and cream, like they serve in the Café de la Mairie with warm bread.

And me, I'm trying to work out what it's best to do, given this virus taking hold. Whether I should leave Paris and go back to Scotland, go to my sister in Greece, where best to work on this book. Like Sadie, like Clara, I know I am lucky to have choices.

Now Notre Dame is undergoing profound reconstruction, the scaffold is intricate and fine like very-large-scale filigree and great wooden beams shore up the buttresses. You can't help but think about history and *patrimoine* and politics and religion and all the different commitments needed for everything and how sad it is when things you treasure burn

And ideas burn
And ideals burn
And people burn

I am on my way to the Shoah Museum in Paris. It will be the third time I have visited. This city survived a brutal Occupation, not unscarred, but determined, and the colours of Paris are from the eternal unique oyster-shell palette of Paris and everything matches and the sun comes out bright against a deep stormy sky and the city looks proud again and hopeful.

I had been thinking and wondering, instead of looking where I was going, it's caused me to go two bridges too far and I now have to turn back. I am on my way to the Shoah Museum in Paris. This will be the third time I have visited, you'd think I'd know my way by now, but people can get distracted.

In a shop window I see some comfortable-looking convertible sofas in crushed velvet, deep cerise, ideal furniture for a temporary contemporary.

I pass the café where Ruth and I stopped for wine that afternoon after we'd been to the Shoah Museum for the first time and neither of us was really talking and we just drank our wine in near silence and when the wine was not even finished we hugged for a long time before we went our separate ways.

On the way along the Quai de Gesvres, a discarded face-mask, the first of many no doubt, the new half-shaded face of normal.

The poplar trees by the river are well into shiny green leaf now. Silver sun sparkles on the rushing water. The *bateaux mouches* continue to sail and make wakes that send smaller boats bumpily sideways. Gulls screech and squabble in the froth of the wake.

I put on the headphones and listen to the testimony, twice, three times, I have to wait each time until Vivette's story comes round again on the reel, repeats itself on the Real. Vivette's brave story.

It's just left for me now to remind Sadie of the crucial importance of testimony, *témoignages*, of voices, of stories, of the necessity of putting stories into waiting and hauling them back out when it's their time to be heard.

PART 6

Echo of the morning, return of the light

Louise Bourgeois
from *Hours of the Day*, 2006

Sadie, goes back to sit on the bench on the Place St Sulpice where she used to sit with László, remembers the *épiphanie* she had at the start of Mass. She'd tried then to tell him how she felt sure nothing like that could have happened had he not been there… But he hadn't wanted to talk, nor to listen; he'd been dismissive, as he often was, made it clear he didn't want to occupy his mind with such things, he had other things now to think about, and anyway he'd be leaving soon. Sadie saw he meant her to understand there are some things that are hers, and hers alone.

She hadn't mentioned any of this to Clara. Some things don't bear analysis, don't bear interpretation; some things—and everything László—belong to worlds other than this one.

Things are winding down with Clara. It is clear they are coming to the close, though Sadie is still not past that internal barrier that is Sangatte, the reason she went to Clara in the first place. The deadline for her submission at the Academy is closing in and she has yet to muster up what it takes to address the work.

You're a coward if you don't put the work out there, Sadie, was László's view. You abandon those people who trusted you.

As if she didn't know that.

You mined their lives and their memories and now you hide all the material, pictures and recordings they in their vulnerable generosity so willingly shared with you... you keep it for yourself... you keep it under lock and key... you keep the voices and the testimonies and the lives of those people all hidden away...

Undo the bandage, expose the wound. The wound must have air if it is to heal.

Selfish, over-privileged Sadie, has she learned nothing.

There's learning and Learning, László.

Sadie sits on in the Place St Sulpice, watching the fountain, the eternal turning of water. It's cold and damp and there aren't many people out this evening and it's dark already. A lady with a little dog crosses the street at the zebra crossing. The cars and buses have their headlamps on, windscreen wipers going, their windows half steamed up. A small group of young people—*lycéens* most likely—cross the square, swinging their sports bags, all legs and arms and laughter.

Sadie had been surprised by László's reverential attitude in the church that day, more than surprised when he'd joined the line to take Communion... The body of Christ... the blood of Christ... Ever since a child she'd found those ideas strangely cannibalistic and had recoiled. Though she had to go through the formalities of Confirmation, Sadie always found it impossible to participate in the ritual of Holy Communion. She hadn't known, she'd never have guessed, that Religion would be a part of László's life.

It's not, László had said. *You misunderstand entirely.*

Sadie had so much to learn, she could see that's what he was thinking.

Haven't you read Tolstoy?

There, László did expect her to know everything.

A Confession?

Sadie hated him when he acted so superior, making her feel small; she hated how he could make her feel like a child, good for nothing, inadequate for everything.

You're the artist, Sadie, he'd said. *These things are important: Faith. The Creation. Humility. Trust. The state of Grace.*

Sadie hadn't understood. So often she didn't understand László until so much later and often too late.

Religions, László explained, *religions use these ideas to talk about their gods. Artists can use the same concepts to talk about Art.*

God is really just a giant muse, he'd added, laughing, *there's a sliver of God in each of us.*

Think on Beckett, László said. *Those guys waiting for Godot. No, he didn't show up. That's because creative inspiration doesn't show up while you sit there and wait for it,* László concluded. *The time's never right. You have to just go at it anyway.*

Sadie stands up, pulls her collar up against the drizzle, and walks around the square. As always at this hour, people are gathering at the bus stop, crowding together under the canopy, trying to keep out of the wet. She hadn't looked up that *Confession* of Tolstoy but she will. She'll re-read Beckett. It's been so long since she's seen László.

90

There was no grand farewell, just the unspoken winding down, the disengage—mutual, though largely unspoken—having already been happening for some while. *Persona* broke them. Clara must now pick up the pieces, learn again the lessons she thought she'd learned with Johannes.

She's taken the break harder than Sadie seems to have done. It was little consolation that she could watch a former patient go from strength to strength, making headway with her art, in fact, no consolation at all when Clara herself was on the very verge of abandoning once and for all her Zuniga project, and possibly also her life in Paris...

Once again Clara remembers those little collages Sadie brought early on into the therapy, how Clara had barely acknowledged their existence, even as she knew, even as she *knew* there would be consequences. That phenomenon when you *know* you should do something, yet you go right ahead and do something else, the opposite even. Ambivalence. The divided self. There'd always been a barrier, a barrier neither Clara nor Sadie, in the end, was able to cross.

And the way, towards the end, that Sadie had blanked her, seeming deliberately to choose a different path. Like the time Clara told her about the Calais, *Testimonies from the Jungle*, expo at the Beaubourg, she brought her the leaflet, it was obviously right up Sadie's street, the very topic she was hooked on… But Sadie's response had been rejecting, angry even: *Stop telling me what to do, Clara.* And as far as Clara could gather, Sadie had not bothered to go to see the expo. Perhaps, as well as Sadie's natural disinclination to engage with the traumatic issues of her past, perhaps there was some envy, some jealousy even, some kind of possessiveness… Someone had managed to make work at Calais… Clara could understand those feelings but, at the same time, she resented that Sadie's rage had been visited on her.

Oh Clara.

Yet Clara feels the losing of Sadie acutely. Yes, it was all tied up with the *Persona* episode and yes, she'd allowed Zuniga to intrude, and yes, her grief—and her mistakes—over Johannes were still too raw. And László, Clara had never quite been able to find room for Lászlò…

Clara, Sadie, László, Paris. Time for Clara to move out of the equation.

91

When Clara had said about the Calais expo at the Beaubourg, Sadie blanched. She literally felt the blood drain down her body like holes had opened up in the soles of her feet.

Sadie was tired of Clara telling her what to do. But not only that; she was sick and tired of Clara crossing boundaries into her world, Sadie's world. Art is Sadie's territory and she wanted and wants to keep it that way. It seemed to Sadie that Clara had taken every opportunity to veer away from Max Zuniga and intrude on Sadie's world. Sadie, the client, who paid for the therapy, had had to carry the responsibility for keeping the therapeutic distance that Clara had stressed at the start was so crucial…

Sadie had got used to these discontents. But the acute pain she felt on hearing Clara's recommendation about the Calais expo was something else. To hear from your therapist that someone had succeeded where you have failed, to discover some other artist has done the same thing as you'd intended but had not been able to start let alone finish… it was all too much. And Clara should have known. It was nothing short of sadistic, the way Clara had announced it. There had been a definite note of triumph at the edge of her voice…

You need to get over this, Sadie. Get over it, shift focus, and move on. We each of us speak from a position of pain.

This is as much as Sadie can tell herself, now Clara is leaving, now László has gone.

This is not about you.

92

No, it's not about you.

Darkness does not name itself, someone has to name it.

Every story has a shadow story where compressed truths emerge as inarticulate or silent screams. In the shadow story, the compressed truths are being throttled.

The shadow story is not an extra story or an unnecessary story, to be forgotten or discarded; the shadow story is what makes the story story the story that it is.

You know about that choking, Sadie, the choking of the shadow story, the inability to swallow, the hold-up in your guts when that which should nourish you becomes stuck.

You know that to maintain silence, to fail to bear witness, is to prolong the scream, is to deepen the shadow, is to condone the throttling, is to compound the wrong. You know Marguerite Duras felt very strongly that one of the main roles of the artist was to bear witness, on every level, to the breakages caused by 'civilisation' itself. She should know, she lived through the Nazi occupation of Paris.

Stories matter. Stories have been used to dispossess and malign. But stories can also be used to empower and to humanise. Stories can break the dignity of people. But stories can also repair that broken dignity—Chimamanda Ngozi Adiche

Your work matters, Sadie, your work counts.

Our lives begin to end the day we become silent about things that matter—Martin Luther King

Tell your story, Sadie. The more stories, the more questions… the better things will be.

93

Diploma submission: **SADIE SARRAZIN**

INTRODUCTION: An Exhibition and its Context

The last of a series of ad hoc refugee camps at Sangatte, near Calais—the 'Jungle'—was dismantled in 2016 and its inhabitants—migrants and refugees, mostly from Albania, Afghanistan, Pakistan, Eritrea, Egypt, Somalia, Ethiopia and Syria— were relocated by the French authorities. The experiences of the flow of inhabitants through the 'Jungle' was documented in Calais: Witnessing the 'Jungle' at the Galerie de Photographies, Pompidou Centre, Paris, Oct 2019–Feb 2020 based on the work of photographer Bruno Serralongue (his Calais Project 2006–18); reports from Agence France Presse; and the testimonies of some of the inhabitants.

An artist drops into a moment in history and bears witness on behalf of anOther who cannot speak. The artist is afraid of trying to enter the consciousness of anOther, but they need to see that what they are doing is not about them, the artist; it's about trying to make heard the voices of the Other which otherwise would be absent or silent. The artist must not see themself as cannibalistic; the artist must try to enter the consciousness of the Other and do the best they can to do it responsibly and to do it justice.

Personal history and personal testimony are not just personal, they are cultural and social and political, alive, vital, necessary, essential; without personal testimony the picture is skewed and incomplete.

An artist can see that something has not been or is not being said because it has not been possible, in all the circumstances, to say it. Circumstances can silence what might, in another time and another place, have been, or will be, heard.

The artist can locate and retrieve and nourish those personal stories and testimonies that have been disappeared or relegated to the sidelines, they can retrieve them from where they wait patiently in the wings for their time and their place. The artist can give those stories their time and a place.

It is absolutely true and correct that no-one has the right to speak on behalf of anOther. But an artist who has been trusted with the stories of anOther has been trusted with a precious gift and is under a duty to respect the gift and to fulfil the promise as truthfully and as sensitively as they are able.

Refugees and migrants are people who have been failed repeatedly. In these bleak days, there is a responsibility on the artist to speak the truth as the artist sees it, to speak truth to power, to give faith and hope that comes by transcending propaganda and lies, glibly told, for political ends; a responsibility to assist in empathy and tolerance and the opening up of human possibilities and hearts.

There is power in the Arts, great power; power to envisage and envision, power to expose injustices and injuries, power to see things getting better.

Art can help heal trauma. It can help heal injustice.

Art, László Száműzetés maintains, *is really only about our struggles to make a world in which we all can live.*

94

CHAPTER 1: Calais: Witnessing the 'Jungle'

CREATIVE RESPONSE

images
that question representation
specifically
the representations of migration

the press reports press reports and reports on press reports and reports tell stories press stories press their stories into being into us into being us

poussez poussez

stories can be made to fit
stand up stand out shift the grander narratives out-shift the big ones
pick up threads weave and weft

pick up pieces pick pick pieces
pick
confirm affirm reaffirm reaffirm
align shape mold tick
tik tok box tick tock

testimonials *témoignages*
tell tales other tell other tells personal tells tales

Ameena

former camp residents speak journeys into microphones, bring traces of encounters, fragments of lives in transit, fragments of echoing lives in transit, fragments of echoes echoing fragments of echoes echoing fragments
of lives in transits of belonging, scattered of belongings scattered transits of belonging among the echoes gathered in microphones, recorded,
record-ed, shadowed lives in transit.

Ameena

place these lives new place displace shift remove move
shift-cap-lock on ECHO echo echo
resonate
displease

here hear the *témoignages* the grander narratives that categorise corral all these lives not recognised
as lives
box and cell them, bars up across around wound around, sound them in with fences, unify valorise categorise normalise

failure
to recognise
Ameena

The artist speaks:

here, the artist says, here a museum space inside whose walls parameters where different grander narratives hold sway
here from the rafters swing little monkey stories tiny tales *témoignages* that make all the difference, that shift the ground

here Art,
the grander narratives of Art slip to the rescue, swallow and display the images of lives outside their usual categories, lives outside their usual lives,
outside their usual shadows

outside the prison of the category prison category
migrant
exists only a person
Ameena

in Art we see the other
in Art we can be the other
Ameena

'Is the evening even taking part in the day'
or does it hive itself off
as extra, as different

which matters most
the answer or the question

Capture capture it in the frame
Retell the story reframe reframe the rupture
Reshape the silence refashion the gaps
Pick it out put it in
Bring it into the frame
Focus
Centre
Align realign calibrate

Recalibrate shame

Lay the facts in a line, tell the story
Move them around, tell the story
push those ones to the edge, tell the story
Pile them up pile them up file them box them lock them up
Tell the story

Ameena

Image maker storyteller
Image maker you record suffering by standing on the outside looking in

There is no outside
only another story
stories within stories

You choose the palimpsest
You choose erasures
You choose the beacons the becomings

Image maker storyteller

Go round on your treadmill
Scrape scrape scrape the barrels of lives

you image-maker you record the suffering you show-
case it for the world which is your job and your duty
you give the world eyes which is your job and your
duty to render the invisible visible
you put it out while the suffering is going on you record
it but you do not put the suffering out you do not lift
up the dying child yours is the shadow over the dying
child *Ameena Ameena Ameena*

you lie on your stomach in the mud adjusting your focus and you ask yourself what it means to be here
to record
suffering; you, recording
suffering

being a recorder places you image-maker story teller
you make suffering visible but it's not you who says
which story shall live and which shall die invisible unheard unhearing

at some time the public will look full-on or squint-eyed
at your images, after the event, even long after, your
story broken into fragments, and no-one knows the
start of it nor the finish

all those people, people,
suffering
lost
lost in the story
Ameena

95

Clara lugs her large suitcase—the one with all her clothes in—and upends it by the door. It's funny, in London, she had two wardrobes and a dressing room, yet in Paris she's managed to live out of a single case, and comfortably. Yes, Paris has taught her that, how it's good to discard baggage, live only with what you can't live without. She thinks of the Catalano men Sadie was so taken with, their missing torsos and their heavy bags, anchoring them to elsewhere.

Next, Clara's work bag: laptop, notebooks, chargers, flash drive, she crams them all in, zips up, sets it down next to the suitcase by the door. The small suitcase—in deep burgundy to match the larger one—Paris has taught her that too, how it's possible to have essential style about the ordinary—the small one is for her personal things—toiletries, camera, photographs, the little bag of talismans, a couple of books she has on the go... She's about to zip the small one up when she remembers the bag of broken glass Sadie foisted off on her some time ago. Sadie had gathered the bits up at the Academy during the clearance for renovation of the Glass Studio—the 'gift' of the potentially lethal shards was viewed by Clara at the time as an act of potentially aggressive purpose on Sadie's part. Clara had stuffed it away at the back of the cupboard and had not since thought about it until now. She reaches into the cupboard and lifts it out.

It's a calico muslin bag from the Æsop store where Sadie used to work on Saturdays. Clara holds the bag to her face and smiles; it still has that lingering trace of that musky Æsop scent that reminds her very powerfully of Sadie. She pulls open the drawstring and looks inside. The bag contains shards of coloured glass, many shapes and sizes. Clara wonders what to do with it. Her first reaction is just to put it back in the cupboard and leave it there, leave it to the next *locataire* to do what they will. She dips her hand in, being careful not to pierce herself on the sharp edges, lifts out a few pieces; one by one she examines them, holds them up to the light, turns them at angles which makes them look different. Something about Cubism edges at her consciousness.

Some of these pieces are beautiful, the way they're coloured and not coloured, transparent and not transparent, reflecting and refracting light. Clara examines a few more pieces, finds some interesting shapes, some pure and unusual colourings. Some of the pieces are textured, some marked with etchings that must have been done with diamond. She'd thought this was just a bag of broken glass, but it's not. It's a bag of beautiful fragments better captured by the French word *éclats*; and, as Sadie would say, a bag of stories, of pieces of former lives, of colours and light and shadows, of things that come from far far away.

Clara tries to remember back to exactly when it was that Sadie gave her the bag of glass. Why would Sadie have brought her such a thing? Right now, Clara can't make the connection. She's doubting though the passive-aggressive impulse on Sadie's part she'd first assumed. Clara can't possibly take the glass with her. They don't allow sharps in hand luggage on planes, and shortly Clara will be on her way to the airport and what use would she have for broken glass for anyway.

It's a pity, but probably best just to leave it behind. She pulls the drawstring tight and lays the bag carefully on the shelf in the cupboard and shuts the door.

Clara looks round the room; only her books left to box and label up for the courier and then that will be her, one last trip to London via Calais, then on her way to Oslo.

Zuniga's *Trauma and Creativity*, the copy Clara bought on her first day here in Paris, stares out from the shelf accusingly. *J'accuse...!* Clara takes it down. Trauma. Creativity. She smiles. Turns out it's much more complicated a territory than she'd imagined. Clara runs her fingers over the cover and feels the smooth texture of it, she flicks through the pages—she'd removed all the Post-It markers some while ago. She looks now at the cover. How odd she's not noticed it before, but the front cover, it's a picture of an Alexander Calder sculpture, one of his mobiles, it could be one of the series she saw in the Cubism expo, it does look familiar... Clara looks closely; this kinetic sculpture, Clara realises to her astonishment, is made from shards of coloured glass.

It begins to come back to her now, to make sense. So, Sadie was ahead of her after all. They'd both taken trips—separately—to the Cubism show at the Beaubourg. Yes. They'd been going through one of the more challenging phases in the therapy... Sadie had questioned Clara's going to the show at all, as if Clara's interest in it were mere posturing and actually invasive of Sadie's boundaries. Sadie had counter-attacked with the notion that we're all engaged in masquerade, performance, spectacle; therapy was no exception, it was little more than a charade, and an expensive charade...

Yes, this little bag of glass tells its own shattered story.

Sadie was blocked in her creative mojo, that's why she'd come to therapy. But she'd generalised to the whole of Art: Art was an irrelevance in the face of human suffering the world over, and there was no point wasting money on therapy trying to force herself to do something pointless... therapy was an expensive self-indulgence in the service of another self-indulgence...

Clara had stepped too quickly into the fray, stepped over the boundary. Intending to encourage Sadie—like you might a friend or a sister—but yes, Clara should have known better. She'd told Sadie she'd been to the Cubism show. She told Sadie she'd been inspired to make an art work herself. Perhaps a mobile sculpture of facets of glass... She told Sadie she'd found a place where you could get broken bits for next to nothing at La Rochère...

Sadie had been silent. Clara had not registered the silence for what it was, but had continued to talk—almost as artist to artist—about what she'd learned about Cubism, about facets and facades and fragmentations, and looking at things from different angles and all sides at once and reflections; how you could exaggerate this or that or shrink things or distort them or put them in the wrong place entirely so they become unrecognisable... Sadie had listened—it seemed with interest—to each and every word...

Clara shrinks now to remember how she'd finished her little spiel: *You should go to the Cubism, Sadie*, she'd said, *you might get inspired too.*

I've already been, Sadie said, *as I already told you*. Sadie's silent anger had filled the room and she'd left early without saying another word. It wasn't like Sadie to be silently angry.

It was not long afterwards that Sadie gave Clara the little calico bag of fragments which, at the time, Clara had neither understood nor puzzled over in any concentrated way, beyond her initial perception of a gift of potentially lethal shards to be a passive-aggressive gesture. She'd shoved the bag away at the back of the cupboard, and forgotten about it until now.

It is sometimes necessary to rewrite History, László remarks, *bring the record up to date, from each new vantage point.*

Clara looks at her watch. She should finish packing the books, order the taxi to take her to the Gare du Nord.

As a last-minute decision—she goes to the cupboard and retrieves the bag of glass, wraps it in a towel and jams it into the big suitcase.

Clara didn't manage to write the Zuniga biography. She was never going to do that. But now—thanks to Sadie—she has material to make something else, a sculpture, a mobile like Calder's of small shards of glass, on wires, carefully balanced, that will move and turn and catch the light and reflect the light and never for two moments will it look the same; it'll be a cubist life, more than one, she'll dedicate it to Zuniga, or Johannes, one or the other or both of them, a mobile for their journeys, together.

Or to Sadie. You could dedicate it to Sadie.

It will be Clara's project for Oslo.

96

Bless me Father for I have sinned... Sadie walks up the steps and into the church at St Sulpice with only half an idea of what she is doing. She stands a few moments on the threshold, fingering the rosary in her pocket, feels the bump, the knot in the chain between the beads where it broke a long time ago and she'd fixed it inexpertly together.

Ever since her visit to the *Witnessing the 'Jungle'* expo, the need for forgiveness, for truth and forgiveness, has been pressing at the heart of Sadie and now she can no longer ignore it.

Her sessions with Clara, she'd tried so hard, in all those sessions with Clara, to get at the truth of things, but it seemed the harder she tried, the more the truth— *her* truth, the *Real*—evaded her until, after *Persona*, she was no longer even sure what it was she was chasing. After *Persona*, what Sadie might or might not believe about herself, what she might or might not care to tell Clara, became an irrelevance. But still, that something inside, was press press pressing at her, like she was no longer seeking unblocking or interpretation or even understanding, like she already *knew* her truths but was somehow refusing to believe them... such had been the confusions inside her until now, what Sadie wanted, she finally realised, was forgiveness. And forgiveness was something therapy could not provide.

It was hard to escape the parallels between the secular psychotherapy she had been through with Clara and the Catholic Confessional of the faith she'd been born into and grown up alongside... yet different truths were made possible in each, different stories feasible, acceptable, necessary. Forgiveness in one, self-acceptance in the other. How often had László said *the hardest thing of all is to forgive ourselves.* How often had Clara exhorted her to be *kinder* to herself... Sadie hadn't understood. And she'd thought László was making a joke when he referred to God as *a giant muse*, the creative force made manifest in all of us... *you don't have to be a Believer to acknowledge God in human truths...*

Such was her frame of mind as Sadie stepped into the church at St Sulpice and made her way to the confession box. *Forgive me Father, for I have sinned.*

97

Sadie tells the Holy Father her story, the story of Sangatte, all the shame and the guilt she's been carrying for the past three years and how they'd got lodged into the core of her... She tells him how she loved little Ameena.

The priest's voice is soothing, he encourages the story. Sadie has never felt that comfort with Clara. *Therapy is not about comfort*, Sadie knows that now: therapy is a different confession for a different purpose. The absolution Sadie seeks now is moral, spiritual, something else entirely.

Sangatte. October 2016. It is night on the third day after Ameena's death. The camps are being cleared on orders from high up. People are supposed to be re-located, but that's not happening. Some haven't slept or eaten since Monday. Frustrations boil over and in some groups the struggle becomes physical. It's dark, but for the bright arc lights that illuminate certain pockets making the surrounding darkness blacker. Police are moving in but there does not seem any co-ordinated plan, they are everywhere. Sadie is there already hesitating when the real trouble starts. It escalates quickly. The crowd surges around her. She is knocked to the ground, trapped and trampled by desperate limbs slipping in the mud as people try to flee. Perhaps she loses consciousness—there's a Red Cross medic down on his knees in the mud beside her, he's talking, he's trying to help her back to her feet, but he's dragged away by someone else to see to a man with a wound to his head, Sadie can see in the torchlight the man's head is gushing blood. The medic is beckoning for Sadie to help him by holding the gauze pad to the man's head while he radios for a stretcher, but Sadie can't do it, she can't she can't she just can't do it, she can't bring herself to go near, can't risk touching the blood or the man being dead like Ameena dead like her father dead and she has to get away, she has to get away...

Her world is going dark, she can barely breathe, there's a crushing pain in her chest as her heart beats too fast...

then she is leaving herself again… everything happening in slow motion… she sees the doctor taking off his gilet, shaking it, retrieving the radio phone from the inside pocket; the pad he is pressing on the man's head with his other hand saturated with blood and the doctor kneeling down to the man and talking into his radio, he's trying to summon urgent help… He looks up at Sadie and she sees the look on his face, a look of frustration that turns to despair then absolute disgust as he shakes his head and looks away and back to the wounded man, giving up on Sadie. Sadie will never forget that desperate despairing accusing annihilating look on the doctor's face and the man lying there bleeding to death.

It is then that she sees the medic's Red Cross gilet is lying in the mud near the bleeding man whose body is twitching. Sadie watches herself pick it up, she's picking up the doctor's Red Cross high-vis gilet; she edges to one side, she backs away from the bleeding man and the doctor and the desperate crowd trying to flee the group of tents and shacks that are now on fire. She edges to the side then she runs, she stumbles forward, slipping in the mud, pushing her way through the crowd, she runs, she's pulling on the bloody jacket as she runs towards the police cordon; she can hardly breathe with the panic and the effort and the smoke and she has to stop to be sick but she keeps on running and it is the jacket that gets her safe passage as the police cordon see the Red Cross and moves aside to let her through while behind her now the little makeshift shelters of the Jungle are burning to the ground.

Sadie is weeping. The Priest waits. It's as though she

will never cease weeping. In three years, until now, she has not had the courage to re-live this experience enough to tell it, even to herself. She is wiping her face with the tissues that are there for penitents but more tears keep coming.

The Priest takes an audible breath and says, *it appears to me, child, that you did wrong, that you did very wrong. I see your own conscience has already told you that you did something you should not have done.*

Father, I have been tormented by what I did for more than three years. I can no longer live with myself.

What is it that you seek, my child?

I am seeking forgiveness.

You seek forgiveness. Without being forgiven, and released from the consequences of what we have done, our capacity to act would be confined to one single deed from which we could never recover...

Yes Father, that is what has happened...

My child, forgiveness must go hand-in-hand with reparation, the priest tells Sadie, *remorse on its own is not enough, I can see you have great remorse, but remorse is never on its own enough.*

A need for forgiveness must not be one-sided, adds the priest.

How can I make reparations to people who are gone... not there... all gone...

We none of us have power over the eventual consequences of our actions, the unintended consequences, says the priest. But perhaps it is enough to think of the small things we can do to make amends, or at least make things better, for others...

Sadie is still weeping, and the priest softens his voice.

When, as in your case, child, we can't make reparations directly to those we have wounded, the most we can do is to change ourselves for the future, to make our behaviour different, to make sure our reparative impulses are used to assist others. Do you so resolve, child, to make Sorry more than just a word?

Yes, Father, I do.

You resolve to make space for reparations, in your own life, and in the lives of others. Do you so resolve?

I do, Father.

In time, child, and with God's help, you will find that you are able to forgive yourself. To forgive oneself is the hardest thing of all.

Deus, Pater misericordiárum, qui per mortem et resurrectiónem Fílii sui mundum sibi reconciliávit et Spíritum Sanctum effúdit in remissiónem peccatórum, per ministérium Ecclésiæ indulgéntiam tibi tríbuat et pacem. Et ego te absólvo a peccátis tuis in nómine Patris et Fílii et Spíritus Sancti.
Amen.

Through the ministry of the Church may God give you pardon and peace, and I absolve you from your sins in the name

of the Father and of the Son and of the Holy Spirit.
Amen

98

PRESS RELEASE: Art Out of Place has been awarded this year's Academy of Art and Design Study Prize.

Art Out of Place (artist anon.) is a multi-media installation at Sangatte positioned on the site of the former 'Jungle' camp near Calais. It is a tribute to those migrants and refugees who made the place their home until the camp was dismantled in 2016. Shown across four large screens, the installation consists, in 3D filmic form, of a giant moving collage.

Film clips and voice-over testimonies from former inhabitants of the 'Jungle' form the core of the work around which the collage has been assembled. The collage depicts shifting groups of people, some in slow motion, some moving at high speed, in and out of the frame and in and out of view in three dimensions. In the words of the *New York Times* critic, the work depicts 'the wonderful and terrible multiplicities of our struggles to remain human.'

Visually, the disparate figures that inhabit the collage are made from fragments of photographs, film stills, ads, media cuttings, and images of works of art by writers, sculptors and painters who lived and worked in the 'Jungle.' The images are accompanied by extracts from recorded testimonies; fragments of music and singing created in the 'Jungle'; and now and again it is possible to hear, in the distance, a young child crying.

There are also flashback references to other Camps in other times and places, most notably from the years when fascism took hold in Europe. On this theme, items recognisable as belonging to the works of artists who fled their homelands or were otherwise exiled punctuate the collage. The *New York Times* critic identified Kandinsky, Max Ernst, Chagall, and Salvador Dali, as well as extracts from the works of writers like Walter Benjamin, Hannah Arendt and Stefan Zweig.

'In all,' says the *New York Times* critic, 'the installation, with its shifting tableaux of multiple visual and auditory references, is shocking, terrifying and moving; shocking in its portrayal of the human capacity for brutality; terrifying in its determination, its intensity and its referencing the repetitions of human history; and deeply moving in its profound portrayal of everything good a human can be.'

This installation marks a moment in the history of Site-Specific Art at the same time as it questions the whole notion of site-specificity. Migration journeys continue long beyond each individual disembarking on a foreign shore, long beyond the stepping from the confines of any Camp. Migrations take migrators out into worlds within worlds for the rest of their lives. The migrations we see here venture across the borders of Art, reminding us these are the journeys—the creative journeys—of each and every one of us; we are all fellow travellers. These people are us. The future is our fault.

The site of the former Jungle Camp, originally a landfill site, is now a nature reserve and a sanctuary for migrating birds.

Note that: the original photographic, video and audio materials have been deposited in the UNHCR Archive where they will remain available for public consultation. The prize money has been donated by the artist to assist the work of the International Red Cross.

99

László had been right all along, Sadie had to get her work out there, she had to use it to help others if she could. She owed at least that to everyone who had trusted her. As she walks round the installation, László's words are playing through the headphones, and Sadie knows they'll play on inside her for as long as it takes.

A photograph does not stand alone. It is part of a wider conversation. As such it can change the world—he's quoting a piece from the *New York Times*

A world without art would not be a world, it would be a small place with four walls, it would be a prison

Art is not just decorative, it is declarative, an expression of humanity's potential to use and transform experience, humanity's intention to remain human, no matter what

Not just declarative: it is interrogative, imperative, genitive

Exclamative!

The Artist has a moral obligation to use and share their gift.

Sadie is coming to the end of her day at Sangatte. It has been the opening—the Private View—today, the opening for the public is tomorrow. Sadie had delayed her arrival, waited until the main body of guests had left; she prefers it that way. She likes how they did the catalogue. She rolls her copy up and puts it into her coat pocket. Soon she'll head back to Paris on the train. She'll just walk round the periphery of the site one more time. If she's not mistaken, someone's left their jacket on that gate-post over there. She'll go and retrieve it, before darkness closes in.

Sadie smiles as she picks up the threadbare jacket.

Ta gueule, László.

100

Epilogue

The last time I saw him he was waiting, waiting in the wings. Someone will carry him in. Or the river will carry him away.

The river is full and thick green with mud; the *bateaux mouches* plough on through, passionless; the poplars on the edges have lost every leaf; the grey sky plunges low and heavy. Crows are perched singletons like ornaments fixed for the season on the ends of branches; strains of Santa Claus music drift across from the Christmas market in the Tuileries; smells of chestnuts, *vin chaud*, *crêpes*, hot dogs, mingle.

He'd learned, in Paris, to fashion *étranger* into something that almost worked for him. The last time I saw him he was waiting, waiting in the wings, waiting for his bit-part, for someone to steady him, reach out, give a hand.

He was waiting in the wings of the morning while, filling the open stage were the jostling lives of shoppers: the phoners the talkers the takers; the wearers of new boots and earrings; the photographers the painters; the sellers the wearers of black; the carriers of bags bags and more bags; the waiters.

The last time I saw him he was waiting, his small green tent tucked away under the arch by the river from where he would hear at night the steady swell and flow of the river.

Up through the Tuileries and all along the rue de Rivoli the party is happening; the marionette people, their mouths opening and closing, the jingle, the big wheel turning and turning and turning.

You can see all this from the Quai François Mitterand, the President who fought in the *Résistance*, who rescued the husband of Marguerite Duras from a prison camp in Occupied France. Now a Quai has been named for him and, close by, tucked away, the little green tent is waiting in the wings, waiting, under the arch, there, by the river.

The sky begins gathering dark to the North; it could almost be about to snow. The crowds have gathered like clouds outside the Louvre, shifting shadows across the giant glass of the pyramid. And for a tiny moment the sun breaks through and people are carrying Christmas in their bags and in their faces and smiling their bared white teeth and their steps and their pockets and everything is Christmas.

Then fat rain drops start to fall and the Africans selling woolly hats and padlocks and Eiffel Towers are gathering up their sheets by the corners and rushing for shelter under the giant arch, slinging all that baggage across their shoulders like they too were refugees again and on the road to some other place.

Then, just as quickly, the rain gives in. Now someone is sketching an Italian. Someone else is selling water, small bottles he keeps overnight in the drain. Someone is sweeping up shit from the Gendarmes' horses. And all across the Tuileries gardens people are walking in all directions. Or is it the gardens that are moving and the people who stay standing still?

In the end, László says, *it all comes to the same.*

The last time I saw him he was waiting, in a place he could neither leave nor remain.

—FIN—

PARIS PAGES

CITATIONS, REFERENCES and FURTHER READING

This novel began its life when I was living solo in Paris in 2019. My days were spent tramping the streets, absorbing the city, writing on the hoof about anything and everything. By the time Coronavirus showed up in early 2020 and I had to leave, I had some 10,000 words-worth of strange little hybrid pieces—neither wholly fact-based nor wholly fictions. I hoped they captured the spirit of the city and my experiences in it. I pulled the pieces together and titled them *Cahiers d'une Flâneuse*.

Crucial in the creation of these small pieces were the ever-present artistic and literary dimensions of Paris and the unique ways that life in the city impacted on me. It affected not only my ways of seeing but seemed to fashion for me new ways of being. The physical displacement I experienced on becoming an *étrangère* heralded another internal, psychological, displacement—new vistas were opening up, older ones transforming; I felt myself changing, I saw it reflected in my work. These dual-edged displacements I came to see as at the heart of my creative process, and this was to become one of the main themes of the novel that I began writing around the core pieces during the Covid Lockdown.

Beyond the city itself, though linked to it, further influences on my work lay in personal encounters with particular works of art—sculpture, painting, literature, all so easy to access in Paris with its rich seams of culture seemingly endless and everywhere. Foremost was my long-standing passion for the works of Louise Bourgeois; her art, in all its forms, spoke to me in ways for which I find no words. Over the years, in many major cities, I have encountered her work and always experience that *frisson* of connection, that excitement of desire, that activation of longing, that peace of sharing some deeper 'knowing' which has the power to catalyse my own creativity. I bought a season ticket to the Pompidou Centre so I could repeatedly visit her works there, and in the library I discovered a whole shelf of Bourgeois books—I queued day after day to study pictures and texts by and about Bourgeois, her life and art, deepening my understanding of what motivated the profound and moving works of this singular genius.

In grateful tribute to Louise Bourgeois, I have incorporated into my novel quotes from her visual and written works that I have gathered over many years and which, in Paris, in the city where she was born, worked their magic to inspire me to transform my own small *Cahiers* into a full-length work of fiction. Full references are included as 'Further Reading' below.

The opening section of *Paris Pages* focuses around Bourgeois' *I do, I undo, I redo*, the title of her Installation at the Turbine Hall, Tate Modern, in May 2000—words that echo a recurring theme in her work, and which I chose as a central motif in my novel, words that have become something of a mantra, capturing the deep significance of the psychological and creative work of repetition—what psychoanalysts call 'repetition compulsion' whereby repressed traumas are apt to surface from the unconscious in repeated attempts at resolution of unresolved conflicts—'the return of the repressed.' In this process, in the repressed traumas of her girlhood, Bourgeois saw the well-spring of her art.

In 2013, at the Fruitmarket Gallery in Edinburgh (see Morris and Larratt-Smith), I visited an exhibition of Bourgeois' *Insomnia* work made in 2010, close to the end of her long life. I encountered these words (line breaks and capitalisations as the original), looking out at me from the wall:

> *I Give everything away*
> *I Distance myself from myself from what I love most*
> *I leave my home*
> *I leave the nest*
> *I am packing my bags*

The works in that show, which I visited several times, reached me apparently unmediated by anything as clumsy as thought or attempts at understanding. In them I recognized my own ongoing preoccupations and felt in them a resistance, an acceptance, and a profound sadness. It became inevitable that the contradictory liberating and painful sentiments expressed in those words would find their place at the heart of my novel. In Paris they took shape in the characters, each displaced from their places and from themselves, each expressing the proxy lives of an eternally displaced narrator who, like the characters, kept on making the same mistakes; *I do, I undo, I redo*.

Wet Sunday Morning in Paris is one of the original pieces from *Cahiers d'une Flâneuse*. The first draft was written not long after my arrival. It was later published as a stand-alone piece in *Postbox* magazine. The piece illustrates how I sought to integrate and incorporate and bring alive in new contexts—and not simply 'use'—not only Paris the place but also works and words of other artists and authors as they resonated with my own through the minds of the characters. This issue recurs as a theme in the novel—the recognition that not one of us stands alone; but culture, film, song, works of art and music and literature contribute continually to making and remaking who, where and what we are... our 'presents,' our 'places', our 'belonging'—indeed our very selves—are multiple, resonating as they do with so many pasts, both personal and cultural; the references I make to a wide range of works I hope reflects this. Many of these come through the mouth of László, the doubtful interrogator, the embodiment of Exile, the personification of the creative spirit.

In *Wet Sunday Morning* I also wanted to point to the essentially 'hybrid' nature of 'autobiographical' writing. Paris, for me, had and has a personal history; what it 'means' to me not only resonates with stories of my own past, but also accords some symbolic significances to the ongoing quotidian activities of myself-in this-place now and on into the future. Already I am not a unified self, but a writing self, a self that is about to fragment into the characters whose desires and conflicts will drive the narrative the novel will become. The enigmatic László appears, then Clara, Sadie, each telling their stories as they criss-cross with my own.

'Real' people—for example at Berkeley Books of Paris, at Red Wheelbarrow Bookstore, at Chez Georges—walk in and out of the text from time to time, interacting with characters in the novel and with the narrator.

In addition to the work of Louise Bourgeois, I have long been an admirer of Samuel Beckett's prose—he of course lived and worked in Paris for most of his life. Beckett's characters are usually beset by insoluble ambivalences, torn between opposing desires, trapped in states of indecision, as they attempt to find meaning amid the absurdities of existence. In this continual searching for something that can never be found, I saw parallels with the repetition compulsions in Freud, the *I do, I undo, I redo* states of mind in Bourgeois, parallels which manifested in the characters' experiences of Paris, and fed into the core of the novel, in particular into the theme of creative process.

It appears that Beckett himself thought in these inherently ambivalent ways; they fed into doubts about his own creative process, as he wrote in a letter to Barbara Bray, his long-time literary confidante:

> *I am in an acute crisis about my work...and have already decided that I not merely can't but won't go on as I have been going on more or less ever since the 'Textes Pour Rien' and I must either get back to nothing again and the bottom of all the hills again like before Molloy or else call it a day ...*

According to biographer, Deirdre Bair, Beckett had ongoing issues with his creative process. He spent a long time trying to circumvent his own traumatic memories in order to be able to write. It was not until he entered psychoanalytic therapy with Wilfred Bion, and encountered Jung's views on creativity, that he realised his best forward path was to embrace his internal conflicts and to use their energies to fuel his work. These pivotal moments in his creative life Beckett was able to capture in his work (for example, in *Krapp's Last Tape*) offering us insights into how our own hidden internal conflicts can provide the motor energies of our creativity, as Louise Bourgeois also believed. These beliefs I donated to the character Clara for her to grapple with in her intended biography of the (imagined) psychoanalyst, Max Zuniga.

Inspiration for the original pieces in the Cahiers, and later as the novel took shape, also came from exhibitions of art works and photographs that I visited during those early months in Paris. One such was to the *Expo Sébastien Lifshitz, Inventaire Infini*, at the Pompidou Centre in which were exhibited photographs of sleeping people. The pieces *Les Dormeurs* 1 and 2 were my direct response to the photographs in that exhibition; I made notes as I looked, and then fictionalised my observations in the novel by giving them to the character Sadie who, as a photographer, was having issues with her own creative practice and the role of photography in bearing witness.

I still haven't been able to decide on the extent to which the Narrator/Writer is itself a 'character' in the novel. As I say in the first section, "its characters are ditherers," and they are, ditherers, in the sense that they—with the single exception of László—find it impossible to step outside or beyond their own ambivalences, and the narrator clearly cannot make up their mind who in fact is the 'main character.' I've included in the novel pieces that belong to the narrator and which speak in its idiom. At times the narrator interacts with the characters in real time or in memory time, as explored in 'All the mirrored selves we are,' published in *3am Magazine* in July 2021. The shifting 'protagonist' of this novel does, at times, take the persona of the writer/narrator itself. A prominent theme is the narrator's own creative process which recognises each of us as more than one, as always more than ourselves.

This idea of multiples inside each of us—and the dilemmas and questions that raises—I found superbly captured in work exhibited at the Louise Bourgeois Artist Room at the Perth (Scotland) Museum and Art Gallery in 2017, particularly in *Cell XIV (Portrait)* made in 2000 when the artist was 80 years old. The red, three-headed fabric sculpture is captured in a metal cage, either for confinement or safety. *Hysterical*, the pink fabric figure of a woman with no arms and three heads was made the following year. Louise Bourgeois concealed layers of wounds under those bandaged *personnages*, with their gaping mouths, their multiple heads, some confined torso-less in cages.

Bourgeois is of course renowned for her stitched pieces, the making and mending, the destructions and reparations, which come back to her *I do, I undo, I redo* mantra of repetition compulsion and the 'return of the repressed.' But the repetitions are not just repeats of the same old story, they—not least because, like the repeated lines in a villanelle, they are in new contexts—they are re-fashionings, re-statements of old ways gradually yet radically transformed and transforming. In her art, literally as well as metaphorically, Bourgeois connected and re-connected the threads of trauma, stitching and weaving, harnessing repressed energies, transforming them into art. Many of her stitched pieces are made of materials that look like bandages. It is this trope that Clara battles with in her attempts to formulate a theory of creativity alongside (but in the absence of) Zuniga, and the guiding principle in her therapeutic interventions with Sadie. I wanted to see Clara try to put into practice Bourgeois' idea that trauma can be transformed into art, and that 'art is the Guaranty of sanity' (sic).

Bourgeois' bald statement that *Art is not about art... Art is about life, and that sums it up*, remained in the back of my mind as I wrote; it generated questions for the characters, such as the nature of the synergies between life and art, and the crucial role of 'memory' in its many guises. Bourgeois said: *I need my memories. They are my documents.* I contrived for poor Clara to remain document-less as far as Zuniga was concerned; no documents, no evidence, no biography, unless you make it up, make fiction. The document about Zuniga's life, when it does arrive, comes via Sadie, comes too late, and has the effect of revealing to Clara, not just a crucial aspect of Zuniga's life, but an unwelcome parallel in her own. Another case of 'repetition compulsion,' perhaps. Freud, in *Beyond the Pleasure Principle*, puts it like this: *The patient cannot remember the whole of what is repressed and what he cannot remember may be precisely the essential part of it... He is obliged to repeat the repressed material as a contemporary experience instead of remembering it as something in the past.*

One of the central dilemmas that traumatised photographer Sadie grapples with in the story is the question of the meaning and usefulness of Art, as both practice and product, in particular in 'bearing witness,' in a world as troubled as the one we currently inhabit. Sadie's concern with the politics and ethics of art arises specifically in relation to her volunteer work with migrant communities in the so-called 'Jungle' in Calais-Sangatte. She's taken photographs and collected testimonies from residents in the Camp, but finds herself questioning the ethics of 'using' such materials in her work. The issues raised in this regard in the novel were directly inspired by my own witnessing of the *Calais: Witnessing the 'Jungle,'* exposition at the Centre Pompidou in Paris in early 2020 just before Lockdown (see Serralongue et al.). My own notes and responses made during my visits to the expo became the core of Sadie's responses and paved the way for the making of her final installation as site-specific art—*Art out of Place*—on the land at Calais where the 'Jungle' was situated.

One of the difficulties in writing a novel with 'creative processes' as a central theme is the challenge of finding an appropriate language (beyond 'art' itself) to talk about an area of human psychological reality that, for each of us, has neither a straightforward objective existence, nor is wholly subjectively constituted. (This was of course a recurring issue in modernist literature, and often addressed by stream-of-consciousness writing.) But this, the enigmatic space where creativities operate, I saw as needing a psychological language to capture it, and I found such a language in the work of psychoanalyst Donald Winnicott. As he put it: *'If we look at our lives we shall probably find that we spend most of our time neither in behaviour nor in contemplation, but somewhere else. I ask: where?'* These words have been a guiding principle of my thinking ever since my undergraduate days and this third space he envisages is the space I have explored in Paris Pages. Winnicott's concept of a 'potential' or 'transitional' space fits well to the thought and creative practices of artists like Bourgeois, and Beckett. It appears too, in the novel, in Sadie's procrastinations, her hoverings around meaning, and Clara's mis-typings—of 'palace,' of 'refuge'—it is Beckett's, *'I can't go on, I'll go on,'* his *'He could have shouted and could not;'* it is Sadie facing herself beside herself, detached, unhitched, unable to locate herself in her mirror. The novel ends in further liminal space, with a final nod to Beckett, as creative spirit László is relinquished by the narrator to go on his way.

References, and Suggested Further Reading

Acker, K., Scholder, A., Cooper, D. (2002) *Essential Acker: The Selected Writings of Kathy Acker*, Grove Press
Anzieu, D. (1989) 'Beckett and Bion,' *International Review of Psycho-Analysis*
Bair, D (1978) *Samuel Beckett: a biography*, Harcourt Brace
Beckett, S. (1995) *The Complete Short Prose, 1929-1989*, (Ed. S.E. Gontarski), Grove Press
Blanchot, M. (1982) *The Space of Literature*, trans. Ann Smock, University of Nebraska Press
Bourgeois, L. (1992) (Cell) *Precious Liquids*, 'art is a Guaranty of Sanity,' Pompidou Centre, December 2019
Bourgeois, L. (1999) Has the day invaded the night ... MOMA https://www.moma.org/collection/works/62542
Bourgeois, L. (2004) 'Rocking to infinity the red skein it will never be interrupted, abandoned or cut. There is one eternal thread and it is you,' see Wade, F. (2016)
Bourgeois, L. (2006) Hours of the Day
Collins, B. (2021) 'Paris in May', *Whale Day*, Picador

Connor, S (1998) 'Beckett and Bion,' Beckett and London Conference, Goldsmiths College

Coxon, A. (2010) *LB: Louise Bourgeois*, Tate Publishing

Day, S. (2021) 'Wet Sunday Morning in Paris, November 2019, *Postbox* magazine

Day, S. (2022) 'All the mirrored selves we are,' *3am Magazine*, July 2021; https://www.3ammagazine.com/3am/all-the-mirrored-selves-we-are/

Dean, Tacita, *Event for a Stage*, screened at The Fruitmarket Gallery, Edinburgh, 2018, with Actor Stephen Dillane.

Faulkner, W. (1951) *Requiem for a Nun*, Random House

Freud, S. (2010) *Beyond the Pleasure Principle*, Pacific Publishing Studio

Greenberg, J. and Jordan, S. (2003) *Runaway Girl: The Artist Louise Bourgeois*, Harry N. Abrams Inc.

Guo, V. (2019) 'Art is not about art. Art is about life and that sums it up.' Hauser and Wirth.

Haus der Kunst, Munich (2105) *Louise Bourgeois: Structures of Existence: The Cells*

Hommage aux écrivains de la grande guerre (2018–9) Mairie de 6e, Paris

Larratt-Smith, P. (ed.) (2012) *Louise Bourgeois: The Return of the Repressed*, Vols 1 and 11, Psychoanalytic Writings, Violette Editions, London.

Love, D. (undated) 'The disquieting muse: Beckett's schizoid fiction,' https://www.academia.edu/11321403/The_Disquieting_Muse_Becketts_Schizoid_Fiction?auto=download

The Marginalian (2019) discusses Rilke, on Love: https://www.themarginalian.org/2018/09/03/rilke-love-marriage/

Moorjani, A. (2004) 'Beckett and Psychoanalysis,' in L. Oppenheim (ed) *Palgrave Advances in Samuel Beckett Studies*, Palgrave Macmillan

Morgan, E. (1990) *Nothing Not Giving Messages: reflections on his life and work*, ed. H. Whyte, Edinburgh University Press

Morris, F. and Larratt-Smith, P. (2013) *Insomnia in the work of Louise Bourgeois*, published on the occasion of the exhibition Louise Bourgeois: *I Give Everything Away*, Fruitmarket Gallery, Edinburgh

Muller-Westermann, I. (2015) Louise Bourgeois: I have been to Hell and back. Moderna Museet, Stockholm

Musée d'art et d'histoire de Judaïsm, (2019) Expo Freud: du regard à l'écoute https://www.mahj.org/fr/programme/visite-de-lexposition-sigmund-freud-du-regard-lecoute-1165

National Galleries of Scotland (2013) *Artist Rooms: Louise Bourgeois: A woman without secrets*

Nixon, M. (2008) *Fantastic Reality: Louise Bourgeois and the Story of Modern Art*, MIT Press

Perth Museum and Art Gallery, Scotland, Artist Room (2017) https://www.artistrooms.org/rooms/louise-bourgeois-perth

Sarraute, N. (1982) *Pour un Oui ou Pour un Non*, Gallimard

Serralongue, B. et al (2019–20) Calais: Witnessing the 'Jungle,' Centre Pompidou, Paris. https://www.centrepompidou.fr/en/program/calendar/event/c4EgAaA

Serralongue, B., Ebner, F., and Rancière, J. (2020) *Testimonies from the 'Jungle' 2006–2020*, texts trans. from the French by Simon Cowper, FRAC Île-de-France

Stanislavski, Constantin (1989) *An Actor Prepares*, Taylor and Francis

Tokarczuk, O. (2017) *Flights*, trans. by Jennifer Croft, Fitzcarraldo Editions

Wade, F. (2016) *Louise Bourgeois, Turning Inwards*. Hauser and Wirth

Weller, S. (2008) '"Some experience of the schizoid voice": Samuel Beckett and the language of derangement,' *Forum for Modern language Studies*, Vol.45 https://doi.org/10.1093/fmls/cqn063

Winnicott, D.W. (1971) 'The place where we live,' in Playing and Reality, Routledge

Wye, D. (2017) *Louise Bourgeois: An Unfolding Portrait,* MOMA, New York

Zigmond, V. (2019) Expo Photographs, Institut Balassi hongrois

GRATITUDES

The pieces that came to form the core of this book—which together I called *Les Cahiers d'une Flâneuse*—were drafted on-the-hoof in Paris in 2019-20 before the Covid pandemic hit. I am grateful to Claude et Frédérique for generous loan of their studio in rue des Canettes over those months. Sections of the *Cahiers* were workshopped at AWOL writers' group at Berkeley Books of Paris, Scriptorium writers' group, Paris Creative Writers, and Birds of a Feather. I am grateful for the feedback I received in those groups from, in particular, Connie Bradburn, Beverley Bie Brahic, Dee Burton, Phyllis Cohen, Anne Depaulis, Ruth Druart, Gray Elliott, Kseniya Navazhylava, Yan Rucar, Veronica Sorace, and Susan Townson. For sustenance and always a generous welcome, thanks to the team at Bar Chez Georges: Comptoir des Canettes, particularly Hugo, Nicolette, Marie, and Guy.

When Lockdown hit in March, I returned to Scotland and used the empty time to think about drafting a novel around the core of Les Cahiers. A crucial time in the development of *Paris Pages*, I was working, not with my feet still tramping the streets of that city, but instead treading the realms of memory—places and pages had begun to be creatively processed. Three characters were already clamouring to have their voices heard.

The second Lockdown was strict. From the distance of a small town in rural France, my Paris-as-place took shape on the page, alive in different ways in each of the characters. With Covid and confinement there inevitably came bouts of spirits flagging and progress was intermittent. Far away in California my youngest grandchild Lola was born and I was unable to travel to her. Those were tough times for so many people in different ways. Then, as the year was turning, I received the very good news that my short story collection—*what are you like*—had won the prestigious Edge Hill Prize. This gave me an enormous boost to keep on going.

Emerging from the second Lockdown, there followed the difficulty finding an apartment in Paris, the one I'd been promised having been suddenly withdrawn. The quest proved impossible and I left to spend the summer off-grid in a cabin in Norway knowing that I did not have a home to return to in France. I mention this here because the uncertainties, the displacements, and the destabilisation fed into the novel, they were built into the place and into the lives and minds of the characters—each grappling with similar issues. In the solitude of Norway I completed the first draft of *Paris Pages* during the summer of 2021. I am greatly indebted to those whose friendship held us and helped us. Particular mention for the late Gerd Isum, and Pål Isum, Rune Haverstad and Hildegunn Klypen, Tulla Bakk and Dagfinn, and Gunvor Midtskog Skurdal. Special gratitude is owed to the late Pål Audun Midtskog who sadly passed away last year just as the snows came; he is very much missed.

Rewrites proceeded through 2022 as I continued to fail to secure an affordable place to live in Paris. Eventually in October I got the keys to my own tiny 6th floor studio, and there I worked systematically on the rewrites. I am grateful for critical feedback at different stages from Anne Bottomley, Charlotte Gosling, Sue Haigh,

Angela Jackson, Anni Walsh, Lindsay Macgregor, Maz Smith, Moira MacPartlin, Carmen Marcus, Rod Miller, Yan Rucar, Andrew Sclater, Catherine Simpson, and Sussi Louise Smith. And huge special thanks to Jacky Collins (aka Dr Noir), Angela Jackson and Bev Bie Brahic for their generous contributions to the launches in Newcastle, Edinburgh and Paris.

I am immensely grateful once again to the awesome team at Red Squirrel Press /Postbox Press, particularly Sheila Wakefield, Founder and Editor-at-large, Gerry Cambridge, designer and typesetter and Colin Will, Editor at Postbox Press, for their continual generosity of spirit supporting me every inch of the way. It's easier to believe in yourself when others believe in you. Thank you.

And, finally, for cover artwork, to my son Nicolai Sclater, @OrnamentalConifer, thank you. It is always such a pleasure to work with you.

A NOTE ON THE TYPES

The text of this book is set in Palatino Nova Pro,
Hermann Zapf's & Akira Kobayashi's redesign
& updating in several weights
of Zapf's classic Palatino, which was originally
released in 1950. Renowned for its legibility,
it takes its name from Giambattista Palatino,
a calligraphy master & contemporary of Da Vinci.

Section markers and other matter are set
in the companion face Palatino Sans,
Zapf & Kobayashi's curved and rounded sans
serif designed as a contemporary
complement to its classic precursor.